THE
PRINCE
& THE
APOCALYPSE

ALSO BY
KARA McDOWELL

This Might Get Awkward

One Way or Another

Just for Clicks

PRINCE

& THE

APOCALYPSE

A NOVEL

KARA MCDOWELL

WEDNESDAY BOOKS
NEW YORK

First published in the United States by Wednesday Books, an imprint of St. Martin's Publishing Group

THE PRINCE & THE APOCALYPSE. Copyright © 2023 by Kara McDowell. All rights reserved. Printed in the United States of America. For information, address St. Martin's Publishing Group, 120 Broadway, New York, NY 10271.

www.wednesdaybooks.com

Designed by Devan Norman
Star universe background illustration by buffaloboy/Shutterstock.com

The Library of Congress Cataloging-in-Publication Data is available upon request.

ISBN 978-1-250-87304-0 (hardcover)
ISBN 978-1-250-87306-4 (trade paperback)
ISBN 978-1-250-87305-7 (ebook)

Our books may be purchased in bulk for promotional, educational, or business use. Please contact your local bookseller or the Macmillan Corporate and Premium Sales Department at 1-800-221-7945, extension 5442, or by email at MacmillanSpecialMarkets@macmillan.com.

First Edition: 2023

10 9 8 7 6 5 4 3 2 1

TO OWEN, GRAHAM, AND EMMETT:

THE BRIGHTEST STARS IN MY UNIVERSE

THE
PRINCE
& THE
APOCALYPSE

PROLOGUE

My sister, Brooke, once told me that your roommate can become your best friend, but your best friend can't become your roommate. She was talking about college dorms, which is why Naomi and I ignored her and signed up to be roomies for our study abroad trip to England. We've been best friends for three years, and I can't imagine anything will happen in the next ten days to change that.

I am, however, already learning new things about Naomi. Case in point? She's obsessed with the royal family. We've been on the airplane for three hours and she hasn't talked about anything else.

Naomi flips the page in an overpriced magazine she bought at O'Hare and points to a picture of the British royal family. "Don't *ever* tell my mom I said this, but I think Queen Alice is the perfect mother."

"Hmmm," I hum noncommittally.

"Look at her! And look at the kids! How do they look so polished all the time?"

"Money." I close my eyes and tip my head back.

"Does it make me a bad feminist if I want to become a princess instead of a girlboss?"

"I think girlboss is an insult these days."

"Oh, it totally is. Does it make me a hypocrite if I want to eat the rich but *also* become a princess?" She sighs dramatically. "Because it would be fun, just for the fashion alone."

I open my eyes. Apparently ignoring her is the wrong tactic. "I think royalty is a human rights violation," I quip cheerfully.

Naomi's eyes widen. "Wren! You can't say that," she whispers, scandalized. She glances over her shoulder to make sure I wasn't overheard. You'd think I'd just announced my plan to murder the Queen.

"Think of those poor children, born into a life of public scrutiny. They have no choice in it. Their parents have no choice. Their grandparents have no choice! It's child abuse all the way down," I say.

"Stop talking," she hisses. "Being born a royal is fate. Destiny." She flips the page to a close-up of one of the yellow-haired British princes and shoves it under my nose. He's waving at the camera, a big corny grin plastered on his face. "Does he look unhappy to you?"

"Eh." I take the magazine and muse over the picture. My feelings about the royals aren't strong enough to keep arguing with her, but it's just so funny. Naomi and I have been best friends since her family moved across the street three years ago, but I've never once seen this side of her. At home in Chicago, Naomi is a fellow Type A. She's class valedictorian, president of the Jewish Student Club, and a future TV meteorologist. As soon as our plane left American soil, however, her brain was taken over by Royal Fever. "What's with the scar through his eyebrow?" I ask. "Did Mummy slice his brow open with the Crown Jewels when he failed to curtsy?"

Naomi's jaw drops and I bite back a laugh. She makes it way too easy.

"I think it gives him a rugged charm." She snatches the magazine back and swoons.

"What about Levi?" I tease. "Are your loyalties so fickle?" She's been pining over one boy at her synagogue for ages.

"I'm allowed to be in love with two people at once," she reasons. "Especially when they live on two separate continents. I never know what fate has in store for me."

"I don't believe in fate or destiny or anything else that wants to steal credit for my hard work," I say. She ignores me, her eyes still on the rich boy with hair the color of straw.

In some ways, I feel like my entire life has been leading up to this study abroad trip. It's been the number one item on my Life Plan since Brooke took the same trip four years ago. But being here isn't *fate*. It's the result of careful decisions and hard work. I spent two years researching transportation and restaurants and museums to create a foolproof itinerary. One of the requirements for the trip was a 3.8 cumulative GPA, so I never let my grades slip. And when my parents said I had to pay for half the cost, I worked at the animal shelter every summer to earn the money.

Fate and destiny can stay in the pages of fairy tales and Greek tragedies and out of my life.

A flight attendant appears at my elbow. "Something to drink?"

Naomi orders a Dr Pepper, her favorite. The plane lurches and my stomach somersaults, bringing a rush of nausea.

The flight attendant gives Naomi her pop and looks at me. "And for you?"

The plane hits another rough patch, and I'm too sick to speak. Naomi comes to my rescue and orders me a ginger ale.

"Are you okay?" she asks. "Did all my royal talk make you queasy?"

I nod once, though I'm sure it's just airplane sickness. "Can you open the window?"

Naomi pulls up the plastic covering, and we both stare in wonder at the clouds below. Only a few more hours until we land at Heathrow. My stomach turns again, this time from four years of anticipation and excitement.

Thanks to my excellent planning, these next ten days are going to be the best of our lives. I've never been so sure of anything.

CHAPTER 1

10 DAYS LATER
DATE: SUNDAY, JUNE 12
LOCATION: LONDON, ENGLAND

ITINERARY
9:00 A.M.: PACK
10:00 A.M.: BREAKFAST AT THE WORLD'S END
3:00 P.M.: FLIGHT HOME :(

I miss peanut butter, salsa, and ice cubes. I miss sunshine and my family. I miss my dog.

But most of all, I miss the girl I thought I was ten days ago, before I realized I'm the worst kind of traveler: the kind who just wants to go home. I flew almost four thousand miles for the adventure of a lifetime with my best friend, and all I got was this lousy homesickness.

Once upon a time, I thought the worst thing an American

tourist could be was obvious. Brooke warned me about all the stereotypes: Americans are obnoxious and loud. They wear gym shoes when they shouldn't. They smile too much.

I vowed not to be that person, even if it meant blisters on my feet and a week of nonstop whispering. I'd *prove* how happy I was to be in London by scowling at people on the street.

I had a plan.

But after spending five days facedown in a hotel toilet, that plan is in tatters. I might as well parade down Abbey Road in tacky sneakers and a Stars and Stripes fanny pack, waving my basic bitch flag. I'd consider it if it meant this trip even remotely resembled the one on my detailed ten-page itinerary.

Nine pages down, one left to go. My eyes stray to the last item on the list as I neatly fold a dirty sweater and place it in my suitcase. *3:00 P.M.: Flight home. Frowny face.* I had such high hopes when I penciled that doodle in, the final touch to my masterpiece years in the making. Now the face mocks me: one more thing the itinerary got wrong. When that airplane takes off from Heathrow, I'll be mentally dancing in the aisle.

The door to our shared hotel room bangs open and Naomi rushes in. I try to ignore the jealous pang that burns behind my ribs over the fact that she was out without me. She tosses her hotel key on the TV stand and collapses, distressed, across my bed. "The prince is missing."

"Which one?"

"The important one," she says seriously, showing me a *Daily Mail* article on her phone. I glance at the headline: PRINCE THEO GLARINGLY ABSENT FROM TROOPING THE COLOUR. WITH NO WORD FROM THE PALACE, WE'RE LEFT TO WONDER: IS THE FUTURE KING SICK, OR JUST PLAYING HOOKY?

"So he skipped an event." I return my attention to the mountain of clothes in front of me. It shouldn't be this difficult to fit them back into my suitcase. I have acquired nothing on this trip except disenchantment.

Naomi sits up, a protective glint in her eye. "He's supposed to be working at this event—"

"Liberal use of the term 'working.'"

"Trooping the Colour is *very* important to the monarch," she says with complete seriousness.

"If that's true, they shouldn't have given it such a silly name."

"Trooping the Colour marks the official birthday of the sovereign."

"I'm sorry—all this fuss is because the prince missed his mom's birthday party?" I pick up Naomi's phone and scroll through the photos included with the article. The event appears to be the height of British pomp and pageantry. There are thousands of guards in silly costumes. Guards on foot and guards on horses. *Guards in a house. Guards with a mouse. Guards here and there! Guards everywhere.* Musical instruments, funny fuzzy hats as far as the eye can see, and, because why not, a whole bunch of cannons. Real goofy shit.

"He's not on the balcony. The entire royal family is always on the balcony." Naomi takes the phone and points to a picture of a crowded mezzanine occupied by a group of polished children whom I vaguely recognize as the prince's younger siblings. The photo holds an air of importance that I begrudgingly admire.

"Maybe he jumped," I say.

"Not funny."

"If this is the royal equivalent of work, then he's been working since the moment he was born. Before, even! He deserves a day off."

"When the royals take a day off, they release a statement. The Palace's silence speaks volumes. Something's not right."

"I hear you. I acknowledge you. Please don't make me talk about the royals anymore."

She drops her phone with a huff as tension chills the air. It's not common for us to get annoyed with each other, but it's been happening more and more the past few days.

"Emily, Tatum, and I are going to walk to Camden Market to shop for souvenirs," she says.

I'm stung by the period at the end of her sentence. The finality of it. There's not even a hint of invitation lingering in the air.

When I was too sick to leave our room for five days, Naomi had to adjust her plans and find other people to hang out with. The strain between us didn't start until I stopped puking and assumed she'd ditch Emily and Tatum so we could spend the second half of the trip the way we'd planned. Turns out she didn't want to do that; turns out European Naomi doesn't like my itineraries nearly as much as Chicagoan Naomi does. After years of working her ass off to be valedictorian, she wanted to let loose and let off steam, not follow another rigid schedule. Initially she invited me to join them on morning walks through the park or evening trips to the pub, but I kept saying no. First out of hurt, and then out of a stubborn unwillingness to let my itinerary die. I'm great at making plans and backup plans, but I didn't have a plan for when my best friend started choosing other people over me. Soon enough, she stopped asking.

"Have fun. I have to finish packing anyway." *There*. Proof that I'm fine without her invitation.

She rolls her eyes. "Why are you going so slow?" She gathers an armful of clothes and shoves them haphazardly into my suitcase, holding the top down to zip it shut. "There. All done."

Okay then. I press my lips into a thin line as I pick up a pen from my bedside table and carefully scratch a line through *9:00* A.M.: *Pack.* "Thanks," I say. I fall quiet as tension bubbles between us. "I'm getting breakfast down by Camden Market!" I announce. Not at all hurt. Not at all sad.

"With who?"

"Just myself."

She sighs and leans back against my pillows. "Sounds . . . fun."

My fist curls tightly around the edge of my itinerary. This trip has been nothing but disaster after disaster. First, the never-ending stomach virus from hell. Then a string of stormy days that canceled Shakespeare in the Squares and ruined our trip to the London Zoo. Even the larcenous British Museum turned out to be a disappointment, but that could have been my fault. I don't have the right disposition for museums; I can only pretend to care about old things for so long. The Rosetta Stone, for example: objectively, a very cool old thing. Props to the French guy who found it! Staring at a midsize boulder with ancient writing on it that you can't even read? *Eh.* Interesting for fifteen seconds. I couldn't even bring myself to get excited about taking photos of the priceless artifact because there must be millions of the exact same photo floating around in the cloud right now. That's not my thing. I'd have been much happier lying in the grass on the lawn outside the museum and snapping candids of the people around me, capturing small moments that exist and are gone in a breath.

But Brooke said that the World's End had the best breakfast she'd ever eaten, and I'm determined to get one thing on my itinerary exactly, perfectly right. The plan may be in shreds, but it's nothing I can't carefully tape back together.

"Brooke ate breakfast at this pub on her last morning of the program. It's a family tradition." Or it will be once I follow in her footsteps.

Naomi scoots to the edge of my bed and stands up, refusing to look at me. "Well . . . enjoy your plans."

"You can come with me if you want! The full English is supposed to be amazing."

"Do you know what's in a full English breakfast?"

"Fried tomatoes and mushrooms and baked beans and—"

"Blood pudding and sausage," she says. "Wren, you're a vegetarian!"

My sensitive stomach revolts. I press my lips together, the memory of my virus so fresh that *I* want to throw myself off the Buckingham Palace balcony. "I won't eat the meat, obviously."

"Do you even *want* to eat tomatoes for breakfast?" she asks.

"Of course!" Defensiveness flares in my chest.

"Just like you *wanted* to ride the London Eye on our first night here?"

"It was—"

"On the itinerary," we say at the same time. In retrospect, the decision to ride London's famous Ferris wheel when I was already feeling nauseous was not my brightest idea. At least my vomit didn't land *on* anyone—except the tail of that bulldog, but he didn't hold it against me. Angus was a total sweetheart when I got off the ride to apologize, though his humans were less kind. I may not have understood all the words they yelled at me, but I felt the venom behind them. No one's ever crocheted "manky git" on a throw pillow, to say the least.

"Not this again. Don't you ever want to change the itinerary?"

Naomi huffs. My inflexibility never bothered her at home, but now it does. Now I can *feel* her roll her eyes every time I consult the schedule.

"Actually, I do." I scribble over the frowny face next to *Flight home* and replace it with a smiling one. "There. Happy?"

She shakes her head with a small sigh. "C'mon, let's get our stuff downstairs and you can walk with us." She heaves her luggage into the crook of her arm and holds the door open for me. I drag my suitcase off the bed and spare one backward glance for my temporary London home. The Grange Beauchamp Hotel in the heart of Bloomsbury sounded so glamorous at the beginning of all of this. *Blooooooomsbury*. The word rolled off my tongue like a name in a romance novel. Even when we arrived, I was enchanted by the brick building with white curtains and red flowers in the windowsills. Now my eyes rove over the threadbare blankets to the window that refused to open and let in fresh air, and my enchantment is nowhere to be found.

"I'm going to miss this place." Naomi says the words I wish I felt. A painful knot grows in my throat. We walk into the hall and let the door thump closed behind us, sealing four years of disappointment inside.

I'm not going to dwell on it. Or on the fact that if this plan was a bust, the future I envisioned for myself might also be vulnerable. I don't want to make new plans. I wouldn't even know where to start.

Downstairs, we step out of the hotel into watery sunlight. After drizzling most of the night, the clouds have finally cleared and the smell of diesel exhaust fights with musty rain-soaked brick. I'm no stranger to humidity, but no matter which neighborhood I find myself in, the air in London is consistently thicker and heavier than what I'm used to in Chicago. It sticks to my lungs, coating them in black coal dust.

We ditch our luggage on the curb with Mrs. Kerr, our English teacher and one of the trip chaperones, who warns us to meet back here at the van no later than noon or "we'll leave without you!"

Emily and Tatum join Naomi and me as we board the Tube near our hotel and exit about twenty minutes later, strolling into the colorful and chaotic streets of Camden Market. They peel off at an outdoor souvenir stall sitting between a tattoo parlor and a vintage clothing shop, and I can't quite meet Naomi's gaze.

My fingers itch to grab my camera and photograph the people around me: a mixture of tourists with selfie sticks and locals in black leather and goth makeup. It reminds me of high school, the way the groups move around each other while pretending the others don't exist. Because there's not time to use my DSLR, I settle for my phone. I point the camera at the crowd of people while the market's curious shop signs provide a vibrant background, snapping a dozen quick shots before sliding my phone back into my pocket.

The smell of damp stone mixes with a curry stall tucked across the street and a mouthwatering fish and chips shop. My feet slow and I can't help but gaze through the floor-to-ceiling windows. For the first time in ten days, my stomach pangs with a craving for the hot, salty French fries. I waver, but the last page of my itinerary weighs heavy in my pocket. Today's the only day I can get completely right. If Brooke can do it, so can I.

My boots clack against the brick as I walk down Camden High Street toward my destination: the World's End.

CHAPTER 2

*B*rass letters reading THE WORLD'S END shine against a red background. It looks exactly the way I envisioned it— except for the glaring CLOSED FOR RENOVATIONS sign in the window. The dates scrawled below indicate it closed this morning.

I sigh and press my forehead against the cool glass, my feet aching from the long walk. I can't believe I'm one day late. When I started this itinerary years ago, it never occurred to me that an iconic landmark that's been around since the 1800s would be closed during my eventual visit. Sure, the World's End opened its doors for Charles Dickens and Radiohead and Brooke Wheeler, but now that I'm here, the curtains are drawn, the doors boarded shut.

What a disaster.

When my sister flew to London, she came home with life-changing stories about Shakespeare, pub crawls, and Harry Styles look-alikes who called her "love." If I can't even replicate one stupid meal, what makes me think I can match any of her other achievements?

Earlier this spring, Brooke made my parents' dreams come true by receiving a full merit scholarship to Northwestern Law. I didn't even know those existed! said absolutely everyone in the comments of my mom's bragging Facebook post.

Not long after she posted, I'd found Mom in her home office and told her that I wanted to be a lawyer like her and Brooke. She'd looked up from her laptop with a beaming smile. "I can see our letterhead now—*Wheeler & Daughters*! No, *Wheeler, Wheeler & Wheeler*." Her smile faltered. "Hmmm. Sounds kind of clunky. I'll have to think on it."

I turned to leave, and my stomach sank as I saw Brooke framed in the doorway. I hadn't heard her approach. "You want to go to law school?" she asked skeptically. "How is that going to be possible when you're planning to major in *photography*?"

"I'm not," I protested weakly. "I'm going to do political science like you." I didn't need Brooke to remind me yet again that pursing photography was impractical, because I already knew; my dream job is the one thing I don't know how to plan for.

"I hope so. No use taking out all those student loans for a career that will never make you any money," she said as my cheeks flamed with embarrassment. She turned her attention to Mom. "Don't print the business cards just yet, Mom. We don't even know if Wren can hack it in college—let alone get into law school." She winked.

She was joking. I *know* she thinks she was joking. But what's that they say about every joke containing a hint of truth?

"We don't know if *you* can hack it in law school either," I said. Brooke laughed, completely unaffected by my comeback, because we all know she's a genius who can and will do whatever she sets her mind to. My future, on the other hand, is not a sure bet. Good grades and a penchant for making plans aren't all that impressive stacked up next to Brooke's National Merit Scholarship and Mensa IQ.

Brooke probably doesn't remember that conversation, but I think about her comment at least once a week and it still knocks the confidence right out of me. I hate that feeling, which is why I never let myself wallow in it. Avoidance is my tried-and-true method: instead of being sad that my sister has no faith in me, I kick my competitive nature into overdrive and blast my "you suck" playlist at top volume for motivation.

Brooke thinks I can't get into law school? Fine, I'll show her by getting a full ride to Harvard!

Good luck to me, I guess. This trip is the first time I've been out in the world on my own and it's been an utter face-plant from start to finish.

I take a picture of the CLOSED sign to show Naomi later. It looks even more pathetic on my screen, and suddenly I can't help but laugh at the absurdity of it all. Which is what I'm doing when a white guy joins me on the sidewalk in front of the pub. He shoots me a quizzical look before frowning at the door. He's wearing a Yankees hat and sunglasses. *American?*

"What's so funny?" he asks in a British accent. I should have known. His gray suede boots don't give off American boy vibes.

I gesture to the sign on the door. "It's called the World's End and it's closed, which feels like the end of the world. I know it's not, but . . ." I trail off with a shrug and he chuckles low under his breath.

I can finally admit to myself that it's time to give up the itinerary. I've been carrying it around as a reminder of my failure for days, and I'm gripped by the sudden urge to destroy it. "Do you have a lighter?" I ask the boy. I would say his shoulders stiffen, but the truth is they've been rigid the whole time. His posture is ramrod straight as he reaches into the pocket of his jeans and retrieves an expensive-looking lighter with an intricate engraving. My eyes catch on his chunky black ring as he flips the top open and a small flame blazes to life.

I pull out the last page of my worthless itinerary. *Here goes nothing.* I smooth the worn paper open and hold the corner to the flame. He swears under his breath but doesn't withdraw the lighter. The paper catches, the flame quickly devouring the edges into disappearing ash. "Ow!" I drop the last corner of the paper on the damp cement and shake my fingers. He flicks his lighter shut and stomps on the scraps of my plans.

"You all right?" He speaks with a posh British accent, his vowels longer and slower than many of the people I've encountered in London. Half the time I hear a local speak, I'm convinced their English is a completely different language than mine, the words crowded together like a tumbled chain of dominoes.

"I'm fine. Just hungry."

"What did we burn?"

"My future, I think."

"Oh good. As long as it wasn't anything important," he says dryly.

We stand in silence for a beat and I try to figure out how old he is. He's got the faintest hint of light facial hair dusting his cheeks, and something feels familiar about his profile. He catches me staring and bristles, quickly turning to face the pub again.

"I'm guessing you didn't know it'd be closed either?" My stomach growls loudly. I'm wasting too much time standing here, but even with my plans literally up in flames, I can't quite bring my feet to move.

"I did not," he confirms. Another long beat of silence.

"This will sound dramatic, but I think this might be the worst day of my life." At least when I was lying on the cold bathroom floor, too nauseous to open my eyes, I still hoped the trip would get better. I still believed I could follow the path Brooke and her genius IQ blazed through our family.

"This will sound dramatic, but I have to agree," he says.

I glance sideways to see if he's mocking me. He's still standing with perfect posture, his hands clasped behind his back, his eyes glued to the World's End. When the corner of his mouth twitches, I take it as an invitation.

"I'm Wren Wheeler. Eighteen. American," I say. He stares at my outstretched hand, his lips turning up in wry amusement.

"How do you do, Ms. Wheeler?" he says politely.

"What's your name?"

"Geoffrey. Nineteen. British."

"Nice to meet you, Geoffrey."

"Tell me about your rubbish day."

"Oh, you know. I just had the mind-melting realization that I'm the family flop." I shrug. "What about you?"

He squints up at the quickly graying sky. "It's supposed to rain today."

"That's it?"

"Some days that feels like enough, don't you think?"

"Only if you've had a very easy life," I grumble.

He winces as if my comment stung a lot more than I intended it to. "You would not be the first to accuse me of such."

"Sorry, that was rude. I know what you mean. I've been grumpy about the weather since—" The words die in my throat when Geoffrey tenses. I turn to see what has him rattled but don't see anything ominous, just a small group of women taking pictures of the World's End.

"If you'll excuse me, I must go," he says, taking measured steps out of the sunlight and into the shade of the awning above the restaurant door. He glances left and right the way my dog, Wally, does when he's cornered. Awareness prickles up my spine; the women aren't taking pictures of the pub. They're taking pictures of *him*.

"Who are they? Who are *you*?" I ask.

He adjusts his baseball hat and my heart stops. It was only a second, but I saw it. A scar slicing his left eyebrow in half. Naomi called it "rugged."

"You're Prince Theo?" I whisper.

When he holds a finger to his lips in silent confirmation, my head spins. Naomi is going to dissolve with jealousy when I tell her I met the missing prince. I glance over my shoulder and see the group waiting to cross the street, still snapping pictures and whispering to each other. They remind me of lionesses advancing on their prey, and that stupid unwanted sympathy I have for this absurdly rich boy flickers in my chest.

"Act casual. They can't be sure it's you," I say quietly.

"Not yet. But they will be in about thirty seconds."

"Then let's go." I grab his hand, and he startles at the sudden contact. I pull him down Camden High Street, away from the pub and the women. We walk as fast as possible without looking suspicious. "Aren't you supposed to have bodyguards or something?" I hiss, dropping his hand.

"I ditched them."

"How?" I thought he was one of the most popular and important people in the country. Like if Taylor Swift had a baby with a Kennedy and that baby grew up to be a teenage heartthrob. It couldn't have been easy for him to slip away from security.

"It's been a hectic couple of days at the palace."

The footsteps get closer. "Prince Theo?" a voice calls out. It sounds friendly enough that I hesitate.

"Wouldn't it be easier to just stop, take a few selfies, sign some autographs, and then leave?"

"Autographs and selfies are prohibited." He lengthens his stride and I jog to catch up.

"Can't you at least say hi?"

"Not today. I can't let anyone find out where I am." His tone is laced with desperation that feels more human than any of the dozens of pictures Naomi has showed me. "Please." His voice cracks.

"Follow me." I turn down a narrow alley between a shop and a yoga studio, and we slip inside a back door into the small, crowded clothing store.

"'Ello there! 'ow can I 'elp you?" the woman behind the counter asks.

"Just browsing!" I say with forced ease. I steer the prince to a corner of the shop behind a large rack of sunglasses and pull his baseball hat off. His golden-blond hair tumbles across his forehead. Too noticeable. I stuff a tweed newsboy cap on his head.

"Ow! Go easy on me." He winces.

"Sunglasses." I hold my hand out and he hesitates for a second before carefully placing them in my open palm. We stare at each other for a heartbeat and my stomach lurches. His eyes are bluer than I expected, and for the first time, I understand why Naomi is obsessed with this guy. It's not just that Theo is a prince; it's that he's a prince who looks like he could wreck my plans—and my life—if I'm not careful.

I drop the glasses into my pocket and switch them out for a different pair. He rests the thick black frames on the bridge of his nose, transforming his face from roguish heartbreaker to bookish college student.

"That's better. Now lose the jacket," I bark. He bristles against the command and my cheeks redden. I must have broken every royal protocol in existence. "Your Highness," I add stiffly. I don't intend to thread a hint of sarcasm through the words, but it's there, and he hears it. He flicks an eyebrow upward as he shrugs out of his navy windbreaker. I toss a long, heavy wool jacket into his arms.

"It's a little warm—" he starts, but shuts up when I put my hands on my hips.

"Can you pay for this?" I ask.

He winces. "I'm not allowed to carry cash." I pull a few bills out of my backpack and leave them on the table next to the hats. The door at the front of the store opens and one of the women who was following us sticks her head inside. Out on the side-walk, the group with her has tripled in size, including what looks like at least one member of the press carrying a camera with a long-range lens. A shudder runs up the length of my spine. I press my hands on the prince's shoulders and force him to the floor. I drop next to him on my hands and knees.

"Is it always like this?" I ask.

"It's usually worse," he muses.

"I'm a terrible bodyguard."

He shrugs. "I'm a terrible prince."

"Back door. Let's go." We crawl quickly to the door that will lead us into the alley.

"Hey!" the woman behind the register shouts. "You trying to nick that hat?"

Prince Theo freezes, his hand in midair.

"Go!" I nudge him in the shoulder blades and to my shock, he listens. He jumps to his feet and opens the door.

"We left money up front!" I yell over my shoulder as I follow him into the alley. The prince makes a beeline for the street, but I yank on the sleeve of his coat to pull him away from the crowd and the cameras. We spin and run toward the chain-link fence at the back of the alley. He climbs faster than I do, reaching the top when I'm only halfway up. Footsteps thunder toward us. He stretches his hand out to me, I place my palm in his, and he pulls me to the top. Together, we jump. My left ankle collapses as I hit the ground hard. I gasp and fall, catching myself on my palms.

Shit. We don't have time to waste, so I push up to my feet and ignore the biting pain. "Let's go."

We run as fast as my ankle will allow, weaving in and out of buildings, crashing through back alleys, and eventually spilling onto the crowded streets of Camden Market. Lines of tourists stretch out of restaurant doors and meander through the streets, making it the perfect place to hide. I avert my eyes from a couple making out on a bench, as does everyone who strides past them, giving them privacy in the middle of a busy corner.

"We lost them," I gasp, doubling over to suck in a breath. The air is so sticky, it feels like breathing through a straw.

"Let's go a little farther, just to be safe," he says. I check the time. I should have left for the hotel by now, but I give myself five more minutes to act as Prince Theo's bodyguard so I'll have at least *one* good London story to compete with Brooke's arsenal.

We slow to a casual pace and wander through the crowd. The prince sheds his jacket and drapes it over the back of a bench in front of a dark shop filled with steampunk corsets and Victorian jackets. I point to a leather-and-chains frock in the window. "Time for another outfit change. Think you can pull it off?" I grin in his direction so he knows I'm joking, but his only response is a straightening of the spine and a pink tinge in his cheeks.

"Paparazzo at ten o'clock," I mutter under my breath. "He hasn't seen us yet." As soon as the words are out of my mouth, the small bald man with a large camera crosses the road to our side of the street. His eyes scan the crowd. Searching for us. I grab the prince's sleeve and drag him against the wall of the goth shop. I press my back against the bricks, pulling the prince toward me to keep his face hidden. "As long as they don't see you, we're okay," I whisper.

"They know what you look like now too," he whispers back, a rush of breath fanning against my ear. Shivers course through my skin, but I don't have time to think about that because the man with the camera is approaching, and the prince is right. His face is hidden, but mine's not. My heart thunders in my chest as the man draws nearer. I have to make sure he doesn't look too closely at us—if he does, there's no telling what kind of mob will form. If that happens, I'm gonna have a hell of a time getting back to the hotel by noon. I feel panicky and claustrophobic, and I can't believe the words that come out of my mouth next.

"Kiss me."

CHAPTER 3

As Prince Theo leans in to hide my face from street view, a lock of golden hair slips free from his cap, falling across his forehead like starlight. It's the last sight I register before my eyes flutter closed and his lips touch mine. We freeze, lips pressed together, our bodies apprehensive, unsure how far to take the charade. And then he moves his mouth against mine, slowly, gently, and heat explodes in my chest. It races outward, down low into my belly and all the way into my aching hands. Everything burns as I reach for the lapels of his absent jacket and my fingers brush against the thin cotton of his button-down shirt. I let my palms rest there, savoring the violent thump of his heart.

He pulls away, taking his radiating warmth with him. "Was that okay?"

My head spins. "Yeah," I gasp, but I am *not* okay. There's not enough oxygen in the whole British Isles. Disorienting electricity races through my blood, and I have no freaking clue why. I've had spin-the-bottle kisses that lasted longer than that.

"My apologies. I got carried away. This is going to sound

like total rubbish, but I'm not myself today." His voice rasps against my skin, raising goose bumps everywhere.

"I told you to do it," I regretfully remind him. I practically commanded the crown prince of England to kiss me. I bet the Queen has rules against fraternizing with girls like me. Eager to change the subject, I glance around in search of the man with the camera. "He's gone."

"Making our snog a successful decoy."

"And nothing else," I quickly add. I don't want him to think I'm some weirdo stalker freak.

"Erm." He glances down at my hands, still spread possessively against his chest.

"Sorry!" I draw back like I've been electroshocked. "Did I just break protocol? Is the Queen going to have me locked up for violating the crown prince?"

"I won't tell her if you don't."

"You *are* the crown prince—correct? What's the difference between a crown prince and a regular one?" Naomi aside, everything I know about the royals I learned from Hallmark Christmas movies.

A drizzle of rain begins to fall, dropping cold, fat drops on my already frizzy hair and breaking the spell. I glance up at the dark sky with despair. As if this day, this week, this *trip* hasn't been bad enough, it's going to end with a walk of shame to the Tube on a busted ankle in crappy weather. Now that the adrenaline of being chased by people with cameras and kissed by a prince is wearing off, the pain in my ankle is dizzying. I lean against the brick wall, worried that I might pass out. "I need to get out of here."

One stunning kiss aside, I cannot wait to put England in my rearview. The sexiest words I can think of right now are

"Boeing 787. Flight 3745. London to Chicago with a layover in New York." *Oh baby*.

Theo straightens. "Let me buy you lunch to repay your kindness. I insist."

"Can you do that? Walk into one of these pubs and buy lunch without being mobbed and without any money?"

He scratches his cheek. "I suppose not. Perhaps you could buy the food for us, although that defeats the purpose of me buying you lunch."

I imagine crouching in the rain and eating soggy French fries—sorry, *chips*—with the future king of England. It's too absurd for words.

I kind of want to do it.

"I can't." Prince Theo is not even a footnote in any of my plans, which I now deeply regret lighting on fire. Playing bodyguard was a fun detour, but it's time to get back on track. I need to get to the airport and go home.

"Thanks for the help. I'm indebted," he says.

"It's not a big deal." My voice is thick with confusing emotion.

He leans close again, suddenly earnest. "It's a big deal to me. It's not too dramatic to say that you saved me. I wish . . ." He blows out a breath.

"You wish what?"

He draws his shoulders back. "Nothing. I shouldn't have—Sorry, Wren. I mean, Ms. Wheeler." He puts another foot of space between us. "If there's anything you need in the next eight days—let me know. I'll call in a favor."

I don't have the mental capacity to think about life beyond my flight home, let alone eight days from now. It'll take me at least a few days to draft a new life plan. "All I need is to catch my flight home."

His brow creases. "What time is your flight?"

I glance at my watch and my stress level ratchets up another notch. "Too soon." I've already missed my deadline to get back to the hotel, which means my classmates have left without me. This is karma for burning the itinerary. "I *really* have to go," I say again, but I don't move.

He stares at me. I stare at him. A royal stalemate. I mentally calculate how much time I have before the plane starts boarding. *Not enough.* I won't move first, though, because if he sees I'm hurt, he might try to do something chivalrous like help me. Screw that. I'm not letting this shitty vacation end with being saved by Prince Charming. Damsels in distress, like fate, are another concept I don't buy into. Girls with plans don't need saving.

"Can I get you a cab?" he asks.

"Without being seen? Seems risky."

"Right. Right." The prince lifts his ridiculous tweed cap and rakes a hand through his hair before placing the hat back on his head. I'm struck once again by his features. Blond hair, blue eyes, dramatic scar through his eyebrow. I'm seized by the urge to take his photo. In one blink he looks like a prince, in the next, like a guy I'd sit next to in calculus. Dazzling, but also real. More human than royal.

Unable to argue with my logic, he instead describes the quickest route to the Tube and tells me which line will take me to the airport. He looks down at me and swallows, his Adam's apple bobbing. "Good luck with your flight," he says seriously.

"I'll try not to let it go down over the Atlantic, but I can't make any promises," I joke. He doesn't laugh, and the intensity

behind his ocean-blue eyes makes it clear I missed his inten-
tion. He wasn't giving me a throwaway line, not the way people
say "Have a safe flight," as if that's something passengers have
any control over.

"I'm serious about that favor. I owe you."

"Right. I'm sure the palace operator will be more than happy
to patch me through. What's the number? 555-THE-QUEEN?"

He puts a hand on his hip and looks away, debating with
himself. Finally he sighs. "I might regret this, but if I give you
a phone number, do you promise not to sell it to the tabloids?"

"Cross my heart."

"Give me your phone."

I do, but it's raining so hard now that he moves under a nearby
awning to program a number. The rain has driven the crowds
under umbrellas and inside shops, but I catch myself worrying
if Theo will be able to make it back to the palace without being
spotted.

I mentally drag myself back to reality. It's not as if this fancy
rich boy needs saving—and if he did, I'm not the girl for the
job. I'm just trying to get home.

He hands my phone back with a grim smile.

"Is this the Queen's direct line, or . . ."

He rolls his eyes. "Goodbye, Ms. Wheeler. It was good to
meet you at the end of the world."

"You mean the World's End?"

"You'll see." He tips his head once and disappears into a sea
of umbrellas.

When he's gone, I test weight on the ankle I've been favoring
and wince as it pulses with pain. Gritting my teeth, I hobble into
the crowd and walk in the opposite direction from the prince.
Rain pummels me and I'm soaked through in a matter of seconds.

Girls with plans don't need saving, I tell myself as I limp across wet pavement.

My current plan? *Get the hell home.* My foot slips out from under me and my ankle turns again. I screw my eyes shut against the pain and bite my lip, refusing to cry.

Girls with plans don't need saving. I don't need princes or fate or destiny, and I sure as hell don't need the hazy golden memory of our kiss. Thinking about it is pointless. I shut it out—refusing to let my brain bask in that warmth. By the time I finally reach the Tube station, I'm not sure I didn't make the whole thing up.

I find an empty seat on the train and cross my bad ankle over my knee to give it some relief. The air is humid and sticky, but I'm just relieved to be out of the rain. The walk here was so slow and painful that I couldn't think about much else, but now worry begins to creep around the edges of my pain. Somehow it's almost two o'clock. Being with the prince dropped me into a time warp; I had no idea it was so late, and I should have been at the airport ages ago. The security line alone could take an hour or more. I chew on my thumbnail, panic rising in my chest. I need a distraction.

I type out a text to Brooke. You'll never believe what just happened. My fingers hover over the send button as I do time zone math and realize it's only 8:00 A.M. back home. I lock my phone without sending the text because I don't want to be the one to wake her. Now that Brooke's home from college for the summer, I can't seem to do anything right. It's like no matter what I do, she only sees me as the annoying little sister. I've got my fingers crossed that following in her footsteps at college will make her take me seriously.

The train screeches to a stop at the next station and a woman's voice coolly announces, *"Charing Cross."* The doors slide open, bringing in a waft of grease, dust, and urine. A handful of passengers exit and more get on, including a bearded white man in several layers of clothing holding an old beat-up duffel bag. He grabs the pole in front of me, fixes his eyes blankly on the front of the train car, and announces, "We'll all be dead in eight days." His voice is eerily calm.

My stomach tightens as I glance at his bag for, I don't know—a weapon or a Bible or a tip jar. Maybe this is a performance? He receives a few curious looks, but most of the passengers ignore him.

"I said we'll be dead in eight days." He's not so calm anymore. "All of us! Poof! Gone!" he says in a raised voice.

I shift uneasily in my seat.

"You can't be talking like that, mate," another man says. Murmurs of agreement follow.

"See for yourself, eh. Look at your phones!" the man shouts back. We *all* avoid his gaze after that. The train car turns into a game of who can ignore him the hardest.

"He's not batting on a full wicket, is he?" an old woman with a floral hijab next to me says under her breath. I smile weakly and check the time again, but it only makes me feel worse. I close my eyes and think of deep-dish pizza and non-frizzy hair. Stealing Brooke's clothes and listening to Dad and my little brother, Cedar, play their acoustic guitars before I fall asleep. The way Mom smooths my hair off my forehead and kisses me good night, every night. I slip my headphones in and cue up my "chill out" playlist, hoping it will dispel some of the dread in my veins. I turn the volume up loud enough to drown everything else out, but I don't take my eyes off the electronic board displaying the upcoming stops.

It's nearly 3:00 P.M. by the time the train finally makes it to Heathrow. I'm first in line at the car doors and I squeeze out onto the platform before they're fully open. I ignore the throb in my ankle and run until I have cell service. I call Naomi, mentally kicking myself for not calling earlier and telling her I was on my way. It rings half a dozen times before sending me to voicemail. I call Mrs. Kerr next and the same thing happens. My stomach drops. The plane is probably already boarding.

I sprint through the nearly five-mile-long airport on a bad ankle. Fortunately, my terminal is close-ish to the train station. Unfortunately, close-ish isn't the same thing as close and time isn't on my side. Neither are the crowds. The airport feels extra congested as I push my way toward security. I stop short when I arrive; the line is Disneyland-long. Tears spring into my eyes.

"My flight leaves in twenty minutes," I tell the agent checking tickets and IDs. "I'm with a group for school. I can't miss it."

"Are you a minor?"

"Not technically—"

"'Technically' is the only thing that matters. Get in line. We're moving as quickly as we can," she tells me in a rehearsed voice.

The line is desperately, painfully slow. In ten minutes, I move ten feet.

I feel the time tick in my bones, until an airport clock hits 3:00 P.M.

"I'm missing my flight," I say to no one. The last item on my itinerary, and the only achievable part of my plan, gone in an instant. All because I met a prince.

In front of me, a Black woman turns around, her eyes full of sympathy. "You're not the only one. Everything's a mess today and it's only going to get a whole lot worse." She gestures to the thick crowd of people, and for the first time since I arrived I pay attention to my surroundings.

The airport is barely controlled chaos, like a pot of water just before it boils over. Around me is a crush of people pushing and running while others scream or cry into their phones. Even freakier is the number of people *praying*. In public.

A suffocating, sinking, falling, drowning feeling fills my lungs.

If there's anything you need in the next eight days—let me know. The prince's posh accent echoes in my head. Those were his exact words. *Eight days.* I thought it was a joke, but then there was that man on the train. *We'll all be dead in eight days.*

It's too much to be a coincidence. I look up at the woman and register the fear mixed with the sympathy in her expression. "What's happening in eight days?"

She tilts her head, surprised that I don't already know. "The end of the world."

CHAPTER 4

Next Monday, a fourteen-mile-wide comet is going to hit Earth. Probably somewhere in the Pacific Ocean, not that it matters much, because a comet that size is an Apocalyptic Event.

The news leaked overnight, spreading like wildfire. Top-secret classified documents were uploaded to WikiLeaks. For a couple of hours, no one knew whether it was a hoax or not. And then NASA confirmed the story in an official press conference this morning. After the initial impact causes the sky to rain fire, dust and debris will fill the atmosphere, blocking out all sunlight and plunging Earth into an impact winter. Nothing will survive.

Within minutes, every news outlet in the world picked up the story. Eight days from now, the world is going to end, and if I can't find another flight home, I'll never see my family again.

My hands are shaking so badly, I can barely hold my phone to call my parents. I try Mom first. The call doesn't go through. I dial my dad's number next, and the phone won't even ring. My heart beats frantically in my chest and my phone slips from my trembling fingers.

"It's not working."

The woman who told me about the comet bends to pick up my dropped phone. "The cell towers are overloaded. I haven't been able to make or receive phone calls since I got here either, but texts work."

I pull up my messages to text my family . . . but I have no idea what to say. What is there to say in a situation like this?

I cry through the rest of the security line.

By the time my body and my bag have been scanned for weapons and explosives, Flight 3745 is cruising over the Atlantic. I've sent every member of my family a text message telling them I love them. I also tell Mom that I missed my flight and that my phone isn't accepting calls.

Mom responds immediately.

> I love you too, Birdie. Don't make yourself sick with stress. The only thing you need to worry about is getting on the next flight home. Go to the help desk and explain what happened. They'll rebook your flight. Use the emergency credit card I gave you.

Mom Mode: activated. She's superwoman in a crisis, never losing her cool when the house floods or the stove catches on fire or one of her new assistants screws up trial exhibits. I'd like to think I take after her in *this* way, at least. Once, when I was babysitting Cedar, he fell out of a tree and cracked his head open on a porch step. Seconds later the back of his shirt was stained bright red. I should have panicked; I was only twelve and knew how freaked out Cedar gets by the sight of blood. But

I didn't see how panicking would help anything, so I pressed an old towel to his head and calmly walked to the neighbor's house for help. That's what Mom is doing now; my entire world is bleeding out and she's pressing a towel to the wound.

Instead of panicking about the world ending, she's given me a way to fix it.

The line at the help desk is twice as long as at security. I shouldn't be surprised; it's an apocalypse. Everyone needs help.

"I missed my flight home. I need to get to Chicago," I quietly tell the harried man at the counter. He looks up in surprise. The surrounding chaos has reached a fever pitch. The giant building is filled with an energy so frantic, I'd swear it could detonate a bomb. For the last hour, almost every customer he's dealt with has been yelling or crying or swearing. In contrast, my voice is flat, my body numb. I can't even feel the pain in my ankle anymore. Every thought in my brain has shut off, with one exception.

Get home.

For the rest of my life, this will be the only plan that matters. And I'm nothing if not good with a plan. If I don't get home, I won't see my family before a giant fireball destroys all life on Earth. I refuse to let that be an option. The man at the counter books me the last empty seat on a 5:00 P.M. flight to New York.

"Thank you so much."

"Good luck." He nods. It reminds me of Prince Theo saying the same thing. Difference is, I think the prince meant it.

"You too. Have a good day." I wince, realizing how silly that is to say. "Sorry. Reflex."

Every seat in the terminal is filled, but I find a small unoccupied space on the floor across from the departures board. I hug my knees to my chest and memorize my new flight number. *Flight 4215. London to New York.* 4215 is my new favorite number.

I update Mom and ignore the other incoming texts on my phone. Sorry, Steven from sixth-grade science camp. If I don't respond to the generic *Happy Thanksgiving!* texts that you spam to everyone in your contacts list year after year, what makes you think I'm going to hit reply when my hours are literally numbered?

An hour later the flight's status changes from *ON TIME* to a bright red *CANCELLED*. It's the first in a line of dominoes. Flight after flight flashes across the board.

CANCELLED

CANCELLED

DELAYED

CANCELLED

It's harder to stay calm as my emotional numbness begins to wear off. I fight to keep my breathing steady as I hug my bag against my chest and limp back to the outrageous line at the help desk. Ninety minutes later I'm booked on a new flight, to Boston, leaving at 9:00 P.M.

After that, I try to take a nap in the corner on the floor, but when I close my eyes, I see flaming fireballs smashing into my family's redbrick home. Wally hides in the corner, whimpering and wondering why his mama never came home.

Two hours later my name is called over the loudspeaker. "Will Wren Wheeler please approach the information desk?"

I bypass the line and go straight to the front. "I'm Wren Wheeler."

The nice man from before is gone. In his place is a giant white man with his hair in pigtail braids, his lumpy biceps adorned with faded tattoos. I crane my neck to look up at him while he scowls down from his tower. "You've been bumped from the flight to Boston," he grunts.

"No!" I can sense a cracking at the edges of my sanity. The plan is failing. I'm so hungry and dizzy and tired and scared and sad that I could drop. "I *have* to go home!"

"Blimey, first time today I've heard that," he says.

"I'm an American on study abroad and I missed my flight. None of my family is here. *Please*," I beg, tears running down my cheeks.

As I suspected, this giant of a man could not care less. "Your seat has been given to a minor. We're giving them priority, since, ya know . . ."

"The world's ending?" I say bitterly.

"Bang on."

"But I'm basically a minor! I still live at home! I graduated from high school last month. I'm not old enough to drink or rent a car or—"

"The kid is thirteen," he barks. "We can't not send a thirteen-year-old home."

I shut up. Cedar is fourteen. If it were him, I'd want the airline to do the same. But it's *not* Cedar. And because of this kid, I might never see Cedar or Brooke or my mom or dad ever again. I can't worry about this random kid I don't know when literally everyone I love is about to die.

"What am I supposed to do?" I ask.

"That's the question, innit?" he says. I start to cry again, and he grimaces. "Wait for the next flight."

"And when that one is canceled?"

He shrugs, looking uncomfortable. At first I think it's because he feels bad for me. Just as quickly, I realize it's because he doesn't. He can't. He's already spoken to hundreds of people today, and if he cared about all of us, he'd break. Everyone *he* loves is going to die too.

"Tell me the truth—am I going to make it home?"

"I don't know." He sighs. "It's all going to pot. Flight attendants are quitting. Pilots aren't showing up for work. Thirty percent of tonight's flights have already been canceled. Who knows what tomorrow will look like?"

"Are *you* coming in tomorrow?" I ask.

He blinks. "Depends on what happens tonight. There's still a chance that NASA could announce they were wrong, and we'll all be fine."

"And if not?"

"Would you want to spend your last week alive at the airport?"

The breath rushes out of me. I wouldn't, and I don't.

"It's not all bad news," he says. "On this side of the pond, you *are* old enough to drink."

It's not much of a silver lining, nor does it make me feel better, but I'm not getting anything else from him. "Thanks for your help. Have a nice—" I catch myself, shrugging once before I walk away. Polite society has not prepared me for how to speak to someone during the apocalypse. I wonder vaguely if there's royal protocol for this. If selfies aren't allowed, I can't imagine small talk about impending doom is either.

I walk to the end of the terminal and stare out at the tarmac. Impossibly, boarding groups are still being called. Planes are coming and going. For now, at least, life is still chugging along.

My phone beeps in my pocket. I push aside a pair of sunglasses to retrieve it. The texts are stacking up—mostly from my mom and Naomi. I open the messages from Naomi. The first few ask where the hell I am and tell me that the van is leaving for the airport. By the time she boarded the plane without me, her messages had devolved into a wall of broken heart emojis and *I'm sorry*s. I should respond. Tell her I don't blame her for leaving without me.

Instead I leave her on read and open the newest messages from Mom.

Update?

Wren?

Did you get a flight?

She's fighting to hang on to Reassuring Mom Mode, but I can tell it's slipping. As much as she wants to save me, she can't do it from the other side of the Atlantic. I have to take matters into my own trembling hands.

I slide to the floor and sit with my back against the large windows and dial. For the first time all day my phone connects to a service tower and the call goes through. I never thought I'd be so happy to hear a telephone ring. And ring. And ring. By the fourth ring, my heart is hammering in my chest.

"Hello?" The voice is low. Male. Extremely British. Every muscle in my body goes taut with awareness.

"It's Wren. I need your help."

CHAPTER 5

"Ms. Wheeler? Shouldn't you be on a plane right now?" The prince's smooth cut-glass accent stirs something in my chest, reminding me that he is a very fancy person, and I am not. It occurs to me that there's likely protocol for this too, and I don't want to risk offending him before I ask for the mother of all favors.

"I don't know the rules for talking to you, but please picture me doing a curtsy, Your Royal—Your Honor—Your, um . . . Majesty?" I groan inwardly. *Nailed it.*

His silence lasts a beat too long. "How may I help you, Ms. Wheeler?"

"I missed my flight and I can't get another one."

"Ah . . ."

"You knew about the comet." I lean my head against the glass, pushing back my instinct to get angry. If I let myself feel mad at the prince, who knows what other emotions I'll have to deal with? Better to bury them all under a layer of laser focus and denial.

"Perks of being a royal," he says flatly. "American allies were alerted a few hours before the news broke."

"You could have warned me."

"It was a state secret. I don't even know you."

I take a deep breath. "Well, I'm cashing in on my favor. You said you'd help me, and I need help getting back to the States."

"I can't do that."

"Your mother is the Queen. You can do anything!"

He laughs. "I can't even walk down the street. When I offered that favor, I thought you'd ask for money or—or—I don't know. Something possible. I can't force the airline to put you on a flight."

"Don't you have a private jet?" I ask shamelessly. I've gone from refusing to let him hail a cab for me to demanding use of his private plane in less than a day.

He's silent for several seconds.

"You *do* have a jet. That's why you're not denying—"

"Hang on!" he orders, sounding so authoritative that I shut up. "I'm thinking."

His thinking takes forever. It eats up time I no longer have. "My phone is going to die and if this call is lost, I might not get another one through," I say finally.

"I have an idea," he says. "Where are you now?"

"Heathrow."

"There's a pub in Chiswick called the Bell & Crown. It's quiet. Meet me there in an hour."

I sigh at the idea of another train ride. At the sheer notion of moving at all. "I can't leave the airport unless you promise you have a way to get me home."

"I won't know that until I hang up the phone and make a call," he says tightly.

Part of me hates the idea of leaving the airport. A different, hungrier part of me needs to stuff something hot and salty in my mouth as soon as possible. We've officially entered "last meal" territory, and if I'm going to get buried under a layer of ash and debris, Pompeii style, future scientists will not find a twenty-five-dollar airport Impossible Burger in my stomach. I refuse.

"Will there be food?"

"Pubs traditionally serve food, yes."

"Fine." I sigh as my hollow stomach pangs. "You're buying." I hang up.

⚜   ⚜   ⚜

The journey to Chiswick is a blur of exhaustion, hunger, and aching pain. The only thing that keeps me moving is the promise of my first meal all day. I lose track of time as the Tube hums along the underground track, and it could be five minutes or an hour later that I drag my bad ankle up a set of cement steps and into a quiet neighborhood. A cool breeze rushes through the empty tree-lined street, causing dark leaves to dance against a purple twilight sky.

The neighborhood is filled with an eerie silence, windows lit behind every curtain. I can't help but wonder if the locals are locked inside, TV news on, bundled in apocalyptic anticipation. I pass old buildings, tall churches, and a small park where a lone pair of black Labrador retrievers wrestle over a Frisbee. I suddenly miss Wally so much, I can't breathe. My family will understand if I never come home, but Wally won't. He'll think I abandoned him. When I brought him home from the shelter, I promised he was going to his forever home and that I was his forever human.

At the end of the street lies the River Thames. Overlooking the riverbank is a small redbrick pub, and contrary to the prince's promise, it's anything but quiet. The locals aren't huddled inside their homes awaiting the apocalypse like I thought; they're all here, getting end-of-the-world wasted. HALF-PRICED DRINKS UNTIL THE COMET HITS boasts a handwritten sign taped to the window. I can't tell if it's a joke or not, and I have no idea why anyone would bother pouring drinks at a time like this. As much as I love my job at the shelter, there's not enough money in the world to bring me to work during my last week alive.

Crowds of rowdy drunks spill out the front doors and fill the sidewalks as a group of white-haired cane-wielding women hunch on the curb sharing an open bottle of liquor with two sobbing goth teenagers. Their emotion is palpable. If circumstances were wildly different, I'd want to take a picture of them. The frat party meets preemptive funeral vibe makes me wonder whether I'd be doing something similar if I were home now. I doubt it.

I pass the women, duck around a fistfight, and scan the crowd for the prince. Around me, raucous laughter mingles with shouting as patrons jockey for a table on the overflowing garden terrace. Standing near the low garden gate is a family of four, both daughters sobbing hysterically while their parents try to calm them, and it's this sight, more than anything else, that hits hard near my solar plexus. I'm struck with a mental image of Mom, Dad, Brooke, Cedar, and Wally huddled together. Instead of their usual bickering, Mom and Dad are comforting my siblings. Everyone is together without me, eating warm slices of the chocolate chip banana bread Mom always bakes during a crisis. My stomach hurts at the thought.

In the corner of the terrace, behind a loud group of red-faced men in suits, I spot a lone figure with his shoulders slumped and his head down. He's ditched the tweed cap for another baseball hat, but a telltale lock of blond hair brushes his collar. I skirt around the family and push through the gate, dodging a spilled beer, a thrown glass, and all thoughts of what I'd do with my last eight days if I were home. Now is not the time to get distracted by pesky, inconvenient emotions.

"We have very different definitions of the word 'quiet,'" I say as I slide into the chair across from him.

"The apocalypse effect. It turns out that certain death makes people want to get pissed," he says. I lean forward to hear him over the din.

"'Pissed' is 'drunk'?"

"Pissed, trollied, sloshed, blitzed, sozzled, buggered—all words to describe the fine people around us." As if on cue, a woman in sky-high heels and a miniskirt flips over the low gate and lands headfirst in a bush. *Now that'd be a good photo*. Half a dozen hands pull her out of the plant, and she emerges smiling and triumphant, despite the smears of mascara running down her cheeks.

"Why aren't *you* drinking?"

"Because I have a plan." He leans across the table, pinning me with his blue eyes. For the first time since our kiss, I allow myself to remember the starlight warmth of his lips on mine. If that was the last kiss I'll ever have, at least I went out on a high note. For the first time in hours, I can't help but grin. It's clearly the wrong move. Instead of returning my smile, the prince clears his throat and sits up, assuming a more formal position than the slouchy one I found him in. "I have a proposal for you, Ms. Wheeler. If I may?"

I don't love being called Ms. Wheeler by the guy I made out with, but I'm too hungry to correct him. "Food first. Plan second."

"They're taking orders at the bar. I'd offer to pay, but as you pointed out earlier, I'm essentially broke."

I open my wallet and slide a handful of bills across the table. Even that is exhausting. The idea of standing up again on my ankle makes me want to cry. I nod to the propped-open door and the dark outline of a beefy man behind the bar. "What is he even doing here? What's the motive for anyone to be at work at a time like this?"

"Where's the right place to be at a time like this?" Theo asks.

"With his family?"

"Maybe it's not that simple for everyone." There's a gravity to his tone that doesn't invite further questions, so I change the subject.

"How does the prince of England know about a quiet pub in Chiswick?" I ask. The question causes his lip to twitch. "What?"

"It's not important, but *technically* I'm the prince of Wales."

"Are you serious?"

"Rarely," he deadpans, surprising me with this unexpected flash of humor. Is it possible the prince is *fun* under all the pomp and circumstance? "But to answer your question, when you're as recognizable as I am, it's good to know places where you can hide. The food is decent too. Get yourself something to eat."

"I can't get up."

"Why not?"

"I screwed up my ankle when we jumped the fence. Adrenaline carried me this far, but please don't make me stand up again."

His eyebrows pinch together. "If you're too hurt to walk to the bar, my plan's never going to work."

"Why not?"

He scrubs a hand over his face. "It requires quite a lot of movement."

"Whatever it is, I'll make it work," I say. He eyes me skeptically. "I'm the girl who plans things. It's my whole brand. I'm great at follow-through."

"Remind me about that paper we burned this morning."

"You're meeting me on a bad day, but under normal circumstances, I'm the itinerary queen."

"These are not normal circumstances."

"I'll do it," I snap. "If it means going home to my family before the world is blown apart, I'll do it." I push myself to my feet to prove I'm up for the challenge. I take one step on my bad ankle and my knee buckles. I gasp in pain and grip the edge of the table. "I'll do it," I say again. Straightening and gritting my teeth, I limp toward the bar.

"Oh bollocks." The prince sighs, startling me with his casualness for the second time tonight. "Sit down."

I let out a breath of relief and drop back into my seat. When he drops the formality, he's not so bad. "Thank you. And I'm a vegetarian, by the way!" I call after him as he moves through the pub with his head down. He waits at the bar for a long time, which is when I realize the beefy man we were talking about is the *only* employee I've seen since I sat down. By the time the prince returns with two glasses of pop and a basket of "chips," I'm ravenous. I shove three fries into my mouth at once, and then three more. I quickly scarf down the entire basket on my own, and savor the last few bites with my eyes closed.

When I look at the prince again, he's staring at me intently.

Snap. I take a mental picture just in case I never get to take a real one. "Tell me your plan."

He clasps his hands together on the table and takes a deep breath. "I grew up spending summer holidays at a home on an island in the Aegean sea," he begins.

Something about the phrase "summer holidays" in a British accent is too much for me to ignore. "See, we are very different people, because I spent my summers watching *Family Feud* reruns."

"Do you want to hear my plan or not?" He looks annoyed.

"Sorry, please continue, Your . . . Royalty? Royalness?"

He rolls his eyes. "If and when the comet hits, I don't want to be Theodore, Prince of Wales. After nineteen years of doing exactly what the Firm has told me to do, when they told me to do it, I want out. I don't want to die surrounded by expectations I'll never meet. All my happiest memories live in Santorini. It's where I want to be when it ends." His eyes fill with an emotion I recognize as the same one swelling in my chest. We both just want to go home.

"Does your family know where you are?"

He shakes his head. "They can't find out."

"Why not?"

"Royals fleeing the country doesn't inspire a 'Keep Calm and Carry On' attitude. If I leave, it'll look dodgy."

"We're in the middle of an apocalypse. Does it matter what looks good?"

"Always." His matter-of-fact reply can't hide the sadness in his eyes.

"What does this have to do with me?"

"The compound in Santorini has a private jet with a full-time pilot. She'll fly you to the States as soon as we arrive."

"Shut up!" My outburst catches him by surprise. His eyebrows rise in what could be amusement or annoyance. "When do we leave? How do we get to the island? Is there a smaller plane that will take us?"

"No. We'll have to take public transport. If everything is up and running the way it should be, it'll take three days."

It's impossible not to think of the crush of frantic bodies at the airport, all those canceled flights. "What are the chances of that?"

"Not good, I'd wager," he says seriously. I wilt. "The sooner we leave, the better."

Even if everything goes perfectly, three days plus a transatlantic flight is more than half the time I have left. "It'll take too long."

He winces. "I wish there were another way."

"I don't understand. This is *your* country. Don't you have a jet *here*?"

"My family does, but I can't ask for their help. If they find out, they'll order me back to the palace immediately."

"But—but—" I sputter, my mind spinning for another way. "Can't the pilot pick us up here? Fly you to the island and fly me home?"

"That's not possible."

"Why not?"

The prince clenches his jaw. "Do you know how private airfare works?"

I shrink in my seat. "No."

"Planes need charters. People will be looking for me, and they'll be watching the skies. If our plane moves from Santorini tonight, they will be tracking it, and they'll be on the tarmac before it lands. They'll drag me off in handcuffs," he says, which strikes me as a smidge dramatic, but what do I know? His face softens. "I need your help as much as you need mine."

"How could I possibly help you? I don't have anything but this bag." I hold up my ratty backpack as proof. I don't even have clean underwear.

He leans back in his seat, appraising me. "You were a decent bodyguard today. If we travel together, I can keep a low profile while you arrange tickets, food, lodging—"

"I can't waste my last days on Earth traipsing across Europe with you. You said you owed me a favor! The flight is the favor."

"You spent an hour or so running from the paparazzi with me, and in return, you're asking me to charter a private jet to fly you halfway around the world during the apocalypse. Does that sound like a reasonable exchange?"

My stomach sours in embarrassment. I know I'm asking for too much, but what other choice do I have? "What if I say no?"

"Then neither of us gets what we want."

I think of the airport and how it was on the verge of shutting down mere hours after NASA's announcement. Public transportation won't run smoothly for long, meaning every hour that passes lowers my chances of seeing my family again. And here I have the future king volunteering to help me get home. It's the best offer I'm going to get.

My heart beats a hummingbird rhythm. It'd be one thing if he were just some random guy, but I can barely wrap my mind around traveling with the *prince*. "If we do this, I can't be worried about royal protocol or what's appropriate or official titles—"

"I don't care about any of that," he insists.

"What do I call you? I don't even know!"

"Theo," he says with such force that I have no choice but to believe him.

"Do you really want to spend your last days on Earth cosplaying as a normal guy, sleeping on trains and eating gas station food? I bet the food at the palace is incredible."

"I *am* a normal guy! I've spent my entire life pretending to be a guy worthy of being bowed to, and I'm done. There's no food worth dying a hypocrite," he says.

Spoken like someone who's never had a deep-dish pizza, if you ask me.

He blows out a breath and makes his final request. "I'm leaving tonight. Do we have a deal, Ms. Wheeler?"

I unzip my backpack and retrieve a notebook and pen. I slide it across the table to him. "All right, *Theo*." His eyes flick up to me when I call him that, but I can't read the expression in them. Despite his insistence, I'm not sure if he can handle "normal guy" treatment. "Make me an itinerary."

He picks up the pen and begins to write. I watch him scrawl the names of cities we'll travel through, including preferred and backup methods of transportation. *Not too shabby for a prince.* He estimates how far we'll travel per day, although the timeline isn't as precise as I'd like. I cut him some slack on that—call it the apocalypse statute—but I don't let him off the hook when he scribbles the name *Stella?* next to the city of Milan.

"What's with this?" I point to the question mark next to the name.

"She's a friend. We might be able to crash at her place for a few hours if we need sleep."

I crane my neck to read the rest of the schedule. I tell myself I'm looking for holes in the plan or possible setbacks, but the fact is, I can't even begin to guess how realistic this itinerary is. I don't know anything about traveling through Europe even when the world's *not* ending. I have to trust Theo on this one, which I'm inclined to do because these are his last days on Earth *too*. He wouldn't risk spending them all with some random American girl for nothing. Why would he bother?

A warning bell goes off in my head, reminding me of one glaring reason why boys lie to girls.

"I'm not going to sleep with you," I say.

"What?" He chokes on his drink, spraying pop across the table. "Why would you say that?"

"Just because I forced you to kiss me doesn't mean I want to do it again, or that I'll do more than that." I cross my arms over my chest. It wouldn't be the first time I kissed a guy and he assumed it'd go further. I'd rather not have to kick Theo in the balls if I can help it.

"Stop saying that. You didn't *force* me to snog you. You helped me out of a rough spot. I have no assumptions or expectations."

"Good," I say. An awkward beat passes. With that out of the way, there's only one thing left to say. "Okay."

"Okay?"

"I'll do it."

"We need to take the train to Paris. If we leave now—"

"Not yet." I hold up my hands to stop him. "First we need to get a room at the inn I passed on my way here."

He frowns and holds up his hands. "I thought we just agreed *not* to have a repeat of this morning."

I roll my eyes. "Not that." I swipe the itinerary away from him and squeeze my own agenda item at the top.

"'Disguise prince?'" He reads my upside-down handwriting and raises an eyebrow. "Should I be afraid?"

I glance up at him. The ends of his gravity-defying blond hair swoop up around the edges of his hat. A dead giveaway.

He'll never make it out of the country looking like this. *Snap.* One more mental picture before I commit a crime against the crown. "Depends on how attached you are to your hair, Goldilocks."

CHAPTER 6

We exit the restaurant terrace through the gate and stand on the abandoned sidewalk, neither of us daring to speak first. This feels like the moment we decide what happens next for us, like everything we said back at the table was nothing more than two kids playing pretend. If I go with Theo now, I'm irrevocably tying my future to his. And that's not *fate*. It's a decision I could still take back.

But I already know I won't. The schedule has been made; the plan is in motion.

I follow Theo's gaze up to the inky sky. "It's strange that I can't see it," he says.

"The comet?" I nod. It seems like something so destructive should be visible.

"No, my hair," he says, removing his hat so he can push his fingers through his golden locks. "I want to see it one last time before you butcher it." He smiles wryly. I *think* he's kidding.

"Did you hear that?" I ask as a breeze whistles across the water, scattering goose bumps along my arms.

"Hear what?"

"The sound of my sympathy catapulting itself off the planet. Say goodbye to your yellow hair."

"Yellow?"

"If mine is brown, yours is yellow." I cross my arms in anticipation of his rebuttal, but I'm distracted by my phone buzzing. I swear, if it's Steven from science camp again, I'm going to crunch him up like the rat bones in the owl pellets we dissected. I pull out my phone and see a text from Mom, begging for an update. "I have to call my family before my mother freaks out and contacts the embassy, and then I'll go to the drugstore to grab makeover supplies. You can go ahead to the inn."

Theo makes a pained face as he stares at the Thames over my shoulder.

"What's wrong?"

He scuffs the toe of his boot against the pavement. "I can't."

"Can't or won't? Should, maybe, but shorn't," I say. It's a nonsensical joke from *The Office* that my dad used to quote when I complained about putting away my laundry or bringing Mom a snack while she worked. Thinking of Dad is a bee sting to the heart. Eighteen years of memories threaten to close in over my head, hundreds of Saturdays when I was woken up by him blasting the *Hamilton* soundtrack only to have him thrust a mop into my hands as I stumbled out of bed. Dad gets high off Saturday chores, and if I think about that fact for another second, I'm going to pass out. I strangle the memory into submission and stuff it into a little box deep in my chest. Drowning myself in memories now won't help me get home.

"I can't get a room without you," he says. "That's the whole reason you're here, innit?"

"Oh, it is, innit?" I mock him in a bad British accent to cover the fact that I forgot my end of the bargain. It's not that I blame him for being, well, *him*, it's just that I truly cannot think of a more inconvenient travel partner. "Hang on, I still have your glasses." I fish around in my jacket pocket for his sunglasses and hand them over. These streets are ghostly, and with the hat and glasses, Theo shouldn't have a problem making it to the inn unnoticed. "Worst-case scenario, someone sees you and thinks you're an idiot for wearing sunglasses at night."

"Worst-case scenario, I end up walking behind a woman and she thinks I'm Jack the Ripper."

"As long as she doesn't think you're a *royal* serial killer, you're golden. Unlike your hair. Which is yellow. Like straw." Nerves make me ramble. I spin and walk toward the river, where I sit on a bench overlooking the water and tuck my legs up under me. I dial Mom's number.

"Wren? Are you okay? What's going on? Do you have a flight yet?" I'm surprised to hear Brooke's worried voice instead of Mom's, and it transports me home in a blink. I close my eyes and imagine her sitting on her messy bed in shorts, a tank top, and fuzzy slipper socks because her feet are always cold.

"Hey, Brooke." My eyes well with tears. Just because our relationship isn't perfect doesn't mean I miss her any less.

"Where are you? Mom's been trying to call, but she couldn't get through. The cell towers are overloaded and she's freaking out—"

"Where is she?"

"In the bathroom. She'll be out in a minute."

"How's Cedar?"

"Quiet. He's been sitting in front of the news all day, but he hasn't said a word," she says.

"Play Nintendo with him."

"I don't know how to play his video games."

"Even better. He hates losing."

"He gets that from you, you know."

"I know." We're both quiet, the silence filled with a million unspoken fears. "How's Dad?"

"Focusing all his attention on Cedar and me to avoid talking to Mom."

"Typical."

"I know."

A familiar quiet stretches between us. All I ever wanted was a big sister to turn to when Mom and Dad were fighting, but Brooke and I never had that. It hurts in ways I can't describe to think we never will.

Brooke breaks the silence. "Dad took Cedar to the store to get him away from the TV and to stock up on whatever they could find. Every store has been ransacked. Hoosier Mama Pie was looted. The windows were smashed open, everything was trashed, and someone took a shit in the glass display case on top of a coconut cream pie."

"Ew! Why would someone do that?"

"Because they can get away with it? I don't know. There's this TikTok trend telling people to post a video of something they'd never do if the world weren't ending."

"But coconut cream is my favorite."

"A fact the looters strangely did not take into account," she says. And then: "Dad will be furious he missed your call."

"Tell him I love him. Cedar too."

"I will."

"Hey, how's Wally?"

"He's—"

"Wren? Is that you?" Mom's voice replaces Brooke's. "Do you have a flight?" My bones ache with homesickness at the sound of her voice.

"Not yet. I'll find a way home, though, I promise. I'll stay at the airport until I do." Lying is the easiest way to keep her from worrying. I'm not sure her heart will survive if she knows I've left the airport to travel across Europe with some boy I don't know—royal or not.

"Don't give up, Birdie."

"I won't." My eyes well with tears. If I don't hang up now, I might never bring myself to do it. "I've got to go."

"Wait—"

"I'll see you soon. I love you all." It's only after I've hung up that I realize I forgot to ask Brooke how *she's* doing. My fingers itch to call back, but instead I hug my phone to my chest and promise myself that I'll get to see them all again.

"You all right?" Theo's voice comes from behind the bench.

Startled, I turn, grateful that I didn't let myself break down. Not yet. I carefully put the phone call in the box of things I won't let myself think about, along with Dad and his soundtracks and his mop. "What are you doing here? I thought you were going to the inn?"

"I can't."

"I told you that you'll be fine with the hat and the glasses—"

"I'm not worried about making it to the inn. But, erm, they'll ask for my ID," he says apologetically.

"So much for royal perks," I mutter.

"Are you going to say that every time my royal status is an inconvenience?"

"Would you blame me if I did?"

"Truthfully, I'd blame you if you didn't."

"Good. We're on the same page, then. You can wait here while I go to the drugstore."

"What am I supposed to do?"

"I don't know. Stare at the river and contemplate our imminent death." I hitch my backpack higher on my shoulders.

"Can I come with you?"

"I need a few minutes alone to think and just . . . wrap my head around everything. I won't be long. Where's the nearest drugstore?"

A pained expression falls across Theo's features. "I can't in good conscience let you walk alone at night. It's not proper."

"I'll be fine."

He glances meaningfully at the out-of-control crowd outside the pub. "I'm not willing to let my bodyguard take any chances. I'll never make it to Santorini without you."

"What kind of bodyguard am I if *you* have to protect *me*?"

"What would you like me to call you? My chaperone?"

"No."

"Attendant?"

"Try again."

"Companion? Entourage? Escort?"

"Stop." I hold up my hands. "These are getting worse and we're wasting time. Call it what it is. I'm your babysitter. Now, where are we going?"

He points across the street from the pub to a large drugstore. "What do we do if it's abandoned?" he asks.

"I guess we just . . ." I trail off. I've never shoplifted in my life. Then again, if society as we know it is falling apart—what even are rules? I take a breath, steeling myself to do whatever it takes to return home. *That's* the new plan. "We'll take what we need."

He winces. "I would prefer to do this without breaking any laws."

"You and me both, but that might be impossible."

He glances up and down the street, his expression wary.

"Are you sure you're up for this 'normal guy' experience, because if not—"

"I am," he insists. "Let's go."

I lead the way across the street. A glass door slides open as we approach the store, revealing a middle-aged white man sitting behind the checkout counter with his head bent over his phone. "If you're here to film a TikTok, bugger off," he growls.

"We're not," Theo says, looking horrified by the suggestion.

"We're out of bottled water and booze. There's a little food left."

I glance beyond the cashier to the ransacked aisles. Dread steals into my lungs, making it a struggle to breathe. It's hard to believe the world is ending until you come face-to-face with empty grocery store shelves, but that's when survival mode kicks into gear. This is high-key zombie apocalypse shit. I want to buy every edible thing in this store and hoard it, in case we have to barter stale bags of "crisps" for clean drinking water and transportation.

"Do we need food? We should bring food, right? We can't be stopping in restaurants all the time. It'll slow us down too much and you'll get noticed and—"

The back of Theo's hand accidentally brushes mine. "We can't carry much, but we should grab what we can." The brush of his skin combined with the soothing lilt of his accent snaps me back to the task at hand.

"We can survive three weeks without food, three days without water, three minutes without air," I say.

"What are you going on about? We're going to be taking a few trains and a ferryboat. We won't be without *air*."

"You never know."

He rolls his eyes. "I'll get food, you get whatever it is you need to make me look different. Meet me at the register in ten minutes."

Theo heads for the plundered aisles while I limp toward medical supplies. I pop the top off a bottle of painkillers and dry swallow two pills before putting the bottle in my basket. I also grab bandages to wrap around my ankle and a few other first aid supplies, just in case. Next I make my way to the hair care aisle. My plan was to shave Theo's head—his golden locks are a dead giveaway that not even a hat can hide. When I can't find hair clippers, I stop in front of a shelf of boxed hair dye. The names on the boxes are familiar to me: Champagne Fizz, Honeydip, Black Licorice. Last summer I helped Naomi dip-dye the bottom of her hair hot pink. When she asked if I wanted to dye mine too, I said no without really considering it. Maybe she had a point about my itineraries.

I pick the darkest brown on the shelf and throw it in my basket. Theo was born with literally every advantage, including his starlight hair. He doesn't get to go from golden to Chocolate Cherry or Cinnamon Stick. He can live with generic Brown. After a brief second of hesitation, I throw in a box of bleach. *Just in case I mess up,* I rationalize.

At the front of the store, Theo is piling a mountain of snacks next to the register. I only recognize half of them.

"I thought we can't carry much?" I raise my eyebrows as he moves to stand behind me, probably hoping to avoid attracting unwanted attention from the cashier. I pick up a bag of something called Hula Hoops and inspect the picture on the front. "At least we won't be hungry when the comet hits," I say.

The man at the counter scoffs loudly as he rings up our purchases. "You sheeple are all the same."

"Um . . . what?"

"Sheeple. People being led like sheep by the mainstream media."

"Being led where? To do what?" I glance around the store in case I'm missing the government officials with tranq darts and handcuffs.

"To be ruled by fear. To panic-buy all the bottled water in the store. And for what?"

"Because there's a massive comet hurtling toward Earth?"

He shakes his head. "I don't believe in the comet."

Behind me, Theo stifles a laugh. "Science is real whether you believe in it or not, mate," he quips. I elbow him in the ribs to make him shut up. If we get caught because he's arguing with a conspiracy theorist, I'm going to kill him.

"I guess we'll see who's laughing a week from now," the cashier says smugly, like *we're* the idiots. He finishes ringing up our purchases and I pay for them with a portion of my spending money. The man sighs like forcing him to count cash is a bigger personal inconvenience than the comet he doesn't "believe in."

We leave the store and continue up the block until we find the old inn I passed earlier, with its redbrick walls, gable roof, and white window frames. I tug on the front door, but it's locked.

"What do we do?" Theo asks.

Echoes of the last hour replay in my mind. A new plan. Less regimented. More spontaneous. *Whatever it takes.*

"Smash a window?" I'm shocked by how quickly the answer comes to me, but if I'm going to get home, there's no doing this halfway. I push onto my tiptoes to look in at the dark lobby beyond the window. I try to yank it open.

"Absolutely not!" Theo insists. "My mum is supposed to release a statement today calling for order and peace. She wants essential workers to keep doing their jobs, and for everyone else to follow the law. My family would be eviscerated by the media if I were caught vandalizing an inn."

"If we're all going to be dead in eight days, what does it matter?"

"I'm not agreeing with the conspiracy theorist, but they conceivably could have done the maths wrong. Or maybe they're right, but they find a way to fix it. It's not over until it's over, and I refuse to go on a breaking-and-entering rampage if we don't have to."

I tug the window again. "I hate to be the bearer of bad news, but I think we have to." I'm glancing around the street for a suitable rock when the front door opens and a young Black couple steps out into the night.

"Wait!" I shout, and leap to grab the edge of the door before it can shut behind them. "Are you staying here? Is there anyone inside?"

"Dunno about the rooms, but the staff all skived off this afternoon," the woman says. "Told us to leave our room key in a drawer behind the desk in case the comet doesn't hit or whatever and they need to come back."

"Perfect. Let's go." I turn to Theo, but he's gone. I hurry inside and find the key to room 108 behind the desk. When I go back outside, the couple is gone, and I find the prince skulking in the shadows of a nearby oak tree.

Our room has a cockroach-brown carpet that would send Dad on a ten-minute diatribe about germs in hotels while Mom rolled her eyes. We drop our backpacks onto the bed and I turn the bag of supplies upside down on the floral comforter.

"What'd you get me?" Theo eyes the pile with interest.

"Brown."

He picks up the hair dye and turns it over in his hands. "This says Dark Chocolate."

I grab the box back, annoyed again. Even the way he says "chocolate" is fancy. I should have been referring to my drab hair as "chocolate" this whole time.

"It's brown. Let's go."

"Do your ankle first," he says, nodding to the bandages.

I hesitate at the threshold of the bathroom. The pills have kicked in, taking the edge off the pain, and I'd rather ignore it for now. I'm scared of what I'll see when I take off my shoe. "Hair first. I'll wrap my ankle while we're waiting for the dye to set."

He joins me in the tiny bathroom, the box of bleach in his large hands. "What's this for?"

"Nothing." I snatch the box and toss it in the empty trash can, embarrassed by my impulse purchase. Theo sits cross-legged on the counter beside the sink, leaning against the mirror while he watches me slide on plastic gloves and mix hair dye solution in a small squirt bottle. His gaze is weighty, his stare making me feel hot everywhere. His body is so big that he takes up most of the confined space. My hands bump against his knee while I work, first on accident, and then on purpose. Theo doesn't readjust his position.

"Is the bleach for you?"

Heat rushes to my cheeks. "No!"

He quirks an eyebrow, looking wildly unconvinced.

"Sit here while I apply this." I motion through the doorway to the edge of the bathtub. Theo takes off his hat and tosses it onto the counter before untangling his long legs and moving to the tub. He sits facing me and I stand in the gap between his knees, my breath going shallow. We haven't been this close since I yanked his body against mine and demanded a kiss. My chest flushes with inconvenient heat. Our proximity combined with the toxic smell of the dye makes my head spin. I blink to clear away the distracting thoughts.

"Erm, what are you waiting for?"

"I just—my ankle. I need to sit." It's not a lie. Even with the slight numbness brought on by the painkillers, my ankle still throbs.

He slides down into the bathtub and sits cross-legged, staring up at me through long lashes. "Now you can sit too."

I sink to the edge of the tub, keeping my knees glued together and angled away from him. "Thanks." I swallow, still hesitant to ruin his perfect hair. "I'm sorry in advance if I screw this up," I say.

"I don't care," he says, too quickly.

"I know a lie when I hear one, but I appreciate the effort." I give the bottle one last shake and squirt a dark stream of hair dye onto Prince Theo's head. Naomi will never forgive me. If our friendship survives her abandoning me in London, it won't survive me ruining Theo's golden hair. With my free hand, I massage the dye evenly into his scalp. I get another unwanted fluttery feeling low in my stomach and bite my lip to keep from sinking too far into any ridiculous fairy-tale fantasies. "Turn around," I say in an embarrassingly husky voice.

He does, and I finish massaging the dye into the back of his head.

When I'm done, it's a herculean effort to stop touching him. "Now we wait. In twenty minutes, you'll be a whole different person."

"Fingers crossed," he says.

I stand and back up as far as the small space will allow to give myself breathing room.

"Tell me the truth about the bleach," he says. I shrug, but then tears spring up, burning the backs of my eyes. I blink up at the ceiling, begging them to go away. We do not have time for this unwanted emotion.

"C'mon," he prods gently. His tone is warm and dangerously sincere. I glance up to see him staring through me with those laser-blue eyes. *Snap.* Another mental picture. I'll take one every time he shatters my preconceived notion of spoiled royalty.

I let out a shaky breath. "I've never had any hair style or color other than this one." I gesture to my frizzy brown locks. "When I saw this box on the shelf, I realized this would be my last opportunity—*ever.* I don't know, I just . . ." I clear the emotion out of my throat. "It sounds stupid. I'm about to die and I'm thinking about my hair, of all things."

"It's not stupid. Let's bleach it."

"I don't know . . ."

"What do you have to lose?"

Nothing that won't be gone in eight days, anyway. When I crack a smile, he leaps up and pulls the bleach out of the trash can. Two minutes later we've switched positions; I'm in the bathtub and he stands behind me, distributing the bleach through my long hair with surprisingly gentle fingers. I sink back against the tub and close my eyes as he massages my scalp. My mind drifts into a stupor until he crouches next to me and his breath fans against my neck. Every relaxed muscle in my body pulls tight, newly aware of his closeness.

The alarm on my phone chimes, snapping us back to reality and alerting Theo that it's time to rinse his hair.

Back in the room, I sit on the bed and bring my ankle up to rest in front of me. I slowly untie my shoelaces, gingerly pull my sock off, and *Oh. Oh no.* This swollen black-and-purple monstrosity is not a human ankle. It's a horror-movie prop. I tear open the bandage packaging with my teeth, close my eyes, and wrap the appendage with all the precision of a toddler wrapping a Christmas gift. *Ta-da!* Out of sight, out of mind. Crisis averted.

I prop my foot on a stack of pillows (it's what my mom would make me do) and wait for the prince of Wales to get out of the shower. (What a sentence!) I'm stuck in the UK on the eve of the apocalypse, but away from the eerie, empty convenience store, the impending disaster feels ten shades of fake. The prince showering on the other side of a thin wall, however, is as hyperreal as the steam curling from under the bathroom door. It's just unhinged enough that I can dwell on it without having a full-blown panic attack.

The shower shuts off and my heart hammers in my chest. I hold my breath and wait. By the time the bathroom door creaks open, I'm once again dizzy with nerves and my scalp burns like someone snuck chili peppers into the hair bleach.

Theo steps into the room wearing the same jeans and button-down shirt he wore earlier, now slightly damp. He's towel-drying his hair and I'm so impatient to see my handiwork that I almost burst.

"Tension, suspense, etc." I motion for him to get on with the reveal.

He drops the towel to the floor. My heart somersaults after it.

CHAPTER 7

Theo's eyes widen as he takes in my horror. "That bad?"

Worse. He looks like a living, breathing fairy tale. A curtain of dark hair falls across his forehead like smooth, stupid chocolate. If I had clippers, I'd shave his head right down the middle. It's not fair that a boy who was born with every advantage also looks incredible with a discount-box dye job.

"It's fine," I wheeze.

He spins and inspects himself in the mirror, self-consciously running a hand through his towel-dried hair as he slumps over the counter.

"It's fine," I say again. "It's brown. Everyone looks good with brown hair."

"You flatter me, Ms. Wheeler," he says dryly.

"You *have* to stop calling me that. If you're Theo, I'm Wren. Regular guy, remember?"

He clears his throat. "Are you ready to rinse your hair?"

"Considering my scalp low-key feels like it's on fire, absolutely."

"Why didn't you say anything?"

"Because everything else in my life feels worse." I swing my legs over the side of the bed and test my weight on my wrapped ankle. *Nope. Bad, bad Wren.* My knee buckles and Theo reaches to steady me. His hand touches my elbow and I discover fifty thousand undetected nerve endings. My heart beats cartoonishly fast.

"You all right?"

"Fine!" I shake off his grip and order myself to keep it together. I don't have the time to be attracted to the prince. Every second I waste thinking about the heat of his hand on my skin is one second that I'll never get back. I hobble to the bathroom, where I lock the door behind me and quickly strip down. I rinse my hair first, keeping my eyes closed while I do because I'm too nervous to look at the new color. I reach around the shower curtain for a towel and am wrapping it tightly around me when a clump of hair slips over my shoulder.

It's bright orange.

I scream and lunge at the trash can. It clatters loudly to the floor as I pull out the dye bottle I used for Theo. Stupid, handsome royal Theo and his beautiful brown hair. The bottle is almost completely empty. Why did I use all the dye? If I'd been less thorough, he'd look worse, and I'd stand half a chance of fixing my Cheeto-bright strands. Win-win. With the amount of brown dye that's left, I'll never be able to fix my hair.

The bathroom door handle jiggles. "Wren? You all right?"

"I'm fine!"

"Is it your ankle? Did you fall?"

"I'm coming out!" I swing open the door, nudge him to the side, and limp to the mirror. I physically *feel* the moment he registers my hair because his shock vibrates through my chest like an atom bomb. Theo rubs a hand over his mouth, his expression glaringly neutral. He hates it. It's obvious. He can't even bring himself to lie about it.

I sweep my hair over one shoulder. Clumps of streaky orange cling to my wet skin as small rivers of water trail across my collarbone. I bite my lip to keep from crying. It's so far from the icy blond I imagined that it doesn't even belong on the same color wheel. Whatever this shade is, it does not occur in nature.

"It'll look better once it's dry," he says unconvincingly. I push past him and lock myself in the bathroom, where I change back into my day-old clothes, pull a comb through my tangles, and blast my hair with the dryer attached to the wall.

When I look in the mirror again, my hair is not only streaky and orange, but thanks to the crappy blow-dryer and the London humidity, the ends puff out from my head in the shape of a triangle. It's worse. Way, way worse.

"Can I look?" Theo asks.

"Might as well." I open the door to let him in.

He cocks his head to the side to inspect the disaster and then opens his mouth. Nothing comes out. I get the sense he's weighing his words carefully.

"I look like Gritty," I moan.

"What's a Gritty?" Hearing the name of the Philadelphia Flyers' mascot in his posh British accent makes me feel insane.

"Of course you don't know who Gritty is. Your life is a castle-dwelling fantasy."

"What's your point?"

"You go to fancy balls and shit. You have servants—real, actual people whose job it is to brush your hair and make your bed! The closest I'll ever come to that is my dog, who licks the crumbs off the floor when I drop food."

"I still don't understand what this has to do with your hair."

"You look like, well, like a *prince*. I look like a cartoon character!" I burst into tears.

Theo watches me warily. "It's literally not that bad." He drops the second syllable from the word: *lit-reli*.

A dam breaks in my chest, releasing all the tears and emotions I've been avoiding today. "I'm going to die with frizzy orange hair!" I wail. It sounds so trivial and absurd that laughter mingles with my tears.

"I'm going to die without playing Monopoly. Or eating shellfish," he muses, which only makes me laugh harder.

"You're better off. Monopoly sucks. *I'm* going to die without ever having gone to law school."

"You want to be a lawyer?"

"Not really, but I want to prove I can." It's the first time I've ever admitted that out loud. I feel somehow lighter, as if that truth has been weighing me down for months. I wonder if another admission will feel even better. "I'd rather be a photographer, but that's a waste of an expensive college degree."

Theo surveys me. "Why do you need an expensive college degree?"

I cannot say *because my sister has one*. And yet it's all that comes to mind. "Honestly? I don't have a clue."

Theo smiles. "I want food. Do you want food?" He retrieves a handful of packaged snacks from the bedroom and drops them onto the floor in front of us. He picks a bag of Hula Hoops and I choose something called pickled onion Monster Munch.

"Why can't you eat shellfish?" I ask.

"Mum's rule. The chance of food poisoning or allergies is too high."

"No offense, but your family is weird," I say as I open the

bag and place a paw-shaped snack on my tongue. An intense burst of vinegar fills my mouth.

Theo takes a deep breath, like he's steeling himself to speak.

"Spit it out," I prompt.

"I shouldn't. It's not . . ." He trails off. I can tell he's struggling with something, maybe with the same thing he's been fighting since we met. Like he can't decide whether he's His Royal Highness, Prince of Wales, a person who is never, ever allowed to step a toe out of line . . . or if he's just Theo.

"Normal guy," I remind him.

"Right." He blows out a breath and stares up at the ceiling. "Blimey. All right, here goes nothing. I'm going to die a virgin."

I choke on Monster Munch. Whatever I expected him to say, it wasn't that.

"I guess you can't relate?" he asks.

"Not technically?"

Theo laughs and glances into his bag of Hula Hoops. He picks out five loops and places one on the end of each finger. "Can I ask you a question about sex?"

Now *I'm* the one feeling awkward as hell. "I'm not sure if we know each other well enough for that."

"A comet is going to blow the Earth apart in a week. Does it matter how well we know each other?"

"When you put it that way, does anything matter?"

"I'm serious. Let's decide not to care. I would love to skip the we-don't-know-each-other awkwardness and jump to the part where we're friends."

We hold eye contact long enough that heat sizzles through my veins. *Friends*. Sure, I can do that. I can be friends with the version of Theo that is sitting on a bathroom floor with corn chips on his fingers.

"Deal."

"Yeah?" A smile lights up Theo's face, and because I don't want him getting too cocky, I make an amendment.

"Why not? You seem decent enough to be friends with for a few days."

He places the Hula Hoop–ed hand over his heart. "A high compliment."

"You've spent your entire life being told you were 'born special.' I doubt you need more compliments." I throw a monster paw at him and I'm pleasantly surprised when he catches it in his open mouth. "What's your question?"

He shifts uncomfortably, the lightness gone from his eyes. "We don't have to—"

"Ask your question, Your Highness," I say. His mouth forms a tight line. "Teasing is a sign of my friendship," I quickly add.

He pushes a lock of hair off his forehead, only for it to slide perfectly back into place. "What's it like?"

"It?"

He clears his throat. "Sex."

My eyebrows skyrocket.

Theo's cheeks turn pink, which he covers up with a glower. "Is it so embarrassing that I don't know?"

"No! Not at all!" I rush to cover my surprise. "It *is* hard to believe that a bunch of rich boys living away from their parents at a fancy private school don't talk about sex. Especially if they all look like you." I flush. Naomi told me about Theo's years spent at boarding school, followed by a year at "university." British speak for college. There's no way he's been completely sheltered.

"Right, everyone brags about shagging girls, but no one talks about anything serious."

A smile plays at the edge of my lips. Theo looks so earnest; I can't help but love this moment. I want to draw it out and make it last forever. I bite my lip and look up at him from under my lashes. "Do I look like I teach sex ed for princes?"

"Now you're taking the piss out of me." He rolls his eyes.

"Sorry," I say quickly. I feel a twinge of guilt for teasing him when he's being vulnerable. I guess that means it's my turn to share.

"To answer your question, his name was Daniel. We dated for five months."

"That actually *doesn't* answer my question, just so we're clear. How'd you know he was the one?"

I consider this. The truth is, I gave the decision to sleep with my senior-year boyfriend an obsessive amount of thought. It wasn't just a decision; it was a plan. Perfectly designed and executed. "My experience was . . ." The word "great" is on the tip of my tongue. *Perfect. Magical.* I don't remember exactly which words I used for Naomi after the fact, but I do remember the bitter taste of dishonesty on my tongue. Even when I was trying so hard to convince myself that the experience was everything I wanted, I couldn't quite believe the lie. "It was anticlimactic."

Theo's eyes widen knowingly. "Oh."

My stomach squirms as I register what he thinks I'm saying. "I don't mean that in a literal sense!" (Not *only* in a literal sense, anyway.) "I built that moment up so much in my head. I planned it out perfectly to avoid all the clichés. I didn't want to do it after senior prom or in the back of his car or fifteen minutes before curfew, you know?"

"You wanted it to be special."

"Yeah." Now *my* face flames as I stare down at my hands. This conversation is spinning wildly out of control, but I can't shake the feeling that there will be something worthwhile at the end of it. I don't want to spend my last week on Earth with a stranger, and I don't want to die with secrets. Being honest is the fastest way to make Theo my friend.

"I planned it for a long weekend when his parents were out of town. He picked me up at my house and we ordered takeout from our favorite restaurant." I wore a matching bra and underwear under my favorite sundress, but I don't tell Theo that. "Everything went according to schedule."

"Hmmm."

"That was a very judgmental 'hmm.'"

"Sorry, but you had a schedule?" His accent turns the word "schedule" to the despicably condescending *shed-ule*.

Defensiveness prickles along my spine. "So what?"

"Nothing. I guess I just imagined my first time would be rather spontaneous."

"I'm not a spontaneous person. Look what happens when I try." I gesture to my hair.

There's not much else to say about my first time. It was over so quickly, I barely knew it had happened. It didn't hurt like I was warned it might. I didn't cry after it was over, either. I just felt deflated, and then confused. He wanted to talk about it, but I couldn't bring myself to have *that* awkward conversation. I threw my energy into ignoring the weird and disappointing feelings I had, assuming that was the path toward restoring the status quo between us. I tried so very hard to be normal! Happy! Fine!

He broke up with me two weeks later, claiming I "emotionally ghosted" him. Naomi called him every mean name from Urban Dictionary, but the joke was on him because I was able to let go of that relationship relatively unscathed. My avoidance issues might have broken us up, but it also saved me from months of heartbreak.

Theo wrinkles his brow. "Were you in love with him?"

"Geez, you're not pulling any punches with these questions." I steel myself for more vulnerability. "My best friend, Naomi, says when you love someone, you just *know*. With Daniel, it never felt that simple," I say. Without thinking, I add, "I've never heard my parents say they love each other. That's weird, right?" I surprise myself with this admission. I'm not used to saying the quiet parts out loud.

"Penny says—"

"Who's Penny?"

"My nanny. My second mum, really. She raised me." He looks pained, and my heart aches for him, and it aches for me, and it aches for everyone on Earth who is missing someone they love today. "She says that when you love someone, you can't help but shout it from the highest rooftop and whisper it in the stillest dark."

"That's beautiful. Was she talking about her partner?"

"No. She's never been married. Never wanted to be, either. But she loves my siblings and me like that." He furiously blinks back tears. "Blimey, I didn't think this would make me so emotional. She says love is an unstoppable force—like a hurricane or a . . . a comet." He glances up at me, so I know that *he* knows exactly what he said.

"That's dark."

He shoots me a sardonic smile. "That's love."

"Love: it will blow your whole world apart!"

Theo laughs softly. "Can you believe it's a *comet* that's going to kill us?"

"I had my money on climate change."

"Same."

We lapse into contemplative silence. The truth is, I don't know anything about love. Between Brooke swearing off dating guys or girls until she graduates and my parents acting like frustrated business partners, it's no wonder my first relationship was a disaster.

I crumple the purple chip bag and toss it into the trash. "We need to leave if we're going to catch the train to France tonight."

"Tonight's trains are full. We leave first thing in the morning. Oh, and I used your phone to buy tickets while you were in the shower."

"Where's yours?"

He reaches into the trash can and pulls out the shattered remains of his phone. "Now we can't be tracked."

Shivers race up my arms. "Have they been tracking you this whole time?"

"Doubt it. They'd have found us already. With all the chaos today, I'm sure my absence went unnoticed for a while."

"But you've been missing since that birthday troop thing yesterday."

He smothers a grin at my royal incompetence. "Nah, I was in the palace yesterday. I just couldn't bring myself to get out of bed." He sees my confusion and adds, "It was a shit week."

"You knew about the comet for an entire week?"

"No . . ." he hedges. "I was just feeling overwhelmed by everything."

"Everything meaning . . . ?"

"Life?" He rubs a hand over the back of his neck self-consciously.

"You felt this way even before news of the comet broke?"

"My mum . . ." He sighs. "Blimey, I'm just . . . It's hard to explain without sounding like a wanker."

"You can tell me," I say, suddenly realizing how much I want him to.

He wrestles with this before saying, "Someday."

Disappointment courses through me. It's hard to take a "someday" promise seriously at a time like this.

"So you left today?"

"And met a cheeky American girl who bossed me around a bit." He winks. "Still didn't have a bloody clue what I was doing. It wasn't until you rang that this trip became possible."

"Because I'm your bodyguard."

"Well, yeah, but also because you're quick on your feet. I get a bit dim when I'm overwhelmed. I start to drown in my own thoughts. You're not like that."

I bite my lip as my body temperature warms, appreciating the compliment a little too much. *I have to get out of here.* I won't survive the night.

"We can't stay here. We have to stick to the schedule."

"Global crisis. Flexible schedule. That's the deal, innit?"

I groan and scrub my hands over my face. This does not bode well for our trip. "So what now?"

"We sleep."

I glance over his shoulder at the single bed in the room. A loaded silence settles over us.

"I'll take the floor," he clarifies quickly.

My dad is paranoid about the germs on hotel floors. When we'd go on road trips, he'd freak out if we let our pillows or stuffed animals touch the carpet. He'd have an aneurysm if he saw where we're sitting right now. I almost choke on the memories. "My dad brought a black light to a hotel once and ran it over the carpet. The thing lit up like Vegas at night."

Theo shudders. "Thanks for that. Now I'm thrilled to be sleeping on the floor." His eyes rove over the water-stained ceiling to the dingy peeling wallpaper as I toss him two of the three pancake-flat pillows. It's only fair, considering. He drops them onto the floor and lies down before reaching up to pull the floral duvet cover off the bed.

"My dad says hotels don't wash those between guests."

"I'll take my chances," he grumbles.

I slip under the tightly tucked sheets and imagine I'm a mummy in a sarcophagus. It was fun when I was a kid. It's less funny now. When I reach to turn the lamp off, I make eye contact with Theo. It's a mistake. My heart hiccups. We stare at each other in heated silence for a beat too long before I pull the chain on the lamp and plunge the room into darkness.

I toss and turn for a few minutes, trying to get comfortable, but it'll never happen when I'm dressed like this.

"I'm taking my pants off," I say.

"Why are you telling me that?"

"Turn over! Face the window."

"Why?"

I peek over the edge of the bed. My eyes have adjusted to the dark enough to see him staring up at me. "What if I have to get up in the middle of the night to use the bathroom?"

"Let me see if I have this right. You get an entire bed to yourself while *I* must sleep fully clothed, on the floor, under a semen-covered duvet. And now you're asking me to sleep with my back to the room just in case you need to use the loo in the middle of the night, and I happen to wake up and see you in your knickers?"

"Correct."

"And you think *I'm* pampered?"

I blink down at him. His answering sigh is loud and long-suffering as he stuffs a pillow between his knees and turns away from me.

"Thank you." I wiggle out of my jeans and toss them onto the floor at the foot of the bed before realizing that I have to wear them again tomorrow. Dad would have a heart attack.

Dad. I try to picture his face, but all I can see are his wire-rimmed glasses and his fingers strumming softly on his guitar. A tornado of sadness tears through my chest.

"I want to see my family again before I die," I whisper into the dark.

"I know," Theo whispers back. It's impossible to miss the soft regret in his voice.

CHAPTER 8

DATE: MONDAY, JUNE 13
LOCATION: LONDON, ENGLAND

ITINERARY: TUBE FROM CHISWICK TO ST. PANCRAS
   INTERNATIONAL STATION
MORNING: EUROSTAR TO PARIS
AFTERNOON: TGV FROM PARIS TO MILAN
DAYS UNTIL THE COMET HITS: SEVEN

Where are all these people going?" Theo angles his body
toward mine to avoid being seen. His voice is still raspy
with sleep, even though we've been awake for almost an hour.
We woke up before sunrise and packed our stuff quietly, stepping around each other as we got ready to leave. We waited so
long for a train to arrive at the nearest Tube station that we'd
nearly lost hope it was still running, but eventually one came.
Now we're in a crowded train car on our way to St. Pancras,
where we'll board the Eurostar to Paris.

I glance up from our itinerary to observe our fellow passengers. There's an anxious, agitated energy in the air and there are more commuters than I would have expected, leading me to believe that the Queen's plea to keep essential workers from abandoning their jobs worked, at least for now. Across from us is an Indian girl with dark brown hair styled in the same space buns Naomi always wears. This time when I feel a twinge in my rib cage, it's not jealousy, but guilt for failing to respond to Naomi's many, many texts. It's not that I don't want to talk, but it's hard to know what to say. Things were uncomfortable between us this past week, and I'm bad with uncomfortable. Ten disastrous days as roommates nearly screwed up three years of being best friends.

"Can I take your picture?" I can't help but ask the girl.

"I guess?" She shrugs as I pull out my camera and loop the strap around my neck.

"Pretend I'm not here," I say as she relaxes back into her seat. I snap the photo and then zoom in on her bright eyes, wondering why she doesn't look as worried as everyone else on the train. "Where are you going?"

"To meet my best friend." Her mouth splits into a smile. "I've been in love with her for ages, and I've never been brave enough to say it."

"Badass," Theo whispers, low enough so only I hear it.

"Oh wow. Good luck." Tears sting my eyes, and I'm suddenly stupidly jealous of the fact that she gets to choose exactly what she wants to do with her remaining time. If I weren't on this trip, I'd have options. I could vault directly over the awkward gulf between us, and Naomi and I could spend an entire day reading in Millennium Park while we share a bag of Garrett Popcorn. Regret threatens to overwhelm me, making me feel awkward and restless in my own skin.

"Looks like we dodged that bullet," I whisper back to Theo.

"What do you mean?"

"We've never been in love, which means we don't have to waste our last days trapped in sappy conversations."

"You think telling someone you love them is sappy?"

In an attempt not to be seen by the other passengers, his face has veered too close to mine. My heart speeds up. I'm not prepared to have this conversation on public transport, so I opt for sarcasm. "Have you ever seen an episode of *The Bachelor*?"

"Do you always reach for a joke when you feel uncomfortable?"

"Yes," I deadpan, hoping he lets the topic die. He doesn't respond. I pull away and refocus on updating our itinerary.

Next stop: the Eurostar. The high-speed underwater journey should take exactly two hours and sixteen minutes. Our train leaves at 8:00 A.M., but we lose an hour crossing into France, so we'll arrive in Paris by 11:16 A.M.

"What are you writing?" Theo asks.

"I'm fixing the itinerary. It's too vague. If we get to Paris shortly after eleven o'clock, do you think we'll be able to get on a TGV by noon, or is that cutting it too close? Are we going to have to go through security again?"

"We'll need to stop for food and essentials in Paris first. I already purchased 4:00 P.M. tickets for the TGV. The website had a big disclaimer saying all travel depends on staffing levels, but we'll stay as long as it takes."

"What essentials?"

Theo ticks them off on his fingers. "Toothbrush, deodorant, underwear."

"I just want to get on a plane home as soon as possible."

"We'll be fast. I'd say we could shop at St. Pancras, but I doubt we'll have time. The queues will be long," he says.

I get flashbacks to the never-ending lines of bad news at the airport and my stomach spins like a top. "What if we can't get out of London?"

Theo eyes me warily and tips his head back against the cold window. "Don't ask me questions like that. If I fall into that mindset, I'll never be able to claw my way out." There's a note of rawness to his words that surprises me.

I scoot one seat away from him and bring my ankle up to rest in the space between us. The pain this morning was worse than yesterday. I sat immobile on the edge of the hotel bed, unable to put any weight on it, terrified that my journey would end before it even started. But then Theo brought me the bottle of painkillers and a cup of water from the sink. And when he offered to support my weight as I hobbled across the room for the first time, I silently accepted, a joke about him not being able to travel without a babysitter on the tip of my tongue. But when I looked up into his sleep-softened features, he appeared so kind and unassuming that I swallowed the sarcastic remark. He was being helpful for no other reason than because I needed help. My ankle loosened up on the walk to the station and now my pain level is down to distracting but tolerable.

"Can I take your picture?" I lift my camera to my eye and focus on what I can see of Theo's face under the hat and sunglasses.

"All right," he says dully. Through the viewfinder, I see a shadow briefly cross his face before he breaks into a frozen smile. *Snap*. I glance at the picture in the viewfinder and hate it. It looks as fake as the ones in Naomi's magazine.

"No Queen's wave?"

"Sorry, we can do another one." He smooths the front of his wrinkled button-down and takes off his hat to run his hands through his night-kissed hair. "Hat on or off?" he asks seriously.

My stomach sours. "Never mind." We pass the rest of the train ride in silence, and I spend one of the last mornings of my life sneaking glances at Theo, wishing everything were different.

⚜ ⚜ ⚜

We're stepping off the train when a man crashes into me from behind and sends me sprawling across the damp platform.

"Bloody wanker," Theo growls as he reaches to help me up. His hand curls firmly around my scraped palm, and he doesn't let go the whole walk to the railway station. The frantic crush of bodies reminds me too much of the airport. Seeing other people panicked and crying only makes me want to panic and cry, which I absolutely do not have time for. I pull my hoodie up to protect my hair from frizzing too badly in the misty rain, and I'm so distracted trying to remain as small and composed as possible that I nearly miss the towering Victorian Gothic building that is St. Pancras. When I finally look up, my breath catches. The massive building is a fortress of rain-soaked red bricks that looks like it's stood here since the beginning of time, and it's impossible to imagine that even a fourteen-mile-wide comet could disturb it.

"Does Dracula live here?" I ask as we pass through a yawning archway into a cavernous hall of glass and steel.

"Worse," Theo says. "Security queues." He points to the
floor below, which is filled wall to wall with bodies.

We board a glass elevator and stand at the back, facing the
doors as people pour in after us. A white man with a handsome
vampire face and an expensive-looking business suit winks at
me. I step closer to Theo. The last woman in the elevator has
long jet-black hair and a suede miniskirt that looks impossibly
chic, and not like she's wearing it for the second day in a row.
What a concept!

As we're getting out on the lower level, the man in the suit
shoulders his way to the front. When he passes the woman in
the skirt, he slips his hand up and squeezes her ass. She gasps.
He chuckles to himself and walks away.

Theo and I turn to face each other in shock. "What do we
do?" he asks.

My stomach churns. "I don't know." The woman peels off
into the line heading to Brussels. It feels slimy and wrong to
keep going, but I'm not sure what a couple of teenagers on the
run could do to help her.

As we're swallowed up into the massive crowd, Theo's agi-
tation only grows.

"Are you okay?" I ask.

"Not really," he says tightly as an unidentified flying ob-
ject narrowly misses his head. I look up to see a drone soaring
above the crowd. As it dips low over a couple in front of us, a
man swings his bag in the air and sends it crashing to the floor.
Theo and I quickly sidestep the scene before a fight breaks out.

I glance around the crowded terminal, searching for a security guard or a police officer to step in, but the nearest guard is several yards away. The expression on his face is one of deep regret. I wouldn't be surprised if he walked out now and never returned. Every person in here is another piece of kindling added to the fire, and I'm worried the entire building is one wrong word from going up in flames.

The barest thread of silver lining is that absolutely no one gives a damn about Theo and me. "You're blending in fine," I say.

"For now," he says. "I'll need to show my passport when we go through security." He stands on his tiptoes to get a better look at the person checking IDs and passports at the front of the line. I can't see through the crowd, but whatever he sees makes his face pale. "This might have been a mistake, but I couldn't think of anything else. No matter how we travel, we're not getting into France without showing our passports."

"Everyone here is worried about themselves. What's the worst that could happen if someone recognizes you?" I lean in close to whisper. The woman in front of us is wearing earbuds, but I don't want to take any chances. I glance over my shoulder and my body revolts. Standing only a few feet behind me is the asshole who stuck his hand up the woman's skirt. I feel sick looking at him.

"Have you checked the news this morning?" Theo whispers back.

"Just the comet stuff. It's still coming, we're all going to die, etcetera. Why? What's going on?" We shuffle forward, drawing closer to the moment of truth.

"My mother released another statement this morning. She urged everyone to stay calm and keep hope alive—"

"A literal 'Keep Calm and Carry On' message?"

"Exactly. She also offered a reward for anyone who has information about my whereabouts."

I stop short. "You didn't think to tell me that? It's hard enough to hide you from the public when there *isn't* a bounty on your head!"

"I was afraid you'd take her up on it," he says plainly.

"What could she possibly offer me that is worth anything? Money won't matter by this time next week. All I want is to go home, and she can't—" I cut myself off, the truth colliding with me like a wrecking ball. I stop breathing and put my hand on Theo's arm to hold him in place. "If I turn you in, would she fly me home?"

He holds my gaze. "What would you do if I said yes?"

The line moves forward, carrying us along with it. If the Queen didn't explicitly announce what the reward was, imaginations will run wild. I think back to the cashier at the drugstore. He'd rather believe in a conspiracy theory than face his own death. It's not a leap to think that British citizens will place all their faith in the Queen. If they find the crown prince, they might think she can grant them some way to survive the comet.

My heart speeds into a sprint. There's no way in hell anyone in this building will let Theo out of the country. "Our entire fate rests on whether or not the person at the front of this line wants to be noticed by the Queen?"

He nods as he spins the black band on his finger.

"Well—what's the plan? What do we do?" I hiss loudly. A man two places in front of us turns around to glare. I glare right back.

"Go without me," Theo says finally.

"Don't say that."

"No, listen." He leans close. I can feel his breath tickling my ear the same way it did when we kissed in that alley. "If I get caught, you go to Santorini without me. Follow the itinerary."

"Like hell." I grind the words out, suddenly furious and frantic. "This plan doesn't work without you. I don't know where I am! And what happened to your noble concern for my safety? You wouldn't let me walk to a drugstore alone, but crossing four countries where I don't speak the language and men can act without consequence is fine?" Brooke has told me too many horror stories about boys who slipped drugs into drinks at parties and got away with it. And that's when the world *wasn't* ending.

"That was selfishness, not chivalry. Can't get to Greece without my bodyguard," Theo says blandly. I'm not sure I believe him.

"And I can't get home without my prince." Theo's eyes flicker at my choice of words. I inch closer. "What if your pilot sees a teenage girl unaccompanied by royalty and decides, 'Nah, I'd rather not waste my last days flying her home'? What then?"

Theo turns the color of Sheetrock. "I don't know."

I bite my lip, hating myself for what I'm about to say, but I have to do something to keep him from giving up. "I know you've relied on your name and your title and your wealth to get you through life, but guess what—you gave that up. You don't want to be the trapped prince who's bossed around by 'the Firm'? *Prove it.*"

As intended, I've hit him directly where it hurts. His body goes rigid as he scans the crowd. "You can cause a diversion while I sneak onto the train," he says.

I soften. "Good. I can work with that." We stare at each other a long moment and I can still see the caution in his eyes. He's terrified of going home, and I don't know why.

If I turn him in, I never will.

I think back to my plane ride with Naomi when I told her that royalty is a human rights violation. I don't even know what made me say that—I was just trying to get under her skin more than anything—but I can sense the panic radiating off Theo in waves. This is bigger than a fight with his family. Maybe he is pampered and spoiled, but if he's willing to grant me my last wish, how can I deny him the same thing? Underneath the title, he's just a boy.

I put together pieces of a plan in my mind. The clock ticks closer and closer to our departure time, my nerves mounting with each step forward. When the woman in front of us steps up to have her passport inspected, Theo grabs my hand and squeezes it once before dropping it quickly. The contact is brief but electric. A rush of warmth spreads through my veins. The woman moves on and it's our turn.

"You go first," I whisper to Theo. He slowly walks to the desk as I kneel to tie my shoe. He withdraws his passport with a shaky hand, looking petrified.

As I bend, the contents of my unzipped backpack spill everywhere and the pervert behind me rushes to help, quickly kneeling in front of me. He takes a generous peek down the front of my shirt. "Let me help you with that, love."

I look into his eyes once.

"Don't touch me!" I screech, and slap him as hard as I can.

CHAPTER 9

A dozen pairs of eyes swivel toward me. I only care about one of them. The woman with her hand out to check Theo's passport gapes at the scene I'm creating.

"I didn't touch you!" The man with the vampire face holds his hands up in a gesture of innocence.

"This is for the woman in the elevator, and every other woman you've ever touched without her consent," I whisper. His jaw goes slack as I put my hands on his shoulders and shove him hard away from me. "I said don't touch me, you pervert!"

"Stay away from me, you bloody trollop!" he snarls. A police officer in a funny hat breaks through the frenzied crowd.

"What happened here, ma'am?"

I glance behind me to the checkpoint. Theo is gone. A thrill of triumph rolls through me. Plan complete.

I turn away from Vampire Face toward the officer. "He assaulted me."

"I never touched her!"

"I don't get paid enough to be doing this during the apocalypse," the officer mutters. "Do you want to press charges?

Because I've got to be honest, only fifteen percent of the force came to work this morning, so it might take a while to complete the paperwork."

"I'd like to never see his face again." I spit the words with as much venom as I can muster. "But no, all I want to do right now is get on the eight o'clock to Paris. It leaves in five minutes." The officer stands by as I show my passport to the woman at security. She waves me through.

"Thank you for being here," I tell her. "I'm just trying to make it home, and if people like you weren't here, it'd be impossible."

"I have a kid trying to make it home too," she whispers. "Better hurry up if you want to make the eight o'clock," she says. And then, to the groper, "You *won't* be making the eight o'clock."

He seethes at me, waves of fury radiating off him. I smile as brightly as I can. "I hope you have one sock that falls down inside your shoe every day for the rest of your miserable life."

"You talk too loud," he says. He turns to the police officer holding him at bay. "She's traveling with the missing prince. He's wearing sunglasses and an American baseball hat. I'd bet that he just snuck past security and is sitting on the train to Paris right now."

My chest turns to ice. My heart is frozen, my lungs won't work. People in the crowd mutter and shake their heads and I'm falling. I take a deep, sawing breath. I don't know what to do.

"Off his rocker," someone whispers, and that's when I realize they're shaking their heads at Vampire Face. *He* sounds delusional and bitter—not me.

"I'm telling the truth," he insists, a vein bulging in his forehead.

I turn to the police officer. "If I miss this train, I won't make it home to see my family before the comet hits. Can I leave?"

"I don't give a toss," the officer says, throwing his hands in the air.

"If I'm right, we can split the reward for finding the prince!" the groper insists.

The officer sighs and motions for me to show him my passport and ticket. "We'll call ahead to the Gare du Nord and have her questioned and the train searched in Paris."

I spin away and run onto the train seconds before the doors slide shut behind me and a cool British voice announces our departure over the speakers. The train looks modern and sleek, but there are piles of trash everywhere. I kick aside several empty beer bottles and make my way through the brightly lit cars to the very back, where Theo's sitting in a plush window seat. I collapse next to him, still buzzing from what just happened, and run my hands across the gray fabric of our seats. "No semen here," I say.

Theo gapes at me. "Pardon?"

"The inn? Last night? Never mind." My soul physically leaves my body, abandoning me for less awkward pastures. "Stress makes me say weird things."

"Well, that was a bloody brilliant idea. You sold it perfectly. I hope that arsehole gets the book thrown at him."

"He won't." I rub my eyes with the heels of my shaking hands. "He'll probably be given a knighthood."

"Why?"

"He heard us talking in line and knows who you are. He told them you dodged passport check." I lean my head back on the seat and groan. What a complete and utter disaster. Someone could be on their way right now to haul Theo away in handcuffs. My skin suddenly feels too tight. "You have to hide. Take your stuff to the bathroom and lock the door. Don't come out for anything unless I tell you to."

Theo narrows his eyes. "Should we do a secret knock, do you think?"

"Just go." I hoist his bag from the floor and shove it into his arms. "I know you were kidding, but my knock will be three fast, two slow."

"Not how I thought I'd be entering the mile-high club."

"That doesn't even make sense."

"Stress makes me say weird things," he deadpans.

Not twenty seconds after the bathroom door shuts behind him, an announcement blares over the speakers. "Please have your passports ready to be checked by a Eurostar employee. We apologize for the inconvenience, but it is a matter of utmost urgency. We would like to stress that none of our passengers are in any danger. Thank you."

My chest tightens unbearably. On the floor is Theo's passport: a glaring neon sign of my guilt. I could hide it in my backpack, but what if they search my stuff? What if I can't stop myself from laughing at their billy clubs and funny hats as they haul me away to British jail for questioning?

I stand abruptly, leaving my bag and passport on the empty chair next to me. The girl across the aisle from me is wearing bulky headphones, absorbed in a sketchbook. Perfect. I step into the aisle and trip over her outstretched ankle. As we make eye contact, I clutch my hands to my stomach and groan loudly. She slides one side of the headphones off her ear and wrinkles her nose.

"Can I help you?"

I moan again and place a hand over my mouth. She grimaces as she draws away from me.

"I think I ate something bad. I might be in there for a while." I nod to the bathroom. She turns her disgusted expression away and fixes her headphones.

At the bathroom door, I do three fast knocks followed by two slow ones. The door swings open.

"That was fast. Did they already check your passport?" Theo slings his backpack over his shoulder. I block the doorway with my body.

"No, I panicked. I'm coming in here with you." I push him back into the cramped room, tucking myself inside and locking us in. There's barely enough room to breathe. Theo and I seem to realize this at the same time. My breath quickens as my eyes fall to his lips. I strangle the memory into submission. I will not allow myself to lust after Theo in a room used for pooping. Whatever the underwater equivalent of the mile-high club is (twenty-thousand-leagues-under-the-sea . . . club?), I refuse to join it.

"You dropped this, by the way." I hand him his passport and hop onto the small counter. One butt cheek dips into the sink, the other hangs off the edge. My orange hair frizzes out from my shoulders and panic sweat drips down my back. I've never felt sexier in my whole entire life. "We'll stay here until the train stops in Paris." I cross one knee over the other, nice and casual.

Theo's eyes bug out of his head. "For two hours?"

"And sixteen minutes. You'd know that if you made a proper itinerary."

He drops the toilet lid down with his foot and sinks onto it. My ankle rests against his knee, which again, I'm not opposed to in theory. It's the cramped bathroom that I can't get on board with. I rest my feet on the wall across from me, creating a bridge over Theo's legs. He stretches his legs out and places his feet flat against the door.

"You might be surprised to know that before I met you, I didn't sleep on dirty hotel floors or camp out in public toilets."

"Of course not. Only the fluffiest feather beds for the prince."

His mouth forms a thin line. "You're the only one who talks to me like that, you know." His steely voice is a glimpse into the future that might have been. I'm tempted to pull my shoulders back and address him as Your Majesty. Even though he's sitting on a toilet, I can picture it: King Theodore. Shivers run up my spine.

"Is that a complaint?"

"Just an observation."

"Your friends never give you a hard time about being *the prince*?"

"Sure they do. But not the first day we met." One side of his mouth kicks up into a heartbreaking smile.

"The world is ending. We agreed we don't have time to sugarcoat our conversations."

"Something tells me you wouldn't have done that even if it weren't the apocalypse."

"Does it bother you?"

He stares at me with unflinching honesty. "No, because I don't blame you one bit. And yes, because you continually beat me to the punch. How am I supposed to play the part of reluctant, self-deprecating heir to the throne if you always get there first? You think it's never occurred to me that my lifestyle is insane? That I don't deserve one-tenth of one percent of the things I've been given? That I don't know the blood-soaked history of the monarchy?"

"What if you didn't play a part at all?"

He scoffs. "I wouldn't even know where to begin."

"Tell me one true thing. Something you'd say if your last name weren't—" I pause, considering.

"I don't have a last name," he says.

"What would you say if you were the kind of person who needed two names?"

"I have four names."

"And you wonder why I make fun of you!"

He holds my stare for a long moment. The rawness in his expression has me itching for a camera. "I don't know how to be anything other than who they made me. I don't know who I am if I'm not Theodore Geoffrey Edward George," he says, his eyes blazing. This naked honesty is the shot I wanted on the subway. As badly as I want to take his picture, I don't for fear of scaring away the truth in his expression.

"Who did they make you into?" I ask, heart in my throat.

A short, sharp knock sounds on the door. "Occupied!" I shout.

A muffled voice carries through the door. "Did you see who went in there?"

I hold my breath and hope desperately that my gross moaning was memorable. I gag loudly next to the door, just in case the girl with the headphones needs a refresher.

"A girl. She was about to be sick," a voice answers. I pretend to vomit while Theo shakes with silent laughter at my performance. I throw in a loud groan for good measure. "That's her stuff," the girl says.

I wilt with relief. With any luck, they'll now be checking the passport I conveniently left on top of my bag and because Theo's stuff is gone, they'll assume I'm traveling alone.

Another sharp knock. "Are you . . . Wren Wheeler?"

"Yeah, sorry, I—" More gagging and vomiting noises.

"Did you see anyone go in there with her? A guy?" I think they're addressing the girl with the headphones again. Theo and I make eye contact. His back goes rigid. His eyes widen, petrified.

"I don't think so. She looked really bad."

The voice draws close again. "Are you in there alone?"

The steel melts from Theo's spine as he drops his head into his hands. Looking up at me, he mouths *I'm sorry*, claps his hands on his knees, and stands. I shake my head and place a palm flat on his chest. *Sit down,* I mouth. I will not let him turn himself in.

"Yeah," I say weakly. "I can open the door if you want to see, but, um . . . it's kinda messy."

We hold our breath as they mutter on the other side of the door. Theo grabs my hand and squeezes hard.

"That's not necessary. Erm, good luck in there."

The voices disappear and we both exhale in relief. I glance down at our entwined hands.

"Why are you doing this for me?" he asks.

"You deserve to die in peace," I whisper.

Gratitude passes across his features as he squeezes my hand again. There's still so much I don't understand about his life, but I don't regret not turning him in.

"If we get caught, am I going to die in jail, an enemy of the Throne?" I ask, only semi-joking.

Theo rolls his eyes. "Mum's tough, but only on me. She wouldn't arrest you."

I think of my own mom and my phone in my pocket, message after message left unread. I wonder if she slept at all last night. "What if she's just worried about you?"

"Trust me, it's not that."

"Maybe if you call her, she'll understand why you want to go to Santorini and—"

"No."

"I'm sure she just wants you to be happy."

Sadness floods his eyes. "She just wants to save face. She's the Queen first, my mother second. Before I left, she accused me of failing our country. She said I'm too weak to lead. *That* was her biggest concern when she learned about the comet. Trust me, it's better for everyone if I don't go home."

"Oh." I exhale. "I'm so sorry." My parents' marriage might be strained, but I've never doubted their love for *me*. It breaks my heart that Theo doesn't share the same conviction.

"Maybe if you call her—"

"I left a note for my brother. He knows why I left," he says with such finality that it slams the gates on our conversation.

I only wish he'd let me into the fortress with him.

⁎ ⁎ ⁎

Hours, minutes, days, seconds, light-years later, I breathe on the bathroom mirror and draw a tic-tac-toe board in the condensation. "Wanna play?"

By the time Theo glances up, it's disappeared. "Play what?"

"Never mind." My stomach growls and I grab another Jaffa Cake from Theo's open bag. "Do you think we're in France yet?" Time is a construct, utterly irrelevant. I measure my life in the number of times Theo's leg has bumped mine: fourteen. Each time a little electroshock straight to the heart. I think we're running out of oxygen.

"I dunno." He looks sad again. He looks *real*.

"Can I take your picture?"

He nods, but by the time I've pulled up the camera on my phone, he's got a big toothy grin plastered across his face. My heart sinks, but I snap the photo anyway.

"You know they're never gonna let you out of the Gare du Nord without questioning you, right? Not if there's a chance you know where I am," he says.

"Maybe the country will have descended into complete chaos by the time we arrive, and everyone will have dramatically quit their jobs in a last-ditch attempt to go viral on TikTok."

"Wouldn't that be a bloody nightmare."

"Well, maybe they won't care. Are you even that popular in France?"

He laughs. "You really don't know anything about me, do you?"

"I really don't, Goldilocks. Sorry if that's a blow to your ego."

He shakes his head.

"Can I ask you a question?"

"Sure," he says.

"What's it like?"

He cocks an eyebrow, an amused smirk tilting his mouth. "*It?*"

I bite my lip, the memory of our previous conversation heating my cheeks. "Paris," I clarify, giving him a smirk of my own.

"You've never been?"

I shake my head. "I just keep thinking about the Eiffel Tower—all the history I'll never see, the history that won't survive without people around to preserve it. Eventually, it will all be gone."

He studies me, his face inked with curiosity. *Snap.*

"What?" I adjust my top, cognizant of the fact that I can't remember the last time I was looked at so intently.

"It never occurred to me to think of the buildings," he says simply.

"I can't think of the people." I swallow a painful lump in my throat. "If I think of the people—of my family . . ." I'm bombarded with the mental image of Dad taking us down to the beach every summer. Of the first time Brooke begrudgingly let me tag along when she went downtown with her friends. Of Mom and me throwing pennies into Buckingham Fountain and riding the Navy Pier Ferris wheel with Cedar. These memories used to make me smile. Now they're too painful to bear. But with every image I swipe away, a new one takes its place. One rush of terrible nostalgia after another. I close my eyes until all I see are starbursts of light. "I can't dwell on it without falling apart. It's easier to think about the Eiffel Tower, because the sadness of never having seen it won't destroy me the way it will if I never see my family again."

"I get that," Theo says quietly.

"Really?"

"I *love* my siblings," he says emphatically. "And Penny." His voice cracks on her name. "Even my mum, despite everything. Thinking about them hurts."

I don't know what to make of this information. If being away from them hurts so badly, why is he so desperate to leave?

"I'm not the best person to ask about Paris," Theo says, bringing me back to my original question. "I've been in ballrooms and state dinners, but I don't get to explore the city much."

"Oh." My shoulders slump.

He bumps his knee against mine. *Fifteen*. "Paris lives up to the hype."

My heart levitates, just a little. I don't know why, but I feel better living in a world where Paris lives up to the hype. If things were different, I'd plan a detailed visit. I'd take pictures of tourists under the Arc de Triomphe and on the Eiffel Tower lawn. When I say as much out loud, Theo sits up, his eyes flickering to life.

"We could do that! If we don't get arrested, we could see the Eiffel Tower."

I shake my head. "It's not on the itinerary."

Before he can argue with me, the train slows down, drawing his attention to our current problem. "What's the plan?"

For a split second my muscles sag under the weight of expectation, but then I shake it off. I'm ready for this. I'm the girl who has plans, and I've spent much of this ride brainstorming another one. He shifts and his leg rests against mine.

Sixteen.

"We'll split up," I say.

"Famous last words."

"It's a good idea," I insist. "They'll be looking for us as a pair, so we have a better chance going solo. Once we're out of the station, I'll run to the store to buy essentials, and we'll meet back up on the train to Milan." (There won't be a passport check between France and Italy. Bless the European Union.)

"Don't be daft. I'm not getting on the train without you," he says.

"Then what do we do?"

His eyes spark as he leans toward me. "We'll meet at the Eiffel Tower."

Oh. My chest burns bright at the idea of it. Which is why I hate what I say next. "It'll take too much time. It's impractical and out of the way and—"

He threads his fingers through mine. "Please, Wren. Meet me at the Eiffel Tower. Let yourself have that, at least." His voice is terribly earnest, and for the second time since we entered this tiny bathroom, I want to kiss him. But this time it's not motivated by incandescent memories or the pounding of my heart when he draws close. I want to kiss him because he's thoughtful. In a world where it would have been easy for him to turn out selfish and rotten, he chose kind instead.

Outside the bathroom door, the hurried sounds of passengers gathering luggage and lining up to exit the train break the moment. Tears prick my eyes as a panic builds in my chest. "What if I never see you again?" I ask.

Theo opens his mouth to speak, but he's interrupted by a loud pounding on the door. "You must leave! The train has stopped."

"Sorry!" I call through the door. "I'm coming." I close my eyes and count to ten for courage. And then I unlock the door and slip out. I walk slowly down the aisle, reciting the plan in my head. *Don't stop. Don't talk to anyone. Get outside and get in a taxi.* With any luck, I'll see Theo again at the Eiffel Tower before the hour is up.

I barely make it off the train before the plan is blown to hell. A swarm of uniformed men surround me as I place my foot on French soil for the first time.

"Wren Wheeler?" one of the men asks in a thick French accent.

I nod, too nervous to speak.

"You will come with us."

CHAPTER 10

'm led from the platform down a flight of stairs, past rows of luggage lockers, to a small room on the lower level of the Gare du Nord, flanked on all sides by cheerful guards who seem deeply dismissive of me as a suspect. They snicker and chat in French over my head as I make the perp walk. I definitely hear the word "orange." *Oh-ronj.* It's a little insulting, if I'm being honest, that they don't think I'm capable of aiding and abetting the fugitive prince, or worse. Who's to say the short American girl with ugly orange hair didn't kidnap the prince for ransom? They should be more suspicious of me, really. They should have me in handcuffs rather than treating me like an insignificant girl.

I'm glad they don't, obviously. But since they gave me an opening, I might as well take it.

They escort me to a windowless room furnished with a thick mahogany desk and a large upholstered chair behind it. The chair has wooden arms carved with swirly patterns, and the wallpaper is lavish. Dark and damask-patterned.

I sink into a slightly less fancy upholstered chair in front of the desk and swing my legs over the side, hoping it makes me seem young and unworried and innocent. I tilt my head back as the team of Frenchmen post themselves around the room. The desk in front of me remains empty.

"Is this really what you want to be doing with your last days on Earth?" I ask.

"We swore an oath to defend and protect France," one of the officers says.

"Yeah, but does that really matter when a comet is going to blow us all up in a few days?"

"The comet is not going to hit," says another guard with very pale white skin.

"What?" My swinging legs freeze in midair. "Did something happen?"

"Not yet, but it will," he responds.

"What does that mean?" Is he in denial? Or does he know something I don't?

The door opens and a Black police officer wearing an odd triangle hat takes a seat across from me.

He taps his fingers on the desk as he surveys me. "You are Wren Wheeler?"

"That's me."

He tilts his head to the side, already skeptical. "We have reason to believe you have information on the missing Prince Theodore."

Here goes nothing. Time to confirm their suspicions about the silly teenage American girl. "Well, I'll tell you a secret if you don't tell anyone."

He clasps his hands on the desktop and leans ever so slightly forward. His eyes dart to someone standing over my shoulder.

"Prince Theo is my boyfriend."

His eyes narrow. "Your boyfriend?"

"Yes. That's why I'm here, to meet him in the city of love. He asked me to come. I got on the first train from London, even though the world is ending. I want to die in my lover's arms."

His jaw clenches. "How did he contact you? Do you have a phone number for him?"

"Oh no. That's too dangerous."

"Did he email you? Contact you via social media?"

"I told you, he can't take that risk. But he leaves me clues all the time. All I have to do is follow the bread crumbs."

The officer's eyes dart behind me again. He clears his throat. "The bread crumbs?"

"On his official Instagram account." Thank heavens for Naomi showing me this account, otherwise I'd be shooting completely blind. "I can show you?"

The officer nods once, so I unzip my backpack with trembling fingers and take out my phone. I swipe aside the notification telling me I have 107 unread messages and pull up the official Instagram of Prince Theodore. I scroll to a random post of Theo volunteering with a children's "football" team.

"Do you see how the prince is wearing a blue shirt in this photo?" I ask. The officer nods again. "And do you see how the ball is white?" He doesn't acknowledge this, so I keep going. "And those flowers on the headband of that little girl there, you see? They're red."

He glowers at me. "What is your point?"

"Blue, white, and red are the colors of the French flag."

"A lot of countries have blue, white, and red flags. Including yours."

"Don't be silly. Theo can't fly all the way to America at a time like this. If you look closely, you'll see that this photo was posted on"—I squint at the date—"April fourth of this year. If you add the dates, four plus four—"

"Enough!" the officer shouts. I bat my eyelashes as I look up at him.

"Don't you want to hear the rest of his message?"

"I do not," he says tightly. "Were you or were you not at St. Pancras station with the prince this morning?"

"Well—not officially. There was this man there, standing next to me in line, and I was practicing what I'd say when I met the prince—"

"She knows nothing," the officer says. "Get her out of here."

I bite back a smile. "Are you sure? Because if you need my help, the prince has sent me a lot of messages over the years. I can show you—"

"Leave," he says.

Victory fizzes in my chest like a shaken-up pop bottle. I have to get out of here before I burst into laughter. A guard opens the door for me. I'm just about to step out when—"Stop."

I turn. The officer at the desk stands, eyeing me with distrust. After a heavy sigh, he pulls a card out of his pocket and slides it across the desk. I pick it up with trembling fingers. "The Palace has reason to believe the prince is . . . *unwell*." His lip curls with distaste.

Fear clangs through me. "What do you mean by unwell?"

He ignores my question. "If you have any real, concrete information as to his whereabouts, the Queen will make it worth your while to give us a call."

I blink at the card. "The world is going to end in a week. What could she possibly do for me?"

"Don't underestimate the royal family," he says, dismissing me with a wave.

I'm escorted back to the main level of the Gare du Nord and unceremoniously left next to a man openly urinating on the floor while filming himself with his phone. I shudder and jump out of the splash zone. TikTok is a sickness. I make myself as small as possible in the aggressive crowd as I search for Theo, but I already know he's not here. We had a plan: meet at the Eiffel Tower. The proposal feels as fraught as it did when I was locked with him in the train bathroom, this time for different reasons. An hour ago I was terrified of never seeing Theo again and getting lost in Paris without a way home. Now I don't know what I'll say when I do see him, or whether I should tell him that a French police officer essentially tried to bribe me to turn him in. I replay the officer's warning and promise in my head as I walk numbly outside, paying very little attention to where I am or where I should be going.

The prince is . . . unwell.

I have no idea what that means. Unwell how? The word is vague enough that it could mean anything. You never know with fancy rich people. The Queen could be making something out of nothing. *Theo? Yes, he's unwell because he doesn't want to die with the hot gaze of public scrutiny beating on his shoulders! Cheeky boy!* Or she could be downplaying a catastrophic secret for the sake of saving face. *The prince? Yes, he's a budding serial killer whose brain is rather "unwell." Fancy a cuppa?*

My brain makes the leap from "Theo is the victim" to "Theo is a monster" in a single effortless bound.

Outside, the sun shines in a bright blue sky streaked with thin, wispy clouds. It's the most sunshine I've seen since leaving the States, and the feel of it on my skin makes me queasy with homesickness. I slowly turn and blink up at the railway station. The Gare du Nord is beautiful. The colossal white building reminds me of a cathedral. White stone columns support a vast arch that has a large clock in the very center. It's after one o'clock. My breath tightens in my chest. Our train to Milan leaves at four.

I'm still staring up at the clock when my phone buzzes.

"Mom?" I answer in a breathless rush.

"I found you a flight."

Her words stop my heart. "What?"

"London to New York, and I've already booked your flight from New York to Chicago," she says.

My vision narrows and the commotion of the city transforms to a dull roar. "But—*how*?" I cross the cobblestones on wobbly legs and lean against a lamppost for support.

"I made a post on Facebook and Twitter tagging the airline. I begged them to find a seat for you and they did. Just in time too, because all international flights are being grounded tonight for security concerns."

"What time does the flight leave?"

"Three hours," she says.

I tip my head back and blink away tears.

"Where are you? They said they'd call your name over the airport intercom. You're supposed to report to the nearest ticketing desk immediately."

"Mama, I can't."

"Of course you can. Don't be silly."

"I'm in Paris."

She sucks in a breath, and then she curses softly. When she starts crying, I can't hold back my tears for another second. We both sob into the phone as I explain a watered-down version of the truth: that I got scared I'd never find a flight out of Heathrow, so I took a train to Paris after someone told me I'd have better luck finding a flight here. I don't know why I don't tell her the full story: whether it's because I'm trying to save myself from a deathbed lecture, or because I'm instinctively protecting Theo. All I know is that I've never felt like a bigger failure in my life. All I feel is pure, breathtaking regret.

"I don't understand," my mom says again. "Why would you leave?" Her voice cracks. Reassuring Mom Mode: deactivated. I broke her.

"Wren?" Dad's uncertain voice replaces my mother's. I didn't realize he was in the room. I suddenly see the scene at home with perfect clarity. My whole family gathered around Mom as she excitedly dialed my number, ready to give me the happy news. "You're in Paris?"

"Daddy." I sob into my hand, stopping only when my nose becomes so stuffed up that I gasp for breath. I swallow the miserable regret simmering in my stomach and slam a heavy door over it. Lock it tight. Throw the key in the Seine.

I wallowed, and now I'm done. Now it's time to keep my head down and stick to the plan. "I'm coming home." I've never meant anything more in my entire life. "Tell Mom and Brooke and Cedar that I am coming home. I *promise*."

"How?"

"Please don't ask me that."

"We love you, Birdie, no matter what. Even if you don't make it back before the comet hits. We're not disappointed in you," he says with such tenderness that it almost cracks my resolve not to spill any more tears on these Parisian cobblestones.

"Don't let me off the hook, Dad. I told Mom I'd find a way home and I meant it."

"I love you," is all he says again. "Here's your sister. She wants to talk to you."

"Wren?" Brooke's voice is calm and clear.

"Don't you dare say goodbye," I threaten.

"How do you think you're getting home? Because if you give Mom false hope, I'll never forgive you."

"Isn't false hope better than no hope, at this point?"

"Is that all this is?"

"No. I can't tell you the details, because you'll think I'm delusional, but I met someone who owes me a favor. They have a plane."

"Is it a boy?" she asks sharply. My answering silence confirms Brooke's fears. "Oh, Wren." She sounds exasperated. All it takes is those two words to make me feel like the kid sister who can't do anything right. "Don't let some good-looking European boy charm your pants off by promising you things he can't deliver. If something seems too good to be true, it is. Don't trust anyone who doesn't deserve it."

"I'm not stupid."

"You're not acting smart!" she fires back. "You shouldn't have left the airport. I wouldn't have."

"Trust me, I know! You're the genius who has done everything right since the day you were born, and I'm the less smart, less successful version of you. I get it!" Years of pent-up frustration burst out of me and shock Brooke into silence.

"Is that how you feel?" she asks after a long moment.

"I can't talk about this right now. Put Cedar on the phone," I snap.

I ask Cedar to save me a game of Mario Kart, and then I say another round of goodbyes to Mom. I overhear Brooke asking to talk to me again, but I hang up before I get pulled into another argument.

My thoughts are a tangled mess and my stomach a bundle of

nerves as I wade through the crowds in front of the Gare du Nord and wave down a black taxi. "The Eiffel Tower, please."

I lean against the window and watch Paris crawl by. The traffic is terrible, the roads crowded with cars and people. My driver has his hands gripped tightly on the steering wheel, tension radiating off him in waves. I wish I could appreciate the sights for what they are, but I can't rid myself of the feeling that I've made a huge mistake. Brooke's warning hangs heavy on my conscience, as do the police officer's last words. But can they both be true? Is Theo unwell, or is he a panty-dropping snake charmer making promises he can't keep?

My stomach lurches. I curl my hands into fists, my fingernails biting into my palms. I'm suddenly nervous—more nervous than I've been since before I sat down in the restaurant with Theo last night. Was it only last night that we agreed to this plan? It feels like an entire lifetime has come and gone since I learned that a comet is going to hit Earth, since Theo offered me the lifeline I desperately needed. Taking him up on his offer was such a clear choice, at the time. Now I don't know what to do.

The clock inches closer to two, and I begin to panic for an entirely *different* reason. Traffic is at a standstill as people pour into the streets. At this rate, it'll take forever to make the four-mile drive to the Eiffel Tower, and that was supposed to be the easy part. How long will it take to find Theo, and how long from there to get to the train? I wish he'd never smashed his phone in the hotel room.

The business card with the phone number of the French police suddenly feels heavy with promise in my pocket. I could turn him in if I had to. I could cash in my favor with the Queen.

I resolve to wait until I see Theo before making any decisions. If I feel uneasy about our reunion, I'll make the call.

The car rolls slowly forward. "Excuse me." I lean forward to be heard over the blaring radio. "How much longer?"

The driver shrugs, just as something slams into the taxi from behind.

CHAPTER 11

My head throbs as smoke and noise curl around the damaged taxi. Outside the car, the driver is engaged in a screaming match with another man. I don't understand a word of what they're saying, though it's immediately clear that they're both furious, but not hurt. I blink stupidly out the window as time slows down. Everything moves like dripping honey.

Time. The one thing I don't have enough of. I shake my aching head, and my brain catches up with the world. I unbuckle my seat belt, push open the car door, and step into the sunlight on my hurt ankle. Bad idea. It throbs worse than my head. I survey the damage of the car wreck. The taxi no longer has a backside, metal folded in on itself. I belatedly remember to grab my bag from the back seat and then I stumble, dazed, away from the accident.

"The Eiffel Tower?" I ask as I'm swept into a crowd that's gathering at the base of a long flight of steps in front of an old church. A man at the top of the steps is shouting. I don't understand the words, but he has the cadence of a preacher, and many of the people in the crowd are holding signs with

Bible verses on them. Someone presses a flame-covered leaflet into my hand. Chanting and singing come from all directions, worsening my headache. "Eiffel Tower?" I yell louder, my voice swallowed by the mass of moving bodies. My ankle can't keep up. I'll drown out here. "Eiffel Tower? Which way?" I shout frantically as sweat drips into my eyes.

A finger points the opposite way the crowd is moving. I push against the current until I'm freed from the tangle of bodies, then move down a cobblestone path. I sink onto a bench to give my ankle a rest and raise my fingers to touch the swollen lump on my forehead. It's incredible that I'm not concussed.

I push myself up, suddenly unsure. I recite a list of facts: "My name is Wren Wheeler. I'm eighteen. I'm in Paris. It's Monday, June thirteenth. The world is ending next week. I'm looking for Prince Theodore."

I sound batshit crazy, but I feel better about the state of my brain. Hopefully it's not too bruised. A wave of stomach-twisting nausea hits, and I realize I haven't eaten a real meal since the pub last night. No one warned me that the apocalypse would involve so much hunger. *Rude.*

The sun is high in the sky, and it's already after two. I push back to my feet and force myself to keep walking. Following the directions given to me by the maps app on my phone, I wander down a narrow street called Rue Montorgueil that's filled with shops, bakeries, cafés, and restaurants. I inhale a deep breath of fresh bread that wafts from a nearby boulangerie, then choke on the mingled scents of cigarette smoke and urine. My stomach still grumbles, though, and when I pass a patisserie with a colorful assortment of cakes and pastries in the window display, my mouth waters. Telling myself I need the rest anyway, I tug on the door, but it's locked. A handwritten sign in the window reads FERMÉ JUSQU'APRÈS LA COMÈTE.

"'Closed until after the comet,'" a woman passing by explains. I dodge past her and limp down the street, ducking around people, hiding my face so they won't see how close I am to losing it.

I walk down so many narrow cobblestoned streets with buildings rising up on either side that I get dizzy. I have to keep stopping to close my eyes and lean against lampposts, benches, and buildings, because I'm afraid if I sit down again, I'll never get back up. Three o'clock comes and goes, then four o'clock, taking with it our tickets out of France. I stumble over my own feet as I get to an open intersection. Across the road is a large white cathedral with a golden dome top and spire stretching toward puffy white clouds. Beyond it, the top of the Eiffel Tower winks in the sunlight.

I run. A car honks at me as I cross the street. I don't even realize I'm crying until tears slide down my neck. I trip over my own feet as I cross the broad lawn in front of the tower, landing flat on my stomach. My nose smacks into the ground and the taste of grass bursts across my tongue. I push myself up, half delirious from hunger and pain and exhaustion along with the stress of missing the train and disappointing my family. Oh, and the end of the world.

My hands and lips are numb as my heart drums painfully in my chest.

I'm having a panic attack.

The lawn is filled with people, a hectic out-of-control energy buzzing in the air. A dozen people are scaling the outside of the tower. Someone reaches the top and unfurls a French flag. A minute later a second figure releases a German flag. I spin in a circle, searching for a lone figure with dark hair and sunglasses. I don't see him. I spin again, slower, because my head swims and I'm afraid I might collapse. *Where is he?*

I search all along and around the base of the tower, but Theo's nowhere to be found. Brooke's words come barreling back to me. *Don't trust anyone who doesn't deserve it.*

No. I'm not ready to admit she was right about him. Or worse, that she was right about me. That this whole trip was a mistake.

I swallow my tears and look up at the wrought-iron lattice of the tower. Shadows move along the first and second floors of the tower and the breath rushes out of my chest as I realize that must be where he is.

I close my eyes and see Theo's smoldering expression when he asked me to meet him at the Eiffel Tower. For better or worse, I trust that he meant it. With one final glance around the lawn, I resolve to climb.

I bypass the unmanned ticket booth and thunder up the stairs. By step fifty-five I'm wheezing. I grab the wall for support and push myself to go farther. My thighs burn as I climb step after step. At step one hundred, I want to turn around and crawl back down. At two hundred, the tears are back. It's 328 steps to the first floor of the tower, and all my limbs are shaking as I reach the last one.

I step gingerly onto the transparent floor, convinced the weight of me will be the final straw that causes it to come crashing down. I test it first with my toe, and then ease my body slowly onto the glass. It doesn't break, which might be the first thing that's gone right all day. I quickly search the observation deck, but the crowds are thin up here and it's obvious that Theo isn't among them. I scan the lawn from my new vantage point, but I still can't find him.

Second floor it is, then.

Back on the staircase, I start my count from zero. I'm so exhausted that I'm beginning to doubt whether I'll ever make it back down. Maybe Theo and I will stay camped out on the second floor of the Eiffel Tower. There are worse places to be and worse ways to die.

I lose track around two hundred steps. Or was it three hundred? My ankle has gone numb to the pain, my legs barely functioning as I crawl the rest of the way to the open-air deck on the second floor. I collapse with relief before registering the fact that the deck is empty.

He's not here.

The truth hits like a comet, exploding my entire world. Theo left me.

I move to the edge of the deck and press my hands against the glass. All of Paris is on the other side. The city sprawls out before me like a love letter to life itself. Vibrant green grass and trees run like ink through the pulsing white city. It's impossible to imagine how different this view will look one year from now. I pull my camera from my bag and steady the image through my viewfinder and *snap*. I rarely take pictures of buildings or landscapes or cities, but this view is as alive as any person I've ever met.

I stay on the second deck until sundown as people filter in and out around me. Two guys who look to be in their mid-twenties get engaged when they both kneel at the same time to propose, and an hour later another couple climbs the stairs in a short white dress and a tux and gets *married*. I watch the whirlwind wedding from my spot on the floor, snapping pictures of the happy couple kissing as fuchsia clouds stain the surface of the Seine in the background. Glowing yellow lights ignite across the city like fairies, and I want to stay and take pictures of them too. But I've ignored my hunger for too long and I've already eaten every snack in my backpack. I put my camera away and push myself up, groaning when my stiff legs protest. I start the long walk down, my mind too numb to form a new plan. All I care about now is food. The more I think about food, the worse my hunger gets. I let my mind wander, and soon I'm thinking of Theo, and whether he took the train to Milan without me, if he caused enough of a distraction to slip aboard unnoticed and hide in the bathroom again. If at this very moment he's eating dinner with his friend Stella, crashing on her couch like he said we could. I try to convince myself that it doesn't matter, that I don't care. He played me for a fool, and I was desperate enough to believe him.

Sheer force of will propels me back down those steps, but when my bad ankle hits the ground, shocks of pain radiate through my foot and up my leg. I gasp and freeze, waiting for the pain to subside. When it does, I open my eyes.

Ten feet in front of me is Theo, his eyes burning in the dark. My body goes still. Every bit of panic, fear, and despair gone, replaced with pure sparkling relief.

This time, when I take off into a run, I know exactly where I'm going. Without hesitation, I throw myself into his arms.

CHAPTER 12

DATE: MONDAY, JUNE 13
LOCATION: PARIS, FRANCE

ITINERARY: ?????????
DAYS UNTIL THE COMET HITS: SIX AND A HALF

Theo wraps his arms around me so tightly, he squeezes the air from my lungs. It feels . . . *wonderful*. Like getting crushed to death by a million bucks.

"I can't breathe," I rasp. When he loosens his hold, I respond by tightening my grip around his torso. "No. Don't let go. I don't need air." The survival books say you can go three minutes without air. Child's play. I could stay here forever, melting into Theo like butter on toast.

"Are you all right?" He pulls away to look at me.

"I'm delirious with relief. Concussed with joy." I've never been so happy to see anyone in my life.

"Are you serious?" His fingers trail lightly over the tender spot on my forehead, sending shivers across my skin. I lean into his touch until his palm is cradling my face, the gentle heat of his fingers unlocking something in my chest.

"My taxi was in an accident and then I had a bit of a panic attack—"

His eyes widen in alarm and his hands fall to my shoulders.

"I swear I'm fine. Just hungry."

"Prove it."

"Bread. Cheese. Ice cream. Pizza. Chocolate. Am I doing this right?"

He shakes his head, a small smile on his lips. "You're impossible."

"And you are Theodore Geoffrey Edward George, a fact I learned for the first time today. There's your proof that I'm not concussed."

"Chuffed to hear it. Can't have my bodyguard feeling poorly on the job." His eyes twinkle mischievously as one hand slides off my shoulder and settles on my lower back. Desire blooms in my chest. The weight of his touch feels electrifying—until I remember what Brooke said about European boys charming girls out of their pants. I jump back, determined to put more space between us.

I want to trust him, but now that the relief of seeing him has passed, I'm not sure that I do.

"Where have you been?" I ask.

He drags a hand over his face. "When I couldn't find you, I didn't know what to do. I felt daft just waiting around, so I doubled back to the Gare du Nord, but you weren't anywhere. Then I headed to the shops and spent forever working up the nerve to nick a burner phone." He pulls out a small flip phone from his pocket. "That's when I realized I didn't have your number.

Eventually I made my way back here. I take full responsibility for being a knob and ruining the plan. I'm sorry."

He sounds so genuine that I feel compelled to believe him. "Daft . . . knob . . ." I tease. "Any other British insults you can teach me?"

His mouth tugs up in a smile as he picks up my backpack from where I dropped it at our feet. He nods toward the Seine. "Tosser's a fun one to say. Gormless. Prat."

"You gormless prat!" I echo in a butchered British accent.

"Ten out of ten, no notes." He twists the ring on his finger absentmindedly as we walk toward the dark riverbank. A group of naked figures streak past us and splash into the river. Couples, groups, and families with kids dive in, some fully clothed, other stripped to their underwear.

"Feel like a swim?" I ask, only half joking. I've never been skinny-dipping.

"Feel like a quick bout of E. coli?"

"Maybe not." The city lights glimmer on the river, making it look like it's full of stars. Now that we're walking and I can keep my eyes on the lights instead of Theo's face, it's easier to talk to him. "When I couldn't find you, I thought you'd gone up into the tower, so I walked all the way to the top."

"I never would have expected you to walk all those steps on your ankle," he says as if it's the most obvious thing in the world. "How's it feeling?"

"Not great, but at least we know gravity works."

He cuts me a sidelong glance.

"It's what my dad used to say when I fell and got hurt as a kid. He'd inspect the injury and say in a serious voice, 'Thanks for performing a gravity check.' I'd laugh and forget about whatever scrape or bruise was making me cry." My chest burns. I wish Dad were here now to tell some corny joke that'd snap me out of my homesickness. "I thought you'd left me." My voice wobbles, betraying my emotion.

"You don't have to worry about that."

"I don't?" I ask. He stares at me hard for a long moment, and then his gaze falls to my lips, and I can't think about anything other than what it felt like to kiss him. An ache runs through me.

I'm about to lean in when he says, "I can't make this trip without you. Wanted man, remember?"

I swallow my disappointment. It's silly, that I would have expected him to say anything else. We were both clear about what we're getting out of this arrangement. Just because I panicked when I couldn't find him doesn't mean this relationship is turning into something else. It's barely even a relationship. More like a business agreement.

Just because he's the best kisser I know doesn't mean I'll ever kiss him again.

"So what do we do now?" I ask.

"Don't hate me, but we're not going to Milan tonight."

"We have to!" At this rate we'll never make it to Santorini in time. "Can't we get tickets for a later train?"

"There are no tickets until tomorrow morning. They're down to one train a day. But don't worry. This time, *I* have a plan." He flashes a wry smile and I feel a twinge of guilt for yelling at him in the train station when he didn't have any ideas for getting through security. "My best mate from school, Will, already bought us tickets for the morning train to Milan. He's crashing with his boyfriend's parents on the other side of the city, and we can head there now."

I furrow my brow.

"There will be food. Beds that don't require black light inspection. Maybe even a hot shower."

That sounds . . . not terrible. "Fine," I say begrudgingly. "I approve of this addition to the itinerary."

He smirks. "I thought you might. C'mon, let's get off the street."

We hail a cab that takes us through the narrow and winding streets to a tall apartment building with a charming cream-colored exterior. Theo grabs both of our bags, and we're buzzed into an elegant lobby where an elevator whisks us to the top floor. Pulsing music blares through a door at the end of the hall: R.E.M.'s "It's the End of the World as We Know It." I press my ear against the door and can just make out the sound of voices—lots of them—beyond the threshold.

"Does he know we're coming?"

"He does." He spins the ring on his finger again. I'm beginning to realize it's his nervous tic.

"Does he know you're basically a fugitive?"

"Indeed."

"Would he plan a massive end-of-the-world party and invite you over anyway?"

His jawline clenches in aggravated confirmation.

"Do you want to leave?"

"I need something from him," Theo says.

I raise an eyebrow. "Something that's worth the risk of being seen?"

His mouth presses into a flat line. "He's making me a fake passport."

Even though we're now in the Schengen Area, where people

can move freely between countries without showing passports, it *would* make me feel a whole lot better if Theo had some sort of plausible deniability.

"Keep your head down," I tell him as I pound on the throbbing door.

It flies open. A boy with dark brown skin who looks around twenty answers the door. "Je vous connais?" he yells over the music ("The Final Countdown." Points to whoever made the apropos playlist).

"Bonjour. Um, we're friends with Will." I jerk my thumb toward Theo, who's attempting his best disappearing trick against the wall.

"Theo! Salut!" He spots him and grins widely. "Arrête de flipper et ramène-toi!" He turns his head and yells, "Will, Theo is here!" He's switched to English with a French accent.

"Could you *not* yell that? He's trying to keep a low profile." A protective spike of annoyance flares in my chest.

"Oh, no one here cares." He waves off my concern. "Come in, Will's in here somewhere."

"Raoul, this is my friend Wren," Theo says in a low voice as he shakes hands with Raoul.

Raoul touches his cheek to mine and greets me with a kiss. "Oh! Um . . . thank you!" I say, and kiss him on the other cheek.

He laughs and ushers us into the foyer. "American?"

"What gave me away?"

"It's cheek to cheek," Theo whispers. "You're not supposed to actually kiss him."

The apartment is a large open space with sparse furniture, wooden floors, floor-to-ceiling windows, massive skylights, and abstract paintings in bright neon hanging everywhere. The place is crowded with people: lounging on couches, playing video games, leaning against the walls, and dancing. I'm grateful for the loud music, dim lights, and clouds of smoke obscuring us from view.

"Will's in the kitchen," Raoul says. Theo and I maneuver through the crowd, past a ladder in the middle of the room that extends from the second floor, and into the kitchen, where a tall boy with red hair and a mass of freckles is holding court over what appears to be a drinking game involving a wine cork and a lit candle. When he sees Theo, he leaps up from his seat.

"Blaze!" he cries in a booming voice.

"Blaze?" I whisper to Theo. He only has time to shrug in bewilderment before the redhead tackles him in a bear hug. "Nice to see you, mate. It's been too long."

"Thanks for letting us crash."

"No problem. Raoul's parents will be back in a few hours. Everyone will be gone by then." Abruptly, he shoves Theo against a white wall and holds up his phone. "Don't smile!" He snaps half a dozen photos of Theo trying not to smile and then pulls his friend back into one of those one-armed half-hug, half-stranglehold things that guys do. This must be Will. When he releases his hold on him, Theo pulls his hat back on.

"I don't think that's doing as much as you think it is, mate," Will says.

"You might have warned me that the apartment would be full of people."

"They're all pissed anyway. Don't worry so much. It's the end of the world! Passport will be ready in a few. In the meantime, have a drink or several." His eyes slide to me. "You look like you could use it."

"Do you have any food?" I raise my voice to be heard over the music.

"Whatever you can find!" he yells back. He looks over his shoulder at the partygoers playing the drinking game. "Everyone out so my friend Blaze can make his girl a meal." He marches out of the kitchen with a beer held high above his head, belting "I Will Survive" at the top of his lungs.

I blink, unsure how to process everything that just happened. "Who is *Blaze*?"

"I have no idea. Will's off his rocker."

"I thought he was your best friend."

One half of Theo's mouth hitches up. "He is. Have a seat. I'll make you dinner."

"You can do that?" I feign shock as I sink onto a bar stool.

"Contrary to your opinion of me, I'm not completely useless."

"Prove it."

He raises both eyebrows, his eyes dancing in the dim, smoky light, and I get the distinct feeling that he likes the challenge. "You're on, American girl."

My heart hiccups again in my chest, one nickname from Theo managing to knock the breath out of me in a way that not even climbing more than six hundred steps up the Eiffel Tower accomplished. I rest my elbows on the marble countertop, drop my chin into my hands, and curl my fingers over my mouth so he doesn't see the grin threatening to break free. Theo rummages through the refrigerator and pantry, returning with a box of spaghetti, an armful of fresh vegetables, bacon, and ground beef. "Mincemeat," he calls it. A disgusting term that sounds charming when he says it.

"Vegetarian," I remind him, pointing at myself.

"Shite. Of course!" He returns the meat to the refrigerator.

He starts off by narrating what he's doing like he's hosting his own cooking show, but over time he goes quiet and falls into a kind of trance, chopping garlic, onions, and carrots with the focus and precision of someone who's done this before. And not once or twice. I picture him in what are likely the cavernous kitchens of Buckingham Palace with a towel slung over his shoulder and an apron tied low across his hips, humming to himself like he's doing now. It's an easy image. He looks more comfortable and confident now than I've seen him yet.

"How'd you get so good at this?" I inhale the garlicky scent as my stomach grumbles painfully.

"Penny."

"Your nanny? I thought you would have had a chef."

"We did. He loathed me." Theo smiles at a memory. "I made his life miserable. I was the pickiest eater and Mum made him prepare special meals just for me. When I was six or seven, Penny had this idea that if I helped prepare the food, I'd be more likely to eat it, but her plan backfired. Instead of helping with meals, I'd tear through the kitchens, making up my own recipes and leaving a tornado in my wake."

"You sound insufferable." I grin openly up at him now.

"You have no idea. But Penny was adamant. And when I had a bad day at school or Mum would scold me really harshly, Penny would sneak me into the kitchen and teach me to bake biscuits or pudding or pie and mash."

He glosses right over the mention of his mom, but I can't help but think about how the Queen called him weak and a failure. At least he had one ally in the palace. "Penny sounds amazing."

"She is," Theo says. "I loved that time with her so much that I agreed to learn more complicated recipes, and eventually her plan worked. Now I eat everything, though I still struggle with washing dishes."

"Would you want to be a chef if your future weren't set in stone?"

His mouth turns down, just a little. "I've literally never thought about it."

The music stops in the middle of Kesha's "Die Young." The TV is switched from whatever video game was being played to a news broadcast.

"Regardez! Watch!" The party falls to a hush as everyone gathers around the TV.

"What's it saying?"

"My French is a bit dodgy, but I understand it well enough." Theo cocks his head and strains to hear from across the loft.

The color drains from his face as the news anchors speak in rapid-fire French. My stomach clenches in anticipation. After several moments, he looks at me with a wide-eyed expression.

"They're trying to save the world."

CHAPTER 13

A Roman candle of hope explodes in my chest. "How are they going to save the world?"

Theo moves his hands wildly as he untangles the French in his brain. "It sounds like your government is going to launch a missile at the comet sometime tomorrow. They want to blow it apart or knock it off course before it enters the atmosphere."

"Will that work?"

He wipes his hands on a towel and offers me a plate of steaming pasta that I was ravenous for less than five minutes ago. I'm not sure I can eat anything now. "They don't know."

We stare at each other. Our plan has strayed so far from the itinerary, I don't know how to comprehend it. "If the missile launch is successful—what would we do? Go back to London?" I picture Theo and I walking hand in hand down Abbey Road with all the time in the world for me to catch a new flight. It's a good picture. I want what future Wren has.

He shudders. "No."

"You still want to run to Santorini? Will you at least tell your family where you are?" I feel a small rumbling of guilt as

I think about his worried mother, but I lock it away with the other things I refuse to dwell on. Like never seeing my family again. Like *the prince is . . . unwell*. Nope. Not going there, especially because right now, with a plate of vegetarian Bolognese that he made himself, Theo looks *happy*.

He ignores my second question and answers the first. "We have to," he says with urgency as he leans over the counter toward me. "If it fails, we'll have wasted an entire day waiting in Paris." He shakes his head. "Unacceptable. Now eat." He tops my spaghetti with a slice of fresh bread and nudges the plate toward me.

I take a bite, and it's the best thing I've eaten in days. Weeks. Years. "I'm going to cry actual tears."

The TV is turned off, but the former "Only the Good Die Young" mood of the party never returns, and soon enough people are stumbling out the front door. Raoul shuts it behind the last guest and then he and Will join us in the kitchen, helping themselves to heaping plates of pasta.

I check out for the first half of the conversation, floating away into a blissful food coma. I only return to reality when Raoul asks me how Theo and I met. "You go ahead," I tell him as I savor another bite of bread. Bread! Does everyone else know how good bread is? I regret every slice of bread and butter I ever turned down. I can't believe I ever worried about the calories in bread, as if at the end of my life the thing I'd care about would be the size of my pants. Insane.

Theo quickly runs through the story of how we met. When he gets to the part where I grabbed his hand and pulled him away from the paparazzi, Raoul gasps. "You knew he was the prince and you tugged him after you like a toddler?"

"I guess so. Is that bad?"

Will howls with laughter. "You're gutsy."

"Why?" I ask warily.

"She really has no idea, mate."

"She really doesn't." Theo shakes his head with a smile.

"Idea about what?"

"Commoners aren't allowed to *touch* him!" Will says with mock severity. At first I think he's mocking me, but when Theo gives him the finger, I realize he's mocking *the prince*.

"I knew it!" I say gleefully. "He tried to convince me that I'm tougher on him than his friends are, but I knew he was full of it."

"Oh, I absolutely take the piss out of him every chance I can, but to be fair to *the prince*, I am his best friend."

"And I'm just some American girl. Message received," I joke.

"Don't get me wrong, I'm thrilled you two are traveling together. He needs someone who can keep him in check. I've never met anyone who walks the razor-thin line between outrageous self-confidence and debilitating self-hatred like he does." He claps Theo on the shoulder. "No one loathes themselves more for being born under a golden star."

"Cheers to that!" Theo says, clinking his glass against Will's.

"Oh! Speaking of—" Will cuts himself off and runs out of the kitchen, returning a few minutes later with a new passport. He slides it across the marble island. "Hot off the presses."

Theo takes one glance at it and glares at Will. "You named me Blaze Danger?"

Will cracks a shit-eating grin. "It suits him, don't you think?" he asks me. "It's the scar in his eyebrow. Did he tell you yet how he got it, because it's a funny story—"

"This is rubbish," Theo says. "No one will believe this."

"No offense, mate, but the passport is the least of your worries. If this missile launch doesn't work tomorrow, you'll be lucky if the entire world doesn't grind to an apocalyptic halt. When that happens, no one will care about finding the bloody prince of Wales."

"That's what I said," I can't help but add. Theo rolls his eyes.

"I told you. Massive ego." Will holds his hands out to mime someone with a gigantic head. Theo flicks water at him.

"Where are you two stopping next?" Raoul asks.

"Stella's house, right?" I glance at Theo.

Will chokes on his water. "Really, mate?"

"No!" Theo glares at his friend. "Not unless the train is delayed or something. We shouldn't have to. No."

My phone buzzes loudly on the countertop and a text from Mom appears on my screen.

Where are you now?

"Aren't you going to respond?" Theo nudges my phone toward me.

I sigh heavily and quickly respond to let her know that I'm still in Paris. I know I should call, but every time I talk to my family, it reminds me of the overwhelmingly scary feelings I'm trying to avoid. "I'll call my mom when you call yours."

"Your mum isn't having you tracked by the police," Theo counters.

"That we know of."

I listen to Theo and Will banter for the next half hour, but eventually I can't keep myself from yawning. I am bone-dead exhausted, even if my brain is buzzing.

"The guest bedroom is available," Raoul says. "There's only one bed, but it's big enough for two, unless one of you wants the couch."

"I'd rather not be seen by your parents when they get home," Theo says quickly. "But Wren can have the bed. I'll take the floor."

Raoul raises his eyebrows and exchanges a look with Will. "Sure. We'll sneak you out in the morning," he says as Will smirks.

Will leads us down the hall to a small guest bedroom with white walls, a large window with dark, heavy curtains, and smack in the center of the room, the most appealing bed I've ever seen. The fluffy white comforter is littered with squashy pillows. My knees nearly buckle and I hold the doorframe for support.

"Are you okay? Is it your ankle?" Theo hovers a hand near the small of my back to catch me if I collapse, presumably. Which I just might.

"I'm swooning over the bed. I think I'm in love."

Will laughs. "The stuff you asked for is there," he says to Theo, pointing to a pile of reusable shopping bags sitting on the gray upholstered bench at the foot of the bed. "We got underwear in basically every size," he says to me.

"You bought me underwear?" It's the kind of thing that might have embarrassed me—in the *before times*. Once you know you're a few days away from dying, embarrassment feels like a wasted emotion. And because I have to keep such a tight watch on my emotions, lest they all erupt like Vesuvius and smother Theo and me in suffocating ash, I banish embarrassment from the list.

"And deodorant, toothbrushes, and a change of clothes. We picked yours based on Theo's unhelpful description."

"How did he describe me?" I ask, glancing quickly at Theo, who is suddenly extremely interested in the books on the built-in shelves.

"You wanna see the text?" Will asks.

"Don't show her the text," Theo says in a bored voice as he pulls a book off the shelf and thumbs through the pages.

"Aw, c'mon. I want to know what you said about me! Did you mention the orange hair?" I run a self-conscious hand through my tangled Pippi Longstocking hair and turn to Will. "He mentioned the orange hair, didn't he? Did he tell you *he's* the one who made me look like this?"

"Gingers unite." Will holds out his hand for a fist bump. "I think you look good. Like Black Widow."

He is absolutely lying, and I love him for it. Grinning, I glance up at Theo to see what he makes of the compliment.

His eyes flick to Will with a warning, which only makes Will laugh. "I've got the text right here—"

"I said you were beautiful," Theo cuts him off. He stares at me evenly for a strangled heartbeat before he reshelves the book. *He thinks I'm beautiful.* My heart takes a stutter step. "The hair is a tragedy, though. Will is a lying bastard."

Will bursts into loud, raucous laughter that echoes through the apartment. "I'll leave you two lovebirds alone." Theo and I freeze in unison. "You and the bed, I mean," Will says to me with a wink. Laughing again, he snaps the door shut tight.

For the second night in a row, Theo and I find ourselves alone in a bedroom, staring at one bed. It wouldn't be a big deal if I weren't still flushed and flustered from Theo telling me I'm beautiful in such a self-assured way. Or if I didn't still have the memory of his hand trailing a line of fire down my back as we almost kissed under the Eiffel Tower. The air in the room is suddenly heavy with tension.

"I'm gonna kill him," Theo mutters under his breath. He crosses the room and empties the shopping bags out onto the bed.

"Give him a break. What kind of best friend would he be if he didn't try to play wingman?" I force myself to laugh as I sort the purchases into a Theo pile and a Wren pile with slightly shaky fingers. I gather the effects into my arms and disappear into the adjoining bathroom, where I set everything on the counter and inspect the simple black underwear with dainty lace trim in a variety of sizes. Not bad, Raoul. He also bought two pairs of leggings and two striped T-shirts. After almost forty-eight hours in the same clothes, this is heaven. I strip down and scrub myself clean with scalding hot water in the shower. *Heaven, Part II*. How have I never realized that a hot shower is the best feeling in the world? I hate every wasted morning when I didn't appreciate the sting of water pounding onto my shoulders or the feel of shampoo lather on my scalp. Like warm bread and butter, I took it all for granted.

When I finally turn the tap off and step out of the shower, my skin is as pink as the toilet paper. I feel human again as I change into the new clothes and brush my teeth. (*Heaven! Part III!*) Theo switches places with me, and by the time he exits the bathroom in joggers and a T-shirt, bringing with him the fresh scent of soap, I'm snuggled in the plush bed. (*Beds!* Who knew?! Forget everything else I said . . . Beds are the real heaven.) It's comfortable enough that white-hot guilt sears my chest as Theo takes his two pillows and lies on the hard wood floor next to my side of the bed. He pushes his damp hair out of his eyes and folds one arm behind his head.

I suppose this is the part where we should turn off the light and go to sleep. Except . . . we don't.

"Can I ask you a question?" I say. I dart a quick glance down at him before looking back up at the ceiling. Loud music and car horns float through the window from the street below.

"Mm-hmm."

"Why did you wait for me when I didn't show up at the Eiffel Tower on time? You could have taxied here, picked up your passport from Will, and gotten on a train to Milan without me."

"I wouldn't have done that."

"Why not?"

"I made you a promise," he says. As if it's really that simple. As if he owes me anything, when we've barely known each other for two days and none of it will matter in a week.

He shifts and I glance over the side of the bed at him and watch him curl onto his side, facing me. It's become something of a bedtime ritual for me, gazing at the prince of Wales over the edge of my bed before I fall asleep. I bite back a smile.

He looks up at me, his blue eyes piercing mine.

"Thank you for waiting."

"I promised to get you home, and I intend to deliver on that. If you weren't here . . ." He's quiet for a long time. My heart pounds wildly in my chest as I wait for him to tell me what his world would be like if I weren't here. He swallows, the bob of his Adam's apple betraying his nerves. "I'm worried I'd give up on myself."

All the air whooshes from my lungs. I want to know what's happened in his life to put that wave of sadness in his ocean-blue eyes almost as much as I want to protect him from feeling it ever again. "I won't give up on you," I whisper. It feels simultaneously like a promise too big to make and the most obvious thing in the world. That's when I realize I *do* trust him. First thing in the morning I'll shred that business card in my backpack.

"Can I ask *you* a question?" he says in a lighter tone.

"Anything," I say, sounding unbearably earnest.

"What did they say to you at the train station?"

I tear my gaze from his and concentrate on the ceiling. "They asked if I had any information about your whereabouts. I said that we were secret lovers, and I was traveling to Paris so I could die in your arms."

Theo barks an incredulous laugh. "What did they say to *that*?"

"They asked how I contact you, and I told them you send me secret clues through your Instagram posts. They let me leave pretty quickly after that."

I peek over the bed at him again. His amused smile is edged with apprehension. "They didn't say anything about me . . . or my family?"

"Like what?"

He shrugs. "Anything."

The prince is . . . unwell. I scrunch my eyes tight against the memory. I hate it. Hate how it makes me doubt Theo, who put his own future in jeopardy because he made me a promise. "Nope," I lie. My stomach twists in sour protest.

"Good." He sighs a breath of relief. This time, when he smiles up at me, his eyes dazzle like city lights on the River Seine. I'm hit square in the chest with the need for more. More time with him, to find out his secrets. More time on Earth, to say goodbye to everyone I love. To eat bread and take hot showers and fall asleep in a perfect bed. I need more time for all of it, and so does he.

"I'm in love with this bed."

"Don't brag."

"It's so warm and comfortable and big."

"I take it back. I wish I'd gone to Italy without you," he grouses.

"You can come up here. If you want." I hold my breath while I wait for his response.

My lungs are burning for oxygen by the time he finally says, "Okay."

He picks up his pillows and flicks off the lamp before rounding the bed to the empty side. He climbs beneath the covers with me, and as the mattress dips under him, I slide a little toward the middle. The entire atmosphere of the room changes.

Breathing is a foreign concept. Thinking is impossible.

Theo shifts. His foot brushes against mine in slow motion. We turn to face each other and lie in the dark, measuring time with our own breaths.

As my eyes adjust to the dim light, I study his features. "Will you tell me the story about your scar?"

"It's proper embarrassing, so plan accordingly. I'll want to know something humiliating about you."

"That's only fair." I grin into the dark.

"When I was eleven years old, I was mad over Sweet and Sour."

"The girl group?"

"Oh yeah. I begged my mum to let me meet them. She made a call and got me invited backstage to their concert at London Stadium. When I saw them in person, I was a goner. Couldn't even remember my own name."

"That's adorable!" I scoot closer and brush my feet against his.

"A randy kid in love with a bunch of eighteen-year-olds? Just wait. We meet and they're lovely. They tell me how cute I am in a pinch-my-cheek sort of way, and then it was time for them to do their show. Zara—the one I fancied the most—put her hand on my shoulder to guide me to my seat, and I lost all motor function. I tripped over my own feet and smacked into a microphone stand."

"No!"

"Yes. Ended up crying and bleeding all over her Union Jack dress. I've never been so humiliated in my life. Up until that moment, I thought I was going to marry her."

It's painful, what this information does to my heart. I've never liked him more. "At least you have a badass souvenir from your first heartbreak." We're nose to nose, our feet tangled up together. I softly trace his scar with my pinkie finger. His eyes shutter closed. "Is it really against royal protocol for a commoner like me to touch you?"

"Will's a git," Theo grumbles.

"Sounds like a yes to me," I tease, pulling my feet back. Theo's hands fly out, capturing me around the waist and tickling me until I gasp for air.

"It's bad etiquette to touch a royal in *public*," he says as I catch my breath. "I was surprised when you grabbed my hand, but not upset. The thing about the royals is—" He cuts himself off. "Sorry, I was about to go on a rant."

"Rant away. I'd like to know more about your family."

He exhales, like maybe he was holding his breath waiting for my response. "In a world of progress, the monarchy does not change. *Ever*. We can't be seen wanting for anything, not even affection. We're not a warm, touchy family. We don't present one to the public and we're certainly not one behind closed doors. No affection, no hugs—except from Penny. My mum was raised to be the Queen—nothing else—and she's raised me the same way. It's an unbreakable cycle." He clears his strangled throat. "I must sound like a weak prat."

Weak. I'm furious with his mother for putting that thought in his head.

I reach my hand across the empty space between us and twine my fingers with his, squeezing until it hurts. "I'm sorry about your mom," I whisper into the dark. "I think the fact that you've made it this far means you're stronger than you give yourself credit for."

He doesn't respond.

"I'm scared to fall asleep," I say, giving him something in return for the secret he gave me.

"Why?"

"Because when we wake up, we'll have one less day."

"Then let's not fall asleep," he says.

"How?" I can already feel exhaustion tugging at my eyelids, but my chest feels fluttery at the idea of missing these hours. Any hours. There aren't enough left, and I don't want to miss a single one.

"Tell me about your family, and then I'll tell you about mine." Theo's hand returns my pressure, flooding his now familiar starlight warmth through my fingers. Starlight, I realize, because it glitters even in the dark. "Fair warning—I have *a lot* of siblings, so I could talk all night."

His fingers relax against mine and I panic. "Don't let go," I whisper, suddenly terrified by the prospect.

In one swift motion, he pulls me flush against his side. He pats his chest with his free hand and I lay my head down, savoring the thump of his heart against my cheek.

"I won't," he promises, his lips softly brushing my hair.

CHAPTER 14

DATE: TUESDAY, JUNE 14
LOCATION: PARIS, FRANCE

ITINERARY: 11:00 A.M. TGV TO MILAN
DAYS UNTIL THE COMET HITS: SIX

I wake up warm. Everywhere but my nose. I snuggle deeper under the covers, pulling the comforter above my chin. I am never, ever moving. The room is dark, save for the first glimpse of dawn seeping around the edges of the heavy curtains in the window.

Next to me, someone shifts, jolting my body from its sleepy cocoon. My eyes fly open as sudden awareness buzzes through my veins. Theo is curled up against my back like a big spoon. We stayed awake until the early hours of the morning, swapping stories about our families and our friends and growing up: how I spent my summers flying kites near Buckingham Fountain and he spent dreary London winters playing hide-and-seek with his younger siblings in Buckingham Palace (Henry, Victoria, Louise, Andrew, Charlotte—names I'm pleasantly surprised I still remember).

Even when the clock read 3:00 A.M. and I was losing my battle with exhaustion, his hand never left mine. When talking about my family threatened to overwhelm me, he kept me tethered. And when his thumb traced lazy circles on the back of my hand, well, I pretended not to notice how good it felt, or how much comfort I took in his presence.

I do the same now. I slow my breathing and lie perfectly still, content to stay in this position awhile longer, appreciating the feel of Theo's breath tickling the back of my neck. Just a few more minutes before I have to get up and face the cold reality of the imminent demise of everyone I love. (*And* everyone I hate, now that I think about it. Like my seventh-grade PE teacher, who caught me talking and made me run extra laps. When I called him sexist because the boy who was talking to me didn't have to run, the teacher loudly announced in front of everyone that I should thank him because, and I quote, I "could use the exercise.")

I'm not saying he deserves to die in a fiery explosion, but I'm not *not* saying it, either.

Theo shifts and his foot knocks against my bad ankle. I let out a sharp cry of pain and twist out of his arms.

"What's wrong? Are you okay?" He sits up, grinding the palms of his hands into his eyes as he struggles to wake up.

"Just my stupid ankle," I pant.

"What can I do?"

"Painkillers, please."

Theo stumbles out of bed, flicks on the light, and unzips the front pouch of my backpack. He grabs the bottle of medicine, and out tumbles the business card from the French police.

"What's this?" he asks, studying it with a troubled frown.

"Pills?" I hold my hand out to catch the bottle as he tosses it across the room.

"Seriously—what is this?"

"Oh. Um . . . a phone number from the police who questioned me." I rack my brain for a believable reason for this and come up empty. When Theo blinks at me, waiting for an explanation, I examine the instructions on the side of the bottle. "I can take up to twelve of these a day? I've been severely undermedicating."

He doesn't take the bait. "Why do you have this?"

I can't look at him. "They gave it to me in case I had any information regarding your whereabouts. I didn't want to tell you how desperate they were to find you because I wasn't sure we could fit in the bed if your royal ego got any bigger." I crack a smile. The joke doesn't land.

"You said they thought you were crazy."

"They did."

"Then why would they encourage you to call with tips?"

"Your guess is as good as mine," I say. It's not a lie, but it doesn't feel like the truth either, not with *the prince is . . . unwell* always looming in the back of my mind. I feel strangely guilty for not elaborating, but the last thing I want to do with my remaining time is dredge up unpleasant conversations.

"Why did you keep it?"

"I don't know. In case you ended up being Jack the Ripper?" I crawl across the bed and take the card from his hand. I rip it in half twice and flush the pieces down the toilet. "Happy?"

"I guess." He frowns at me. It feels wrong. This whole morning feels off. I want to go back to the way things were last night, when it was just us tangled together telling stories in the dark.

I flip the light off and crawl back into bed. I pull the comforter all the way up over my head. "Wake me up when it's time to leave."

"Oh shite." Light floods the room again, invading my dark and comfy cocoon. "Our train leaves in an hour."

"What?" I bolt upright and check the time on my phone. It's 10:00 A.M. How is it 10:00 A.M.? It's still dark outside. I limp to the window, pull back the curtains, and squint into the blinding sunshine. "Why didn't you set an alarm?"

"Why didn't you?!"

"I don't know! I forgot, or I assumed we'd wake up in plenty of time." I scrub my hands through my hair. I never should have convinced myself that it was a good use of time to stay up so late. If we miss our train because I was too distracted by the feel of Theo's hand on mine, I'll never forgive myself. I run to the bathroom and quickly apply deodorant and brush my teeth. I stuff spare clothes into my backpack. "Can we make it there in time?" I ask, gathering my Pippi orange hair into a high ponytail.

"It's going to be close," Theo admits as he bends to tie the laces on his suede shoes. "By car, maybe."

"Let's ask for a ride." I swing the door open wide, but Theo stops me with an outstretched hand.

"I can't go out there if Raoul's parents are around."

"Seriously? We're going to miss our train!"

Theo's expression is pained. "Please, just check."

Out in the main room of the apartment, Will, Raoul, and an older Black couple who I can only assume are Raoul's parents are watching the news from the couch. Raoul is folded up into Will's side with a mug of something steaming clutched in his hands. "Bonjour," he says. "How'd you sleep?"

"Okay." I glance down the hall, where Theo hovers in the doorway like a shadow. He's shockingly good at making himself invisible when he needs to.

"Maman, Papa, this is our American friend Wren."

I awkwardly wave hello as I bounce anxiously on the balls of my feet. Raoul's parents greet me warmly, and I know I'm probably being rude, but we don't have time for this. Our train now leaves in fifty minutes.

"Do you want to stay and watch the missile launch with us?"

"Actually—" I glance at Theo again. He motions his hands for me to hurry up. *I'm trying!* I mouth back to him. "Our—my—the train leaves in less than an hour. If I don't leave now, I'm going to miss it." I make big pleading eyes at Will.

Will jumps to his feet. "I'll drive." He bends to kiss his boyfriend goodbye and whispers something in his ear. Raoul grabs the remote, turns it up, and speaks in very quick French to his parents while gesturing wildly at the TV. I guess this is as good of an opening as we're going to get. I wave Theo forward. He has his hat and glasses on again, but he keeps his shoulders hunched, his head ducked, and his footsteps light as he flees through the apartment, past the open living room where Raoul and his parents are, and out the front door. I quickly follow behind.

"Did they notice?" Theo asks as the three of us jog to the elevator.

"Doesn't matter now," Will says as he stabs the button to bring us to the ground floor.

Out on the street, Will eases a small blue electric car away from the curb. He drives so quickly and erratically, it makes me nauseous, and after a few minutes my empty stomach (why is it always empty?!) protests. I lean my head against the window and close my eyes for relief. After a few minutes of silence, Will speaks.

"Your mum called last night." Music from the radio grows louder as one of them turns up the volume. I tilt my head so my ear is facing the front seat and strain to hear their voices over the music.

"What did she say?" Theo asks.

"You know what she said," Will says without a trace of his usual good humor.

"Not everyone here does," Theo says. It sounds a hell of a lot like a warning. And maybe a red flag. Is he talking about me? They must think I've fallen asleep. "What did you say?"

"I lied for you. Told her I didn't know where you were."

I peek one eye open and look at Theo in the rearview mirror. His face is tight and completely unreadable. "I owe you. I know I'll never get to repay it, but we'll both go to our graves knowing I owe you, which is almost payment enough," he says.

"I regretted it as soon as I hung up," Will says quietly, ignoring Theo's attempt to change the subject. "Are you sure you don't want to go home?"

"I can't. You know I can't."

"Can't and won't aren't the same thing, mate."

A crushing silence settles over the small car. Even with the music playing, Will's and Theo's unspoken words are louder. Unable to take it any longer, I yawn, pretending to wake up, and open my eyes as we approach the Gare de Lyon. I can't wrap my mind around the conversation I just heard. Why can't everyone leave Theo alone? If the comet hits and scientists are correct in their predictions, it won't matter whether he's in London or Santorini. I understand why a mother would want to say goodbye to her son, but the way he tells it, the Queen wants him to come home only to save face with the country. I might be able to buy that (as little as I know about the royal family), but why is his best friend trying to convince him to return to the palace? Is it because he wants Theo to be surrounded by family, or is it something else?

And does any of this have to do with what the police officer said about Theo being "unwell"?

I can't shake the foreboding feeling that there's something Theo's not telling me. When we pull up to the curb and Theo helps me out of the car, I don't know how to react when his hand clasps mine. I gaze up into his eyes, and I believe them. His hand feels steady in mine. I trust what he's telling me. But why is his friend trying to push him to die in the palace he hates, and does his insistence have anything to do with how paranoid and weird Theo got about the business card this morning? I shake off the thought. I'm reaching—making connections where none exist. Our brains are trained to do that, especially in times of extreme stress or upheaval. It's why conspiracy theories take off, why that cashier clerk (and maybe millions of others) believes the government is lying to him about the comet.

Will climbs out of the car and gives Theo a hug goodbye. They both have tears in their eyes when they separate, but there's no time for long drawn-out goodbyes, and soon we're sprinting toward the railway station. We get there just as a lone employee is locking the front door.

I knock on the glass. "We have to get inside!"

"Je suis désolé. The last train just left."

I check the time: 11:05. Five minutes too late.

Five minutes of pretending to be asleep while Theo curled around me in bed. I liked the feeling of his body close to mine a little too much, and now we're screwed.

"I can't believe there's not another train. Who knew the apocalypse would be so inconvenient?"

"I mean, I could have guessed," he says dryly.

"Well, I'm not dying in Paris, so what do we do now?" I pull out my notebook with the original itinerary, which I have now scratched out and corrected so many times, it's almost unreadable. I point to something illegible scrawled next to *TGV to Milan*. "What does this say?"

"That's just a different train line. That one didn't have *any* trains available for the day."

"And this?" I point to yet another line below the second.

"A third train."

"Your entire plan was trains? What century is this?"

"Do you have a better idea?"

"Actually, I do." I point to a sign on the station window, written in French with the English translation underneath. RENTAL CARS. An arrow points the way. "We'll drive."

CHAPTER 15

DATE: TUESDAY, JUNE 14
LOCATION: PARIS, FRANCE

ITINERARY: DRIVE TO MILAN (TEN HOURS)
DAYS UNTIL THE COMET HITS: FIVE AND A HALF

The rental car place is covered in graffiti. Spray-painted swear words and dicks as far as the eye can see.

"It's comforting to know that graffiti's the same no matter where you are in the world," I say. But I'm lying. There's nothing comforting about today. There's a vibe in the air that makes me shiver. An eerie sense of wrongness that I was too stressed to notice this morning. On our walk here, Theo overheard someone say that three people died trying to scale the Eiffel Tower last night, and there are bullet holes in shop windows all over the city. Sirens blare in the streets. It feels like the whole city is balanced on the tip of a knife, and there's nothing but danger no matter which way you look.

We approach the door to the car rental building, and my heart collapses when I see the doors are locked and the lights are off. "No!" I shout, banging on the glass door with both fists. *This can't be happening.* Behind me, Theo is quiet. "I'm not dying in Paris," I say through the sting of tears.

"It doesn't have to be all bad," he says. "We could make a bucket list and do whatever you want. I'd even swim in the Seine with you, but maybe not until the last day. A bout of E. coli might have me wishing for death."

"No," I insist. "We need to regroup. I'll think of a new plan. I'll—" My words die in my throat as a light turns on inside the building. "There's someone in there. Hide before they see you." I pound on the door again until a figure moves toward me.

"Nous sommes fermés," he says through the glass.

"They're closed," Theo translates behind me.

"Yeah, I got that," I snap. "Please open the door!" I plead to the man on the other side.

He turns a lock on the door and props it open with his toe. "Rot op! We're closed," he says again, this time in English with an unfamiliar accent. "Because of the comet." He's white, very tall, with a long blond ponytail and a strong smell of marijuana wafting from him. He has a lanyard in his front pocket. The name tag hanging out reads DIRK.

"You speak English!" I'm relieved that I won't have to navigate a language barrier. This is the first thing all morning that's gone my way.

"I'm Dutch," he says by way of explanation.

"You work here?"

"Not anymore. I quit. *Because of the comet.*" He says this last part like it should be obvious.

"Then what are you doing here?"

"I left gras in my locker."

"Grass?"

He mimes smoking a joint. *Weed. Got it.*

"Well, since we're both here, I'd like to rent a car." I hold out my passport, ID, and Mom's credit card.

He sighs heavily and glances over his shoulder to the front desk. "Nee. I'm retired."

I push the credit card toward him. "Your fastest model, please."

"Your hair is orange."

"Yep."

"Sorry—it's just that I've never seen hair so . . . *orange.* Is that . . . on purpose?"

"The car?"

He sighs again. "ID?" I hand it to him. He squints at it and then smirks at me. "Nee. Not twenty-one."

"Who cares?"

"Rules are rules." He glances over his shoulder again.

"So what? Break the rules! You're gonna be dead soon any- way!" I shout.

He blinks at me with a dazed expression. "Verdomme."

"Are *you* even twenty-one?" I ask. He looks Theo's age at best.

"Almost. But I'm not the one trying to rent a car."

"Please? My friend and I have to get to Italy *today* and we missed our train. Isn't there anything you can do?" *Like accept the fact that the world is ending and just give me a car because none of this even matters?*

"I have an idea," he says, and my heart soars. "Take the train tomorrow." He looks proud of himself for coming up with such a brilliant plan.

"The trains are completely sold out, and chances are good

they won't be running anyway. Please, just give me something small and cheap. I'll take literally anything."

"Nee. Rot op!" He nudges me backward and shuts the door in my face. The lock turns with a decisive click.

I trudge around the corner of the building to where Theo is waiting.

"What are we driving?" He rubs his hands together, his eyes shining with excitement.

"Nothing. He says I'm not old enough to rent a car."

"Does that really matter right now?"

"That's what I said! But apparently yelling at him that he's about to die didn't change his mind."

Theo looks at me like I'm insane. "Did you really say that?"

"I regret it now!"

"Try again. Don't yell at him this time, and maybe don't mention his imminent death."

I groan. I've never been good at sweet-talking people. I'm more of a bulldozer in situations like this. "What if you tried?"

"Why? What influence does Blaze Danger have that you don't?"

"None, but Prince Theo does have influence. The place is empty. If you go in there as the crown prince, he'll have to help you."

He cocks a skeptical eyebrow. "And if he doesn't?"

I wave my arms in front of me, frustration mounting. "Can't you, like, order him to listen to you?" I almost can't believe the words coming out of my mouth. Me, the same girl who just a few days ago was railing against the monarchy. Desperate times, desperate measures, I guess. It's comforting to know that in a time of crisis, my beliefs will crumple at the first sign of inconvenience.

"No."

"Then what good is being the prince?"

"No fucking good!" he declares. His chest heaves like there's a physical weight on it and he's fighting to breathe. "This isn't my country, and these aren't my people. But even if we were in England, I would never order someone to help me." His words blaze with a conviction that makes me ashamed for even suggesting it.

"Sorry." I raise my hands in a gesture of surrender. "I won't suggest it again." We stare at each other for a moment, something like understanding passing silently between us. His relief is palpable, and I wonder how many of his decisions he has a say in. Not many, I'd guess.

"I'll try to talk to Dirk again. Any advice for sweet-talking a stoner who's too lazy to find me a set of keys?"

"You could try flirting with him," Theo says, his face lighting up as he cracks a shit-eating grin. As if the thought of me flirting is so outlandish.

"I *will* flirt with him," I shoot back, annoyed for a new reason I can't quite understand. "I'll flirt so hard, he won't know what hit him." I stroll back to the entrance and knock for the third time.

"Let your hair down!" Theo calls to my retreating back. "He won't be able to resist those kumquat tresses!"

I flip him the bird over my shoulder as I continue to pound with one fist. It takes Dirk a lot longer to answer this time, and when he does, he looks pissed—the American kind.

"Hey, Dirk," I croon.

He responds with, "Still closed."

My brain stalls and I suddenly have no idea how to flirt. It's not that I never do it, but I'm just as likely to make fun of the guy I like as I am to laugh at his joke or whatever.

I rack my brain for universally translatable flirting methods. I could take Theo's suggestion and flip or twirl my hair, but Dirk doesn't seem impressed by its carrot-esque hue.

"I like your . . ." I scan him for something to compliment. "Name tag." He raises his eyebrows. "I mean your name! It's really . . . nice." *Face-palm*. I suck at this. I bite my lip, hoping I look coy. "So what are you up to tonight?" I tilt my head down and look up at him from under my lashes. I flutter them twice.

"Are you okay?" He squints at me.

"I'm great." I trace his arm with my finger, cringing when I hit sweat. "How are *you*?" I make my eyes go big and round.

"I'm flattered, but I don't go for American girls," he says bluntly. My pride is wounded as I pull my arm back. "And I prefer blondes."

I think I'm having an aneurysm. If I can't get my hands on a car key, I'm going to die here as Dirk insults me. "'Blond' is just a fancy word for yellow," I snap. Over Dirk's shoulder I see the light flick off in the back room. My heart stutters. "Who else is here?"

"No one."

"Someone just turned the light off." I nudge him to the side and push my way into the building. "Who is it?"

He sighs. "My manager," he whispers.

"What are they doing here?"

"Listen." He stops me with his hand. "Between us, I'm about to . . . you know." He raises his eyebrows meaningfully.

"Oh!"

"I've waited a long time for this. She is way out of my league, but no one has time to be picky when the world's ending."

Lovely. "I'd like to speak to her."

"What?" He blinks in surprise.

"This is a business, I'm a customer, I want to speak to the manager."

His face adopts a pleading quality. "C'mon. This never happens to me. I was just here to grab my gras and she also came in to get stuff from her desk, and one thing led to another, and now she's not really in a position to see people, if you know what—"

"I'm not leaving until I've spoken to her, so if you have any chance of having sex today, tell her I'm here."

"Fine," he huffs. "She'll need a few minutes to get dressed. Wait here." He drags his feet into the back room. As the door shuts behind him, I slip around the counter. I scan the desk in front of me but don't see any car keys. I open the drawers, as if I expected this large car rental place to keep all their keys piled in one giant junk drawer. *C'mon, Wren, think.* On the empty counter space next to Dirk's station is what looks like a rental agreement with a key lying on top. Probably from someone who dropped off their car before they closed. I search for the model on the paper, a Peugeot RCZ, and snatch up the key. I've just hopped over the desk again when Dirk comes back. I clutch the key to my chest and run.

"Hey! Where are you going?" he calls.

"Changed my mind! Have a nice life!"

I push the door open and wave the key triumphantly in the air at Theo.

"It worked?" he asks incredulously.

"Yes, *Your Highness.*" I curtsy.

He rolls his eyes. "What'd you do? Pretend you were hiding your identity and ask him to kiss you?"

If my cheeks flush slightly, it's only because of the warm

Paris sun. Not because thinking about kissing Theo makes my blood heat. "Unnecessary. My flirting game is hella strong."

"No one with a strong flirting game would ever utter that sentence out loud. So what are we driving?"

"A Peugeot RCZ. I'm not sure which one. Or which color," I say. This earns me a sidelong glance that I vehemently ignore. When I try to open the first RCZ in the parking lot, Theo's brow scrunches.

"This will take too long. Just lock it a couple of times and see which car beeps and flashes."

"There's no electronic key fob."

If possible, his brow furrows even further. "Let me see it again."

I hold up the key for him to inspect. "Are you sure you heard him correctly? This opens a Peugeot?"

"He might have been confused," I concede, although I clearly remember reading *Peugeot RCZ* on the rental agreement. "He was enraptured by my 'kumquat tresses,' after all."

"I'm sure," Theo says with a heavy dose of sarcasm. I think. His sense of humor is so dry, it's difficult to tell. "Where's the rental agreement?"

"The thing about the rental agreement is that we don't have one."

"This key will not fit in a Peugeot, to my utter disappointment. Whatever car this key belongs to is very, very old."

"Like, vintage?"

His gaze travels over my shoulder to the front of the garage and his face drops. "Like *that*." He points to a faded-yellow car that looks like the French version of a Volkswagen Beetle. "A Citroën 2CV."

"It's cute!" I manage, and it is. In a scary sort of way. It looks like it's one tight turn from falling apart. It's perfect for a quirky Instagram backdrop. Less perfect for a cross-country road trip. "I wonder how fast it goes."

"Not fast enough. But at least we don't have to worry about damaging it," Theo says as we take in the sagging bumper and dents in the doors.

I toss Theo the key. "Wait, do you know how to drive?" I ask, hoping the answer is yes. I'm not a confident driver. He slants me *a look*. "I'm serious. You're not chauffeured everywhere you go?"

"Not everywhere," he says primly as we open the doors to the car.

A crumpled receipt falls to the ground. We stare in horrified confusion.

"Maybe they didn't have time to clean it before everyone quit," Theo says diplomatically.

The car is filled with stuff. The back seat is littered with empty water bottles, a thick hoodie, crusty socks, and a long glass tube that I'm pretty sure is a bong. Not the kind of stuff you leave behind in a rental car, I realize with a sinking feeling. I pick up a used Starbucks cup with a name scrawled in black marker on the side. *Dirk*. Uh-oh. I spin the cup toward Theo, whose eyes widen. Then he bursts into laughter.

"You stole his car key?"

"Not on purpose!" I hiss.

He laughs harder. "I knew you didn't flirt this out of him."

"What do we do?" I ask. The door to the building opens and Dirk walks out, his face slack with confusion. When he sees us standing next to his car with the doors open, the confusion quickly turns to anger. "That's my car!" he shouts.

"Get in!" I yell to Theo. We leap into the car and slam the doors shut behind us. "Go! Go!" I buckle myself into the passenger seat as Theo steps on the gas. We don't so much *peel* out of the parking lot as *putter*. But we're faster than Dirk, which is all that matters.

My heart hammers hard and fast in my chest as we speed from the scene of the crime. We quickly hit traffic in the crowded, narrow streets of Paris, and I'm convinced that every random driver and pedestrian we pass knows exactly what we did, even though rationally I assume that everyone is probably out committing their own crimes.

We've been in the car for twenty minutes when we finally pass a sign that says A6 and merge onto a highway. It's only then that some of the tension in Theo's shoulders releases. He relaxes his fingers on the wheel and lets his body settle back into the driver's seat.

"I always thought if I stole a car, it'd be something faster than this," he muses. "It should be a ten-hour drive to Milan. In this, we'll be lucky to get there in twelve."

"Why would you steal a car?" I ask, my heartbeat still erratic. "You can buy anything you want."

"Which takes all the fun out of it," he says. I have no idea if he's serious or not, and I can't spare an ounce of mental energy figuring it out because *we stole a car*.

Objectively, it was the wrong thing to do. Stealing is bad. Blah, blah, blah. In this situation, I can't muster anything beyond the vaguest whiff of remorse. For one thing, we didn't hurt anyone. For another, Dirk has access to any car of his choosing. He can drive one of the dozens of Mercedes or BMWs we saw in the parking lot for the last five days of his life. So even though

I was plagued with guilt for even *thinking* about stealing a pack of Ice Breakers breath mints from the grocery store when I was six, I'm surprisingly okay with grand theft auto.

Like I realized before, it's comforting to know all my core beliefs are crumbling. At this point, there's nothing I wouldn't do to get home to my family. I need to give Wally a kiss, beat Cedar in a game of Mario Kart, prove to Brooke that I'm not a gullible idiot, and hug my parents. All before the world ends.

CHAPTER 16

DATE: TUESDAY, JUNE 14
LOCATION: SOMEWHERE IN THE MIDDLE OF FRANCE

ITINERARY: MORE THAN EIGHT-HOUR DRIVE FROM
   PARIS TO MILAN (IN A STOLEN CAR)
DAYS UNTIL THE COMET HITS: FIVE AND A HALF

Would you really have spent your last week alive helping me cross things off my bucket list?" I ask an hour later as we're cruising through the French countryside. To every other car on the road, speed limits and traffic laws have become mere suggestions. Our tin snail, on the other hand, would fall apart before breaking the speed limit. I have my feet on the dash and the window down, and although Theo grouses every three minutes about the wind resistance and aerodynamic drag, it's not the worst road trip I've ever been on. Theo loathes this tiny French car with its weak engine, but with wind in my hair and sunshine on my face, I'm kind of in love with it. It might be my favorite car of all time.

"It's not like we would have had many other options," he says.

"It's always nice to hear that spending time with me is a last resort."

He darts a glance my way before refocusing on the road. "It would have been my honor to help you with your bucket list, Wren Wheeler," he says sincerely.

"Oh." My cheeks heat.

"What would have been on it?" he asks.

I've been thinking about that a lot, about what I'd be doing with my time if I weren't so focused on getting home. Whenever we cross paths with someone who is still working, like those people on the trains in London, I can't help but wonder what the hell they're doing, and why they're not out crossing off their own bucket list items. But the truth is—I don't have the slightest idea what I'd be doing.

"So much of my mental energy over the last four years has been focusing on my future. Now that I don't have a future, I don't know what I'd do with one final week in Paris," I admit. In a world without consequences, I'm not sure what would make me happy. I hate admitting this. It makes me question everything I thought I knew about myself. If I'm not the girl with a plan, who am I?

Theo's quiet for several seconds before he responds. "I think I understand what you mean. I've spent my entire life running away from my future."

"We're quite the pair, aren't we? Alone in Europe without parental supervision and we haven't been skinny-dipping even once."

"You're not going to let that go, are you?"

"I'm really not."

He laughs. "I don't know what I'd put on my bucket list either, but I know it'd be simple. I want to eat good food and listen to music that makes me cry and watch reruns of *The Office*—"

"The UK or American version?"

"American, but I'll deny it in public."

"Fair enough." I laugh.

"Most of all, I'd want to spend time with someone who makes me happy." He glances sideways again.

"Too bad you're stuck with me."

"A tragedy."

The radio station switches from music to an English news report and Theo doesn't miss a beat before he turns it off.

"You don't want to know what's happening with the missile?" I ask.

"Not really," he says, avoiding eye contact. "Do you?"

"No. It's too important to think about." I'm so desperate for the launch to be successful that I'm too scared to listen to news reports or watch live update feeds. It's like whenever I took a big test at school. I didn't check the results of my SATs until four hours after they were emailed to me because my score was too important. If I didn't open that email, I could still imagine I lived in a world in which I got a perfect score. This is the same thing, on a more epic scale. "If I don't know what's happening, I can convince myself there's a chance the world won't end," I explain. I don't want to live in a world without hope. I wouldn't know how.

"Schrödinger's comet," he says.

"Exactly! It's my only form of self-preservation. For now, the missile launch is locked away tightly in a box of things I won't think about." It sounds silly when I say it out loud, but he nods thoughtfully.

"Have you ever taken a road trip?" I can't smother my curiosity about him. Every answer he gives me brings up a dozen new questions.

"First and last." His smile takes on a sadness that makes it difficult for me to breathe. I'd be a completely different person if my family hadn't packed our SUV every summer and driven north through Michigan up to Mackinac Island or east to Raystown Lake in Pennsylvania. All my best childhood memories are packed in the back of a tight car, smooshed between my siblings while we played the alphabet game with road signs and searched for every state's license plate.

I hate that Theo never had that.

"Stop at the nearest gas station," I say.

"Why? We're okay on fuel."

"Don't argue with me, *Prince*," I say insufferably. I know he hates it, but I can't stop myself.

It's a miracle that he listens. He pulls off the highway into the parking lot of a BP, where a yellow Labrador that reminds me of Wally is leashed to a post outside the store. He whines at me as I pass, so I kneel to give his big blocky head a pat and promise I'll grab him a treat. The gas station is abandoned and the windows are smashed, but I'm relieved that there's still food left. I grab every edible-looking packaged snack on the shelves, a dozen different kinds of drinks, a bag of dog food, and two slightly suspicious, probably day-old deli-style sandwiches on a crusty, golden-brown baguette labeled *Jambon-Beurre*. I won't eat the ham, but hopefully the bread is good. My mouth waters in anticipation as I hustle out of the building and kneel beside the dog. Aside from our car, the lot is empty.

The dog practically climbs into my lap when I check his neck for tags. "I'm so sorry you were left here," I tell him. "You're a very good boy and humans are rotten." He licks my cheek in agreement. I stroke my hand across his back and promise myself I'll wait an extremely reasonable twenty minutes before I do anything rash.

Thirty seconds later I untie his leash and usher him into the back seat of the car. I tear open the top of the bag of dog food and scoop out a handful, which he licks up eagerly.

"Tell me you're not nicking that dog," Theo says.

"I'm rescuing him." I wipe my hand with a napkin, squirt it with some sanitizer I found in the store, and buckle myself into the front seat, bags of food at my feet. "Let's go."

Theo stares at me, his foot still on the brake. "We can't steal a dog."

"He was abandoned! What am I supposed to do—leave him?"

"Yes."

"No. I'm not letting him die alone."

"This is going to end badly."

"True, but it doesn't take a psychic to figure that out."

Theo slants me an unamused glance as he pulls the car back onto the highway. "What's his name?" he asks after only two minutes of silence, which is how I know he's not as annoyed as he's pretending.

"I don't know yet. What do you think?"

"Comet," he says.

Comet the apocalypse dog. It's morbidly hilarious. "Deal." I lean back to tip a bottle of water against Comet's mouth. He laps it up quickly.

"You got anything in those bags for us?"

"Do you even have to ask?" I'll never understand how people "forget to eat." I've never forgotten a meal in my life. "This is officially a road trip. We'll live off candy and chips and these sandwiches." I unwrap the *Jambon-Beurre* and peel off the meat before taking a bite. "Oh my gosh. I can't believe I wasted my entire life eating stupid flavorless American butter."

"We'll remedy that at the next stop. We'll buy a big tub of French butter that you can put on everything," Theo says as he grabs his and takes a bite.

"Yes. Excellent. I'm not eating anything but French butter for the rest of my life." An unspoken understanding of how short that life will be passes between us in a blink. "Music! Every road trip needs music!" I turn the radio on, and the moment passes as we fiddle with the old dial until we find a station playing pop music in English.

Two hours later I'm slouched sideways in the passenger seat with my feet hanging out the window while Comet snoozes in the back seat and Theo and I sing Lady Gaga. Theo only knows thirty percent of the words to these songs, but that is not stopping him from belting them out at the top of his lungs.

A large bag of Gouda-and-cumin-flavored chips sits open on the console between us. We both go for a chip at the same time and our hands brush against each other's in the bag. A shock zips through my fingers. I pull my hand back quickly and duck my head so he won't see what I'm thinking. I've tried not to be so aware of him since we got in the car, but it's becoming impossible not to notice every little thing, like the way his voice cracks when he strains for the high notes, or how after that happens, he lowers his register about twelve octaves and sings like Gaston from *Beauty and the Beast*.

It doesn't help that the space is so small and he takes up *so* much of it. Our knees are practically touching, I notice. It would take no effort at all to reach out and brush his hair off his forehead, I notice. His eyelashes are dangerously long, I notice. His lips, stupidly kissable. And when he switches lanes, he puts his hand on the back of my headrest, giving me a view of the lean muscles in his arms, which I can't help but *notice*.

When we get tired of singing, I ask Theo to describe his family vacations—ski trips in Switzerland and weekends spent in the Scottish Highlands. When he tells a story about the time he and his brother Henry, only eighteen months younger than him, got drunk and led half a dozen horses into their Scottish castle, I can't help but think about my first week at the animal shelter. I was left alone for an hour and accidentally let thirty dogs loose at the same time, but Brooke came to my rescue and helped me get them all back into their cages. It was one of the most ridiculously stressful and fun afternoons of my life. Sometimes I forget that being Brooke's sister can be *fun*. Regret over our last conversation simmers in my belly. When it comes to Brooke, I'm always on the defensive, and honestly? I'm sick of fighting. Of struggling to keep up. I hope I get home in time to fix things between us.

I lose myself a little bit in the way Theo speaks so fondly of Penny and his siblings. It's obvious from Theo's stories that Penny is more than a nanny—she's been his family since the day he was born. And when he talks about the way she still cares for the little ones, Andrew and Charlotte, his mouth tips up in an easy, unaffected smile. I sneak out my camera to try to capture the expression on film, but by the time I *snap*, he's remade his face into the rehearsed one that's so familiar.

A Dua Lipa song ends, and a newsbreak cuts in. We're still on the English station, so I reach to turn it off, but my fingers still when I hear Theo's name. *"The search for Prince Theodore continues across Europe as the Queen admits that searches of their homes in Santorini and the Swiss Alps were fruitless. She urges anyone who has seen him to—"*

Theo brushes my hand away and turns the radio off.

"Don't you want to hear what they're saying about you?"

"No."

I don't understand how the answer can be so easy when the situation is so complicated. "What did your mom do to you that you can't forgive?"

His scarred eyebrow slants inward. "What do you mean?"

"You love your family. It's obvious when you talk about your siblings."

"I'd do anything for them," he confirms.

"Except stay with them when it matters most."

"You don't know what you're talking about," he says dismissively.

"Careful. Your royal snobbery is showing."

His hands flex on the steering wheel and his jaw tightens. I get the sense that he's weighing the costs and benefits of telling me the truth.

"I'm depressed," he says.

"I'd be surprised if you weren't, given the circumsta—"

"No. I suffer from clinical depression. I have for years," he says.

I reconsider the last few days. Theo telling me he couldn't get out of bed. Saying he was afraid he'd give up on himself. The Queen calling him weak. I flash back to a room on the bottom floor of the Gare du Nord. *The prince is . . . unwell.* Is that what they meant?

I want to say a hundred things, to tell him that his mom is wrong. I start with "I'm sorry."

"My mum has known for years, but she doesn't—" He clears his throat and tightens his grip on the wheel. "I'm not allowed to get help. The royal family does not show weakness, and she takes our history very seriously. She says no one will respect a king who is in therapy or takes medication. She thinks that this is just some teenage phase I'm going through. I'm allowed to discuss mental health as charity work, but I'm not allowed to acknowledge that I have mental health issues of my own."

"That's bullshit."

"I don't disagree."

"You can't let her control you like that. If your mom is as cold as you say she is, your brothers and sisters need you right now."

"It's better for them in the long run if I'm not in London when the comet hits."

What "long run"? I don't understand what he's talking about. How could it be better for them to die without their big brother? "What does that mean?"

"Z in 'Switzerland,'" Theo says in a tight voice that ends our alphabet game and our conversation. He points to a road sign announcing the Swiss border in five kilometers.

"I didn't realize we'd have to cross the border." My life flashes before my eyes as I imagine appearing in an episode of *Locked Up Abroad* for stealing a forty-year-old car.

"It's not a big deal," Theo says. "They don't do border checks. We won't even have to show our passports," he adds, reading my mind.

"What's that?" I point to a small line of cars and the uniformed officer standing on the side of the road, speaking to a driver through an open window.

He frowns. "There's not supposed to be a checkpoint. I don't understand what's happening."

"The radio said they were searching for you across Europe. Maybe they're looking for you?"

"No. No way. Even my mom can't override the entire EU."

"And if you're wrong?" We come to a stop at the back of the line of cars. Theo's lack of response tells me everything I need to know. We're in trouble. "Can you get in the trunk?"

"Now?" he asks incredulously. "I don't bloody think so. He'll see me if I try." He points to the officer only three cars in front of us.

"Switch seats with me," I say. We unbuckle our seat belts and Theo climbs over me. For one heart-stopping breath he's braced over me, and when I glance up at him, his lips hover inches above mine. My throat dries. "If he recognizes you, you have to kiss me," I breathe, because that's who I am. Always reaching for a joke. Masking my feelings under ten layers of sarcasm. Theo laughs as he falls sideways into the passenger seat.

By the time our car reaches the officer, we're both buckled in and acting reasonably normal.

"Passe," the white officer says. I hand both of our passports over while Theo pretends to snooze against the door. His hat is pulled suspiciously low to "block the sun from his eyes," but his night-kissed hair is visible underneath.

"Is there a problem?" I ask. The officer hears my English and glances at my passport. He switches to English.

"No problem, madame." He gives my passport photo a cursory glance and then checks Theo's. I swear his eyes do a double take at *Blaze Danger*.

"Is this about the comet?"

"The comet will be destroyed before it hits Earth," he says. I guess his faith in NASA explains why he's still working. "Is your friend okay?" he asks, motioning to Theo.

"He's been driving most of the day and he's tired."

The officer studies the passport again with a puzzled expression, before returning both and dismissing us with a wave. I breathe a giant sigh of relief as I take my foot off the brake pedal and the car rolls forward.

"Stop!" the officer commands.

I slam the brake as shocks of terror travel up my spine. The officer frowns at me as he opens the back door of the car. I turn around and my stomach plummets.

Comet is sitting up with Dirk's glass bong held like a bone between his teeth.

The officer leans into the car and pulls out a bag of weed that I didn't notice before.

"It's not mine!" I insist. "I don't want it. Please, I'm trying to get home to my family before the comet hits. I'm so scared, I just want them to be okay—" I'm babbling incoherently, my voice rising several octaves. The officer silently pockets the contraband and waves me forward without another word.

I grip the steering wheel with shaking fingers. "Holy shit. I thought we were going to get arrested!"

"I could tell. Your voice hit a register only Comet could hear." Theo laughs.

"Shut up!" I slap his shoulder. "That was traumatizing."

"I take it you didn't get in much trouble growing up."

I swerve the car to the shoulder of the road. "Approximately never. Which is why *you* have to drive again."

We drive for hours, dodging the news and any talk of the comet or the coming apocalypse. I know we'll have to face it eventually, but for now, it's nice to pretend it's just Theo and me on a road trip through Europe. I snap pictures of Comet in the back seat and our piles of snacks and my feet on the dashboard.

The photos aren't impressive or anything, but that's what I like about them. They're simple and mundane and yet somehow tell the craziest story of my life.

It's late when we cross the (thankfully unmanned) border into Italy. Theo yawns and my head bobs as I struggle to stay awake. I'm afraid if I fall asleep, he will too. "We have to stop and sleep," I say.

"I know." He pops open the tab of a Red Bull and takes a long drink. "We're getting close."

"To Stella's house?"

Theo frowns at the dashboard. "Yeah."

"Is something wrong?"

"No, I'm fine," he says quickly. "I just wish I could get you to Santorini faster." It's too dark in the car to see his expression, but I can't shake the feeling that there's something he's not telling me. My eyes droop closed before I can ask.

The next time I open them, it's after midnight and Theo is pulling the dying little French Beetle to a stop in front of a small house.

"This is it," he says. "My ex-girlfriend's house."

CHAPTER 17

Suddenly I'm wide awake. "You dated Stella?"

"Briefly," Theo confirms.

"You said she was a friend."

"She's a friend who also happens to be an ex."

"Why are you telling me this now?"

He looks at me across the dark car. For reasons I can't quite explain, my heart is in my throat. "I didn't want you to be ambushed," he says.

I'm not sure what to make of that.

The street is dark and ominously quiet as we exit the car in front of Stella's two-story ivy-wrapped home, the leafy green plant creeping around the white stucco exterior and climbing up toward the slanted black roof. Flower boxes filled with cheery pink blossoms sit in the windowsills and a wrought-iron balcony hangs off the second story. Behind the house, a slope of tilled green fields stretches into the dark.

"This is Milan?" I ask Theo, nudging Comet awake in the back seat. The dog jumps out, runs three quick laps around the driveway, then pees in the grass.

"Just south of. We're technically in Lombardy," Theo answers through a yawn.

"Have you been here before?" I ask. *How serious was your relationship with Stella?* is what I mean.

"Nope," he says, declining to provide further details.

Theo's hair is delightfully rumpled from the long trip, his body languid. *Snap.* I'd call this photo, *Boy Who Is Not at All Nervous About Visiting His Ex.* Next to it on the gallery wall, I'd put a self-portrait titled, *Girl Who Is Definitely Equally Chill.*

"I don't think the missile worked," I say, ending our unspoken agreement not to mention anything comet-related. Now that the road trip is over, it's like the spell of avoidance we cast around our little car is broken. Back to the real work of doomsday clocks and ex-girlfriends.

"Why do you say that?" Theo's eyelids are barely open.

"I think people would be celebrating." As it is, all the windows on the quiet residential street are a depressing shade of midnight black. We've left behind the wild chaos of Paris and stumbled into a different mode of coping with the apocalypse.

"And on that bleak note—" He opens the white gate and holds out his arm.

"One second. I should check in with my parents." I fire off quick texts to every member of my family so they know I'm still alive, and then I walk past Theo up the brick path, through the large courtyard, and to the front door. He knocks quietly.

The girl who opens the door is short, barely five feet, with olive skin, a curtain of long honey hair, and thick eyebrows. "Theodore!" She throws her arms around him and squeezes tightly. "I missed you."

They hug for a long time. An awkwardly long time. And if I feel annoyed by that, it's not because I'm jealous. *Nope*.

"Come in but be quiet," she whispers. "My nonna's asleep." The floor is reddish-orange tile. The rooms and hallways are small and filled with old, dark wood furniture. She sees my wandering gaze and frowns at the floral curtains. "She won't let me redecorate."

"I like it," I say truthfully. The house has a cozy vibe that feels like home, even if it's not *my* home. I walk to the redbrick fireplace in the front room and run my fingers over the mantel.

Stella takes one look at Theo's exhausted face and points to one of two small, floral couches in the front room. "You can sleep here."

"Thanks, Stel." He drops his bag and without even bothering to take off his shoes, folds himself into the love seat. He drags a crocheted blanket over his shoulders and is asleep within seconds.

Stella gives me a swift once-over before saying, "You can take the other couch. Put the dog in the backyard. We have a fence. The bathroom is down the hall." She turns her back and disappears down a dark hallway. *Well then*. Looks like Stella and I aren't going to become Apocalypse BFFs.

I fill a dish from the kitchen with water for Comet and let him out back. He whines when I try to shut the door, but after a sloppy kiss on my cheek and a promise that I'll come back in the morning, he paces the yard until he finds the best spot of grass and lies down. I hate the person who abandoned him, but at least this trip was good for something. It helps ease the regret I still feel whenever I think about the plane out of Heathrow.

In the bathroom I brush my teeth, freshen up, and change into the same leggings and T-shirt I slept in last night. The fact that Theo and I were in Paris just *last night* is unthinkable. Time has been an unreliable narrator ever since I realized the world was ending. Every minute feels like an hour, every day like a year. At the same time, I'm pretty sure I blinked and was transported from Heathrow to Milan. None of it makes sense. I've known Theo for forever and barely at all. I lie on the couch across from his and pull a throw blanket over my legs.

I stare at the ceiling and count the ticks of a grandfather clock in the corner.

Despite the exhaustion burning through my bones, I'm having the same problem I did last night. My mind races with images that keep me awake. Naomi and I riding our bikes to the beach on summer afternoons. The fancy sushi dinner my family ate to celebrate Brooke's LSAT score. Mom pulling me out of school as a surprise to take pictures on Navy Pier. Me being a bitch about it because my math class was preparing for finals. Theo No Last Name helping me burn my itinerary with his lighter. I linger on each memory until it becomes unbearable, before swiping it away for a new one, masochistically cycling through an image gallery of my life.

Unable to stand my endless thoughts for another second, I retrieve my phone and pull up my texts, finally opening the handful from Naomi.

Text me when you get on another flight.

I'll wait for you at O'Hare

Did you book a ticket yet?!!

What's going on????

I'm so sorry I left you!

Please answer me

I'm scared

Wren?

Are you okay?

I suck. I'm the worst. I'm a bad friend.

I'm so sorry. I miss you. I hope you're okay.

Please call me.

I have no idea what time it is at home or whether she wants to hear from me after so much silence, but I finally answer her.

Hey

My phone buzzes with a reply almost immediately. Can I call you?

I can't talk but I can text, I respond.

Her next response is even faster.

Are you okay?

I mean, I know you're physically okay

because I've been bugging Brooke for updates

but like, are you okay?????

I smile at the way she splits one thought into multiple texts like her fingers are working faster than her brain. Sometimes I'll put my phone down for an hour and come back to forty-five texts from her about her latest TikTok obsession.

Mentally? I add a skull emoji.

Do you hate me for leaving without you?

No. I promise. I hit send.

She responds with another flurry of messages.

Good

Because if I had to die

Knowing you're mad at me

I'd fling myself off a cliff

I send her a heart emoji, knowing it's not enough. There's more to say about how much I love her and regret what happened in London, but I'm too exhausted to say any of it right now.

Another round of texts comes in.

Oh

And I don't want to tell you what to do

But Brooke misses you

I scrub my hands over my face. She's not wrong, but again, I can't face it all right now. It's too much. I bolt upright. Being careful not to wake Theo, I tiptoe to the kitchen.

I startle when I see Stella sitting at the table with an open bottle of red wine. Like a full adult. It's bizarre. I know the drinking age in Europe is lower than in the States, but *wine* feels so sophisticated.

"Do you always drink wine in the middle of the night?"

She huffs a laugh. "No, but the world's not always ending."

"The missile didn't work?" I ask numbly, as much as I hate to check on Schrödinger's comet.

"The weather wasn't right for a launch today. It was delayed until tomorrow. Want a drink?" She holds up the bottle. "My nonna won't care. She has a whole cupboard full of them. At this point, I plan on being wine drunk until the comet hits."

I've had tastes of alcohol here and there, at a friend's party or stolen from Mom's champagne glass on New Year's Eve. But I've never been drunk, because I've always stayed far away from anything that could derail my plans. I've been on a single-minded mission—graduation, Northwestern for undergrad, law school—for as long as I can remember. I didn't have time for anything that could mess that up. Even now, with five days left to live, I waver on the edge of uncertainty. If Theo and I oversleep and miss our ferry, it's over. For both of us. But I'm also tired of being so responsible all the time. I just want to be numb for a little bit, and we already set our alarms to wake us up—I check the time—five hours from now. *Oof*. It's gonna be another rough morning.

"What's it feel like?"

"What? Being drunk?" Stella asks in a surprised voice.

I nod.

"Find out for yourself."

She pulls two wine glasses off a shelf behind her and fills mine all the way to the top. "Cheers, I guess." I raise my glass to Stella and then take a small sip. I pinch my face. It's tarter than I expected, like a handful of sour berries. I quickly take a few more drinks, and when the glass is empty, I hold it out to Stella for a refill.

"So how long did you and Theo date?" I ask too quickly, not at all off-the-cuff.

She raises a dark eyebrow. "What did he tell you?"

"Almost nothing. Just that you're his ex-girlfriend."

"Dai! Veramente?" She laughs loud enough that I'm worried Theo's going to wake up and hear us talking about him. "No. Sorry, but no. We never dated."

"Oh." Now I don't know *what* to think. "Why would he lie about something so random?"

"He's not lying. I think we just have vastly different interpretations about what happened," she says. "We hung out for a few months during the first semester of uni, but he was so paranoid about the press finding out. We couldn't do anything together, not even grab dinner or study on the quad, because he was terrified someone would take photos and sell them to the tabloids."

"Would that have been so bad?" Pictures of the golden-haired prince and his honey-haired girlfriend studying on the quad seems like dream PR.

"Exactly what I said! I wasn't fussed one way or the other if people knew about us, but he insisted. He said the press would ruin my life and he couldn't do that to me." She takes another slow sip of wine. "We 'broke up' before we were even together."

I trace my finger over the rim of my glass while she talks. Her description of him fits with what I know, but it makes me sad for them both. I wonder if he would have found some of the happiness he obviously craves if he hadn't sabotaged their relationship from the beginning. "How'd you two meet?"

"It was the first week of classes. He was staying in a dorm room. Trying to be 'normal,' you know, even though he had security guards tailing him constantly. He's obsessed with the idea of 'normal.' It was the first Friday night of the semester and I was feeling homesick, so I stayed back to do my laundry. When I went to the laundry room, he was in there cursing up a storm because he couldn't figure out how to get the machine to turn on. I taught him how to do laundry and we played an improvised game of beer pong while we waited for our clothes to finish. It was . . . nice." She smiles, her eyes lost in the sweet and uncomplicated memory. A surge of jealousy climbs up my throat. Or maybe that's the wine going to my head. I close my eyes and wait for the room to stop spinning.

When it (mostly) does, I drain my glass again and push it across the table for another refill. "That's extremely wholesome," I say with a heavy dose of sarcasm.

She blinks in surprise. "Is there a problem?" she asks.

"Theo's been on the run since the moment I met him." We'll never have a wholesome meet-cute because we're fugitives and also the world is ending. We'll never have anything but terror.

"He does that," Stella says. She stares at me thoughtfully, almost accusatorily. "What I don't understand is why you're helping him run."

"You should have seen the lionesses," I say through a hiccup. Stella's brow scrunches in confusion, which makes me giggle. "Not literally." For some unfathomable reason I pronounce *literally* in a British accent. *Lit-reli*. I giggle again. I think the wine's going to my head. "People spotted him. He wanted to be left alone, so I helped him run. And hide. Hurt my ankle in the process." I hold up my leg as proof, revealing where my ankle bulges under my sock. It's still wrapped in an Ace bandage, and now that I think about it, I haven't rewrapped it in forever. It suddenly feels tight, like it's cutting off the circulation to my toes. I'm going to be *so mad* if my toes fall off. I say as much to Stella, but she doesn't think it's likely. At least, I assume that's why she ignores me.

"Hmmm," Stella muses. Her brow is still scrunched, her eyebrows like caterpillars wiggling across her forehead. It's the funniest thing I've ever seen. I try to tell her this, but I'm laughing too hard to explain it right. "Theo thought he needed to save me from the paps, but what he needed was someone to save him," Stella says. It makes no sense.

"I didn't *save* him." I laugh hysterically at the thought. *Imagine!* Me saving a prince! "Not bloody likely," I say, and oh dear. The bad accent has returned. I glance over my shoulder to make sure that Theo's not listening. The house is quiet. "Theo! Theo! Go back to sleep!" I whisper. Just in case.

"You saved him once, you can do it again," Stella says.

"Sure, Jan." I burst into laughter and slosh wine over the rim of my glass, which makes me laugh harder.

"Who's Jan?"

"It's a meme." I'm still laughing.

We drink the entire bottle of wine, although I spill my last gulp and then fall out of my chair. My limbs feel sluggish and heavy as I drag myself up off the floor and back into my chair. "I think I'm drunk," I try to whisper.

Stella rolls her eyes at me. "You don't have to yell."

I double over in laughter again, but when my head hits the table, I'm not sure I'll be able to pick it up again.

"Look at me."

I glance up at Stella through bleary eyes. Hers are laser sharp as they burn through me. She doesn't look drunk at all. *How's that fair?*

"You know, I think what you're doing is really shitty," she says at last, as if she can't keep it in anymore. Her thick eyebrows draw together. I love her eyebrows. And her *earlobes*. I want them on my own face. I reach out to touch them and grasp at the air between us.

"Wh—why—" I can barely get the word out. I don't understand what she's talking about or how she's not drunk or why she's mad at me.

"Do you really not know what's going on?" she hisses under her breath.

I open and close my mouth, completely lost.

"You could save him, but you won't," she says.

"How?" My brain feels like it's filled with bees. Maybe she's drunker than I thought. She doesn't remember about the comet. Poor girl. She doesn't know. I have to remind her. "The comet's gonna kill everyone, even him."

"Not if he's in the bunker."

I shake my head. It doesn't make sense. She's way too drunk. "There's no bunker," I say sadly. I grab her hand in mine. She yanks it free.

"The UK has an underground bunker that the royal family will be in when the comet hits. Why do you think they're scouring the globe looking for Theodore? They're trying to save him."

A bunker? I shake my head again. This can't be real. I would have heard about it on the news. Not that I've listened to any news in days, but Theo would have told me. "I don't believe you."

She slides her phone across the table to me. I squint to read the headline from the *Daily Mail*: ROYAL FAMILY PREPARES TO HUNKER DOWN IN COMET BUNKER, BUT WHERE'S THE MISSING PRINCE?

My stomach churns and Stella must see something on my face, because she shoves a trash can in front of me.

"What's this for?" I ask indignantly. She rolls her eyes, and I vomit into the can.

CHAPTER 18

DATE: WEDNESDAY, JUNE 15
LOCATION: MILAN, ITALY

ITINERARY: FRECCIABIANCA TRAIN FROM MILAN
   TO BARI, BOARD FERRY FROM BARI TO GREECE
DAYS UNTIL THE COMET HITS: FIVE

I t's time to wake up."

Theo's bullhorn voice is a rope around my ankle, pulling me out of sleep and back to him. I tug a blanket over my head and turn over, trying to summon my dream. It was him and me swimming in the Chicago River, which had been dyed green even though it wasn't St. Patrick's Day.

"Wren. It's time to go."

Theo puts his hand on my shoulder and gently shakes me. It might as well be an earthquake. My head feels like it's filled with grinding gears, my stomach is churning, and my bones are made of lead. If the comet hit now, I wouldn't complain.

"Wren. Get up!" Theo shouts.

I pull the blanket off my face and glare at him. "Why are you yelling at me?"

"I'm literally whispering," he says. *Lit-reli*. My heart stirs.

"Fine." I squeeze my eyes shut to ward off a swell of nausea. The last thing I need is to vomit in Stella's home. How embarrassing would that be?

I stretch my hand out to Theo. "Will you help me up?" I've forgotten how my legs work.

He grabs my hand and helps me into a sitting position, which only makes the headache worse. I drop my head into my hands.

"Wait—are you drunk?" he asks. He leans closer and makes a face. "You reek of wine."

I want to crawl under the couch cushions and die.

"Did you and my ex-girlfriend have a nice time talking about me?"

"She says she's not your ex. Not technically. Or something." Last night's fuzzy at best.

"So you *did* talk about me."

"Mostly we drank."

He swears under his breath. "I'm going to kill Stella."

"You better do it quick, or the comet will do it first," I say.

Now that my eyes have adjusted to the soft predawn light streaming through the open curtains, my brain gears don't feel so rusty. Theo kneels in front of me and slides my foot into a shoe, his face obscured by his hair. His stupid freaking hair. If *we* were photographed studying together on the quad, he'd look like a midnight dream and I'd look like a rodeo clown.

"It's tragic," I whisper.

"The comet?" he asks as he gently unwraps the Ace bandage

binding my ankle. His fingers skirt lightly over the navy bruise that stretches across the span of my foot.

"My hair," I whisper back. "It looks so ugly."

He chuckles softly and shakes his head. "Open up." He drops two pills into my mouth and tips a water bottle to my lips. "For the ankle and the hangover." He lowers the bottle and returns his focus to my injury. I watch as he winds the beige bandage tightly with careful precision and unmatched concentration. I slip my fingers through his hair and push it back off his forehead while my heart pounds in my ears.

He stops moving, his hands going utterly still against my foot.

Whoops. Maybe his concentration wasn't unbreakable after all.

"Sorry if that was weird," I whisper, though I'm not at all sorry. His hair feels perfect, and I'd do it again.

"No, it's okay. You can touch me. I mean, my hair. I mean—" He cuts himself off and blushes scarlet as he carefully slides my other foot into my shoe and ties the laces. A swell of painful emotion starts in my chest and builds up past my throat. Tears burn behind my eyes and an unnamed and unexamined emotion crashes through my body. When he's done, he claps his hands on my knees and sits back on his heels.

"I packed your toothbrush and stuff from the bathroom. Comet is in the car, hopefully not eating our breakfast. Are you ready to go?"

No, I almost whisper. For the first time in three days, I consider what'd it be like to stay here with him, in a charming house in the Italian countryside. It'd be so simple. I could move on from the dangerous emotion of hope and mourn my family. I could sit on Stella's sun-soaked brick walkway in the courtyard, surrounded by flowers and ivy while I make daily video calls to everyone I've ever loved. I could lean my head against Theo's shoulder and fall asleep with his hand in mine.

I'm so tired, and part of me wishes I could stop running, stop hoping, stop wanting things I'll never have.

Theo's ocean eyes are clouded with concern as he gazes at me.

"I'm tired," I whisper.

"You can sleep on the train."

"We still have so many miles to go."

"I promised not to give up on you, Wren." His voice cracks with raw emotion as he wraps my hands in his and pulls me to my feet. I sway unsteadily. He holds me in his grasp until I can stand on my own. "You don't want to stay here."

"How do you know?" My ankle trembles and I consider the cost of dropping back onto the couch.

"Because I know you," he says simply.

My brain is still full of rusted, grinding gears, but I'm pretty sure that's not true. How could he know me?

"No, you don't," I say, and I recognize the taste of a lie on my tongue. I don't know what the truth is; I only know what this moment feels like. And right now it feels like no one knows how badly I want to get home as well as Theo No Last Name. "Fine. You're right. I'm ready to go."

Half of his mouth tilts up in a cocky smile. "Say that again?"

"What? You're right?"

"That's the one." His half smirk turns into a full grin. "Not so useless now, am I, American girl?"

My heart beats double time. Brooke might have inspired British boys to call her "love," but I don't care what anyone says. This is better. "I'm sorry I implied that you were useless."

"You two have a problem." Stella appears at the opposite side of the room.

"Is it the fact that Wren's hungover? I blame you," Theo says disapprovingly as he shoulders both of our backpacks. I notice Stella notice this.

"She's a big girl. She can make her own decisions," Stella says. "But no, that's not the problem. You've been spotted."

"Where?" I ask.

"St. Pancras. Drone footage was posted on TikTok and a bunch of the commenters spotted you and your fancy new hair."

Theo's face goes white.

"Can you see *my* hair?" I reach up to push an orange lock behind my ear. We'll be too easy to spot if people know Theo's traveling with Gritty.

"Theo's blocking all but the side of your face. Your hair is hidden under a hoodie."

"Okay!" I breathe a sigh of relief. "That's not so bad, as long as they don't know where you are now," I say. I give Theo's hand a reassuring squeeze. He swallows heavily.

"Be careful out there. Now that people know you're using public transportation, commenters are saying they're going to stake out train stations and look for you," Stella warns.

Theo's fingers lock around mine.

"No one's going to waste their time doing that. It'll be fine. I'm sure it'll be fine," I say with as much confidence as I can muster. "Does that mean the trains are still running?" Theo and I haven't dared to talk about what we'll do if they're not.

"I doubt it," Stella says. We walk together out into the humid morning air. Across the street, a startled cat darts around a trash can before disappearing underneath a car.

"Way to inspire confidence, Stel," Theo mutters.

"I'm just calling it how I see it."

"I'm not worried," I lie. "Someone will be there, either because they want to help or because they're in denial or they don't know what else to do." I flash Theo a grin to cover the inky foreboding thrashing in my stomach.

It's not a sign, I tell myself. We'll board the train without being spotted, and this time—for the first time—everything will be fine.

I duck into the passenger seat of Dirk's car. Comet lunges forward over the center console to give me a sloppy good-morning kiss on the cheek. I return the kiss and move to pull the door shut, but Stella's hand shoots out to stop me. Her deep brown eyes cut through me like a laser. "Think about what I said last night." She flashes one last disapproving look and slams the door in my face.

"What did she say last night?" Theo asks as he starts the car.

I rack my brain. Last night is hazy. The only sharp memories I have are the tangy taste of my first sip of wine and the harsh slant of Stella's eyebrows. Based on that expression—and the way she just slammed the door on me—I'd hazard a guess that she's mad at me. If only I could remember why.

"I think we talked about you . . ." I say slowly, fragments of our conversation floating back to me. "How much you hate the press and tried to hide her—"

"*Protect* her."

"Either way." I wave my hand in the air, trying to remember more. Wine. Lots of wine. And giggling. And—*oh my gosh*. I gasp as the memory clicks into place. My hands fly to my mouth.

"What is it?" Theo gives me an uneasy glance.

"I threw up in her garbage can and then I stumbled out to the couch and fell asleep. I probably didn't clean up after myself. No wonder she hates me." I tip back against the seat with a groan. What is it with me and vomit on this trip?

Theo's shoulders relax. "She won't hold that against you," he says, but based on Stella's irritated expression, I'm not so sure. "I take it you're not a big drinker?" He lifts a hand off the steering wheel to pass me a paper bag filled with pastries and my water bottle.

"I'm underage, remember?" Regret pools in my stomach. Only five days left to live, and I'm spending one of them with a hangover. I'm *never* drinking again. "If you didn't force me off that couch this morning, I wouldn't have gotten up. Thank you."

"You would have gotten up eventually." He shoots me a grin. "We would have missed the train, but knowing you, you would have found some other way to get us down the coast."

I can't help but return his smile. He's right; I would have found another way, but I'm thankful I won't have to. "I, for one, am looking forward to one uneventful leg of this journey," I say.

"You know you jinxed us by saying that, right? Now the train will be beset by robbers and we'll get pulled into a jewel heist or something."

"If it means the trains are still running, I'll take it."

"I'm not worried about the trains running. If the public thinks there's a chance that I'm on board and they can find me and win a favor from my mum, every transit worker will be on the job today," he says.

"Wow." He's kidding. I think he's kidding.

"You nervous?" he asks.

"Nope. Just when I think I understand the size of your ego, you surprise me again."

"You're the worst."

"But you love me anyway," I say, laughing.

He rolls his eyes, his mouth hitching up in a smile. "Dream on, American girl."

CHAPTER 19

DATE: WEDNESDAY, JUNE 15
LOCATION: SPEEDING ALONG THE ADRIATIC
COAST

ITINERARY: FRECCIABIANCA TRAIN TO BARI
DAYS UNTIL THE COMET HITS: FOUR AND A HALF

Well, damn. Theo was right. Twice in one morning.

I swallow my fear as we stand at the edge of a massive crowd. In front of us, a teenage girl holds a sign with Theo's face on it. "We're screwed," I say.

"No, we're lucky," Theo says. "We can use the chaos to our advantage." He grabs my hand and pulls me into the crowd. I hold tight to Comet's leash and keep him close. When Theo jostles into a second girl holding a sign that says SPOSAMI, PRINCIPE, I quickly mutter an apology. She rolls her eyes at the back of Theo's head. It's incredible what a hat and a pair of sunglasses will do to disguise the most famous fugitive in the world. No one gives us a second glance as we elbow our way through the station and board the high-speed Frecciabianca train.

The whole country is abuzz. "Cometa" is the word on everyone's lips. Theo roughly translates snippets of conversation for me, and it feels like everyone is teetering on the edge of a meltdown, all of society stitched together with cotton candy thread. If the missile fails today, all bets are off.

I don't think about that. I think about the fact that we made it this far. For once, the plan went off without a hitch.

We settle near the back of the train, where we're alone except for a few days of built-up trash, a toddler who runs up and down the aisles screaming every few minutes, and the exhausted mom who follows her. I leash Comet to the table; he turns twice on the train seats before falling asleep with his head in my lap.

Italy is beautiful. What I've seen of it, at least. It's hard to pay attention to the series of beaches and small towns dotting the Adriatic Coast with Theo launching a two-pronged offensive inside the train cabin. We're playing Speed with the deck of cards I found in my backpack, and it's becoming a problem. For one thing, his hands are faster than mine. (I blame the hangover.) For another, it's almost impossible to concentrate on what's happening on the table (let alone out the window) when what's happening under the table is way more interesting. I can't make my brain concentrate on anything other than the idle circles his fingers are tracing on my knee.

"You're not playing fair." I refuse to look up and give him the satisfaction of knowing how flustered I am.

"I play to win."

"And distracting me is the only way you can win. Admit it."

"Distracting you is as good as winning," he croons.

Oh no. If he adds a charm offensive to his card skills and his under-the-table skills, I'm toast. I bite my lip and widen my eyes. Like I can stare *harder* at the cards and make them fall into place through sheer force of will.

His fingers still on my knee. "I'll stop if you want me to," he whispers.

I bite my lip as goose bumps race up my arms. I look up at Theo from under my lashes and he's grinning because he knows he has me beat. He took off his glasses a while ago, so it's easy to read the cocky satisfaction in his eyes. He pulls his hand away and I reach out to grab it. I lock my eyes on his and slowly draw his hand back to my knee. His eyes light up in surprise.

"I'm going to prove I can beat you even with you distracting me," I say, which earns me a laugh. And then he beats me. And it's my fault, because I couldn't bring myself to ask him to stop the maddening swirls on my knee or tapping his foot against mine. The light, easy contact went straight to my brain, making me feel as drunk as I did last night.

But as much as I hate losing, I can't find it in myself to be upset. Not when a charming British boy is grinning at me on a high-speed train hurtling along the coast of Italy.

"I'm afraid that knowing you is very bad for me, *Your Highness*." I feel my resistance to him slipping, just like it did in Stella's living room this morning. I'm growing to regret the dwindling number of hours I have left to spend with Theo. I wish I'd never met him. I wish I'd met him sooner.

"Why are you looking at me like that?" He runs a hand self-consciously over his chin, which is growing more dusted with stubble every day. It helps with the disguise. His eyes soften from smug to wary in a single swift bob of his lashes. The sun streams in from the window next to him, highlighting his cobalt eyes. *Snap.* It's heartbreaking to think of all the pictures

I'll never take of him. Even worse, to think of all the photographs that have been taken of him that have failed to capture an ounce of the vulnerability in his ocean-deep eyes.

"Nothing," I say quickly. I don't want to have these thoughts about him, don't want one more person to mourn. "I'm just tired." I put my backpack against the window and rest my head on it. I can feel Theo's gaze on me even with my eyes closed, but I force myself not to react. And when he moves his foot away, I don't reach mine out to him, no matter how much I want to.

I sleep for a few hours, and plan on sleeping for longer, but when I'm switching positions to relieve a kink in my neck, I don't see Theo in the seat across from me.

I push myself up, suddenly wide awake, and search the train car, but he's nowhere to be found. I'm teetering on the edge of panic when he walks through the door at the end of the car with an armful of food. My muscles go slack with relief.

"Where'd you get this?" I ask as he sets a salad/sandwich combo in front of me. I tear the top off the packaged salad and take a bite of the first green vegetable I've seen in days. I close my eyes, ready to savor it, and . . . it sucks. The tomato is squishy, the lettuce limp. I give myself five seconds to internally weep over the fact that I am traveling through all of Italy and I'll never eat a scoop of gelato, and then I let it go and stuff my face with wilted lettuce.

"The dining car," Theo says.

"When I woke up and you weren't here, I might have panicked a little bit."

"Oh yeah?" He glances over his shoulder.

"Yeah," I tell him, but he's distracted, too busy spinning the ring on his finger to pay attention to what I'm saying. "I can't get home without you, remember?" It's the same thing he said to me at the Eiffel Tower. I hated it then, but it feels even less true now. For those brief but paralyzing couple of minutes he was gone, I didn't think once about my ride home.

If Theo cares or even remembers, it doesn't show.

"Please wake me up next time," I say around a mouthful of soggy croutons.

"What? Oh yeah, sorry. You looked so knackered. I wanted to let you sleep." He frowns at his untouched food.

"What's wrong?"

"Nothing," he says quickly.

An announcement in Italian echoes from speakers in the ceiling.

"What's going on? Are we in Bari?" I glance out the window in search of a harbor. Bari is a port city where we'll board a ferry to Greece.

Theo's frown deepens. "I don't think so."

"What did they say?" I ask.

"Uh—'stay seated,' I think. We're safe. They're inspecting the cabins."

My blood runs cold. This is too reminiscent of what happened on the Eurostar to be a coincidence. "Did someone see you?"

Theo's throat bobs as he tries to swallow his fear. "I think the woman at the bar counter recognized me. She didn't say anything, but I don't know, I got this feeling . . ."

Shit. My eyes rove over the coach, searching for a place for him to hide. Across from the occupied bathroom is a closet to store carry-on luggage. I shove him inside and shut the doors behind him before making a beeline for the dining car.

Behind the bar, an olive-skinned woman in her thirties or forties with a face full of thick makeup is scrolling through her phone. I slide a handful of euros across the bar and ask for a pop. She delivers a lukewarm flat drink that I pretend to enjoy for a few minutes before I ask the question I've already typed into Google Translate. "Perché ci siamo *fermati*?"

She looks around and, finding the car empty, leans toward me eagerly. "Il principe e sul treno."

My heart plummets. I don't like the sound of *principe*. I look helplessly at Google Translate. I wouldn't even know how to begin to type what she just said. "I'm sorry. Uh—mi dispiace. I don't speak Italian."

The woman waves away my apology. "Prince Theo is on this train."

"How do you know?"

"He ordered food. He dyed his hair, but it was him. I almost didn't come to work today, but I saw that the prince was spotted at St. Pancras, and I thought maybe he'd be here! I didn't actually believe I'd find him, but what did I have to lose?"

"Are you sure it was him?" I ask, but I've already checked out of the conversation because I only have a few minutes to come up with a new plan for getting Theo and me off this train unnoticed.

"Sì. I recognized the scar." She points to her own eyebrow. "I told the conductors immediately. When they find him, I'm going to ask the Queen for a place in their shelter."

This snags my full attention. I snap my face back to hers. "Their *what*?"

"Their riparo . . . the bunker. How do you say it?" She snaps her fingers. "Underground! The one that's going to save them from the comet. When I save her son, the Queen will have to save me."

The train coach spins in my vision as snippets of last night come hurtling back to me. Sitting at a table with Stella, drinking wine. And just like that, I remember. With the last of my hangover brain fog gone, all the pieces fall into place. She wasn't mad at me because I puked in her trash can; she's mad because I'm helping Theo run to his death.

Theo has a way to save himself and he's not taking it.

All I want is more time. Time to spend with my family and figure out who I want to be and eat bread and chocolate and pasta and climb the Eiffel Tower and sleep in feather beds and take hot showers and fall in love. Time to *live*. He has it, and the fact that he doesn't want it makes me dizzy with disgust.

I can't believe I was naive enough to think that one of the oldest and wealthiest families on the planet wouldn't find a way to cheat death. Not even the apocalypse can touch royalty.

"I have to go." Something in my stomach urges me to hurry, but I can't. I walk in a daze back to our seats and stop when I see a train employee checking passports. He searches the empty bathroom, and then turns to open the luggage closet where Theo is hiding. A small, vindictive, *betrayed* part of me wants them to find him and drag him kicking and screaming back to his safe bunker with his rich, powerful mummy and all their servants. The other part of me, the part that makes plans and sees them through, knows if I let that happen, I don't stand a chance in hell of seeing my mom or my dad or my sister or my brother or my dog ever again. And not even the fucking prince of Wales is going to keep me away from the people I love.

I glance one last time at the closet where Theo's hiding, and then I pass out.

CHAPTER 20

DATE: WEDNESDAY, JUNE 15
LOCATION: BARI, ITALY

ITINERARY: TWENTY-FOUR-HOUR FERRY FROM
BARI, ITALY, TO SANTORINI, GREECE
DAYS UNTIL THE COMET HITS: FOUR AND A HALF

*G*uarda, Mamma! Guarda!" The screaming toddler lived up to her reputation, her little lungs shrieking loud enough to alert the whole train. I fought to keep my expression neutral when the train employee came to my rescue, especially when he bumped into my bad ankle. I had to bite my tongue to keep from kicking him in the balls. A first aid kit was retrieved, smelling salts were passed under my nose, and I "woke up" groggy and confused. After a conversation in mixed English and Italian, it was determined that I would rest in first class.

Passing out has its perks.

"Wait! I need my dog." I point to where Comet is still leashed under the table, straining to reach me.

The employee unleashes Comet, then escorts us to first class. I assume he'll resume his search after I'm settled, but with any luck, he'll forget to return to the luggage closet where Theo is hiding.

Up in first class, Comet and I are served a cold drink, a tray of congealed lasagna that looks to be at least a week old, and a solid hour of alone time to stress about whether Theo's been captured.

Just before the train stops at the station in Bari, I'm filled with the familiar instinct to find Theo and make sure he's okay. But I'm swept up in a current of moving bodies and off the train before I can think of a plan to sneak him out unnoticed. He can fend for himself on this one. If he's hell-bent on dying in a fiery life-ending explosion, he can figure out how to get off a train without being seen.

I hear Mom's voice telling me that I can't take home every puppy in the shelter, that I can't save the prince from every stupid scenario he walks into. If he gets caught—good. *He deserves it*. I don't deserve to be caught, though, which is why I cross my fingers that he can manage this on his own.

A strong sea breeze hits me in the face as Comet and I step outside the railway station and hustle toward the ferryboat to check on our departure status. The harbor stretches in front of us, loud music and fireworks sailing off the docked yachts with party lights strung between boats. Laughter carries over the water and I realize that spending my last hours at a big party with family and friends sounds kind of amazing. If I were home, that's what I'd do.

Miraculously, the last ferryboat in the harbor is boarding passengers without bothering to check passports. They wave aboard anyone who wants to come, making warning calls in several different languages that this is *it*. The last chance to get to Greece before the comet hits.

I check the time. It's been at least fifteen minutes since the train stopped. I'm starting to feel sick, thinking about Theo crouched in a luggage closet like a criminal.

Where is he? I try to call, but his burner phone takes me to a voicemail box that hasn't been set up yet.

I sit on a bench across the dock from the boat and just as quickly jump to my feet. I can't sit still. My hands shake. I grip Comet's leash tighter and I'm so freaking thankful he's here because I feel suddenly, terribly alone.

I pull out my phone and call my mom.

She answers immediately. "Wren?"

"Hey, Mom." I blink back tears. Just the sound of her voice saying my name makes me feel like a kid again.

"Thank goodness. Where are you?"

My stomach swims with guilt. "In Italy. About to board a ferryboat that will take me to Greece, where a plane will take me home."

"How?"

"I'm tired. I'll explain later."

"We *miss* you, Birdie." Her voice cracks on the nickname I've had since childhood. "I can't understand why you haven't called more."

"My phone battery sucks and most of the trains have terrible service and—and—" My throat swells with emotion. I don't know how to tell her that talking to them makes me feel worse because it brings all the feelings I'm trying to avoid straight to the surface. "I'm sorry. I'll do better. The ferry doesn't have service, so I'll be off the grid for twenty-four hours, but after that, I'll call. I miss you all too, and . . . I love you."

I've paced back up toward the train station during our conversation, and I end the call just as the door pushes open. I hold my breath—only to see an older woman step outside.

My hope deflates like a slashed tire. "Excuse me! Did you see a boy? About six feet tall, dark hair?"

The words die in my throat as he emerges with his backpack slung over his shoulder and his head down. I expected to feel annoyed when I finally laid eyes on him again, but all I feel is maddening, bone-loosening relief.

He finds me in the crowd and drapes his arms around me like he can barely hold himself up. I squeeze him once before quickly stepping away. Confusion flits across his brow, but he doesn't say anything. Neither of us speaks until we're walking away from the station and toward the sea and a horizon stacked with dark gray clouds.

"Looks like you saved me again," he says in a low voice that rubs like friction against my frayed nerves. He throws me a self-effacing smile that I think is supposed to be charming, and *there it is*. My annoyance flares to life. "Are you all right?" he asks.

I open my mouth. Nothing comes out. I'm a jumble of dissonant emotions. I feel like an idiot for not realizing that Theo had other options this whole time. I'm jealous that he could choose to live if he wanted to, and I'm heartbroken that he won't. I can't wrap my mind around the fact that he's going to die alone at a beach house in Greece when he doesn't have to. *That's how this story ends?*

Theo watches me expectantly, but I can't give him any answers. *No, I'm not okay, and no, I won't tell you why.* The prospect of putting words to these emotions makes my skin prickle. I don't want to have a confrontation about the bunker, because it would betray how wrapped up in him I am.

"Let's just get to the ferry."

What Theo chooses to do when I'm gone is none of my business. And anyway, I'll be dead in less than five days (!!!!), which means the nauseating guilt working its way up the back of my throat won't haunt me forever. He dies, I die. That was the bargain. Just because I *could* save him isn't a good reason to back out now.

I've never been on a ferryboat, so like everything else I've done in the last four days, this is one more thing to check off the bucket list I never got around to making, because if it didn't involve straight A's and admittance to a fancy law school just to prove I could, I wasn't interested. When I let myself wonder what else I missed out on, it's enough to steal the breath clean out of my lungs. So I don't wonder. Problem solved. The box full of things I'm not allowed to think about is getting precariously full, but I'm still putting one foot in front of the other, so it must be working. I might be the smartest person on the planet. Avoidance as a coping mechanism is an extremely handy tool. I wonder if anyone else is as smart as I am and has already figured this out.

The ferry is big. And old. It looks like a cruise ship from the outside, but once we're ushered up the boarding ramp and into the boat, there's not much to see but some couches and chairs. Theo starts to explain that he'll find us a cabin where we can store our stuff and sleep tonight if we want ("Totally optional. I can sleep on a couch or the floor or against a wall. It's no big deal"), but when I shoot him my best laser death glare, the words dry up in his throat.

So maybe my box of off-limit emotions is cracking a bit at

the seams. Nothing that can't be solved by physical avoidance! Once the ship has set sail, I push my backpack into Theo's arms, claiming the need for fresh air. Comet and I climb a set of stairs to the outer deck and gulp in the heavy, salty sea air.

An entire day of my life—one of the last ones I'll ever have—on an old ferryboat sailing through the Mediterranean Sea. What am I supposed to do with all this uninterrupted time with my thoughts? Ostensibly, this would be the ideal place to, I don't know, *think about things* or *deal with my emotions*, but I can't think of a single topic that I haven't banned myself from examining.

I'm not allowed to think about my family or Naomi or my home or dying or the comet or the missile launch or Theo or his bunker and whether there is space for me in it, which leaves me with . . . the sky. The sky! I can think about the sky—as long as I don't think about the comet hurtling through it. But really, the comet's not in the sky. It's in space. Totally different. Even still, every time I stare at the ominous gray clouds above, I get a queasy feeling. So naturally, the sky goes into the box. And then I don't have to think about it anymore! Did I mention what a genius I am?

I turn my eyes to the water. A breeze churns up whitecaps of foam in the bottomless sea. I can't keep my eyes off them. I lean against the rail and stare at the water and let my mind go completely and utterly, blissfully blank.

I have no idea how much time has passed when Theo joins me, leaning his forearms on the rail. The warmth of him makes me realize how chilly I've become with the sea breeze whipping my citrus hair into a tangle. I'm struck by how sad it is that I hated my old plain brown color. So much time wasted disliking something that was so unimportant.

"I found us a cabin. Room 113. I don't think anyone cares about reservations, but hopefully we can get some rest before tomorrow."

"Okay."

"We still have food in our bags. I'm thinking of going to the cabin and eating dinner."

"Okay."

He hesitates as he stares at the gulf between our arms. "Do you want to come?"

"No."

"Did I do something wrong?" he asks.

I angle my face out to the water to keep him from reading the lie in my eyes. "Nope."

"Did something happen on the train?"

"I'm not hungry, okay?" My stomach chooses this moment to growl loudly. We both stare at it.

"Tell me what's wrong." He moves closer, bringing his spell-binding warmth with him. He pulls his sunglasses down to his nose, his eyes searching mine for the catastrophe that has robbed me of my appetite. The wind blows his dark hair into a frenzy that stirs emotions I don't want to feel. I turn my back to the water and cross my arms over my chest.

"I'm about to die, Theo, and there's nothing I can do about it. My entire family is going to die. Everyone I love wiped off the face of the earth. Forgive me if I don't have much of an appetite."

His face falls as he slowly steps back. I hold my breath, wait-ing in preemptive fury for him to commiserate or lie through his teeth and tell me he *understands*, as if his entire family won't be safely hidden underground at the moment of impact. If he lies to me again, nothing will be able to stop me from pushing him overboard.

"I'm sorry, Wren. If you want to talk about it—"

"I don't," I snap. "Take Comet with you. He needs to eat."

Theo loops the leash once around his wrist and presses a cabin key into my hand before tugging Comet after him. And just like that, I'm left with a brain full of thoughts I won't let myself examine and a sunset over the sea.

I turn my back on the water and take pictures of the other passengers as they cross my path. I snap a pregnant woman who paces up and down the deck with her arms crossed over the small of her back, and the frantic man who trails after her, looking helpless and terrified. When all my pictures become dark smudges and the sky is fully black, I take my sad, empty stomach and find our cabin. Comet and Theo are asleep inside. Theo is wedged in the rib-crushing space between the bed and the wall, with only Comet draped across his feet for warmth. A pile of dirty clothes is wadded up under Theo's head, and I fight the instinct to slide a real pillow under his ear and drape a blanket over his legs.

I slip off my shoes and briefly consider changing clothes, brushing my teeth, and washing my face, but the sheer effort of it all seems utterly exhausting, especially when my eyes have landed on something much more interesting.

On the small table next to the bed, a stash of gas station snacks is waiting for me. I pick up an unfamiliar bag of chips and a chocolate bar and tuck my legs under me on the bed while I eat. The chips aren't as good as my favorite (salt and vinegar) and the chocolate bar is warm and melty, but they're both better than the soggy salad and cold lasagna that I ate a billion years ago for lunch.

Homesickness careens through me, and a tear spills down my cheek. A swell rocks the boat, causing me to smear chocolate all over the duvet. I finish the candy and then drape the dirty blanket over Theo's shoulders. I can't help myself.

I hug a pillow to my chest and screw my eyes shut tight as the swaying of the boat intensifies. For the first night since news of the comet broke, I hope I can sleep through this. I've already puked enough on this cursed trip.

The last thing I register before falling asleep is a roar of thunder tearing the sky in half.

CHAPTER 21

DATE: THURSDAY, JUNE 16
LOCATION: ON A FERRYBOAT IN THE MEDITERRA-
NEAN SEA

ITINERARY: DON'T FALL OFF THE BOAT
DAYS UNTIL THE COMET HITS: FOUR

'm woken up by a loud thump and a whimper from Comet. I leap out of bed and land barefoot on a messy candy bar wrapper. The boat lurches again, throwing me back toward the bed, and I brace myself against the headboard. When the boat rocks violently for the third time, I grip the edge of the mattress. On the floor, Theo rolls into the wall.

He sits up with a grunt and rubs the spot where his head hit the wall. "Whasgoinon?"

"There's a storm. It feels like the boat is about to capsize."

"Boats this big don't capsize."

A deafening thunderclap vibrates through our cabin, followed by howling wind.

"Maybe we're capsizing," Theo concedes, bracing his hands

against the wall. "Wouldn't that be an ironic way to go." He huffs a sarcastic laugh as the boat rocks again.

"I'm not dying on a ferryboat four days before the end of the world." I grit my teeth and prepare for another swell. "I've seen the *MythBusters* episode about *Titanic*, so if I end up floating on a door, you better believe I'm dragging your royal ass up there with me. Much to your disappointment, I'm sure."

"Why would you say that?"

"You know why."

"Enlighten me." He throws me a careless grin that doesn't quite reach his eyes, his effortless charm in action even on the brink of total disaster.

"I know about the bunker."

Our gazes lock as another clap of thunder rattles the stars. Theo is thrown onto the bed as I roll off and smash into the wall. He leans over the edge of the bed and wraps his hands securely around mine, pulling me up next to him. We press our backs against the headboard, our hands still clasped together. His knuckles are turning white and my hand aches from how hard I'm holding on, but I'm too scared to let go. My heart beats wildly against the mounting panic in my chest.

Comet whines and rests his paws at the end of the bed. "Come on up, boy," I tell him. He jumps up and settles his shaking body on top of our feet, his head nuzzled against my calf. I release one of Theo's hands from my grasp and bury it in Comet's fur.

"I did not sign on to help you with your suicide mission." My voice strains from all the fear and hurt lodged in my throat.

"That's not what this is," he says desperately.

"What else could it be? You have a way to survive and you're throwing it away—"

"I don't want to die," he whispers.

His hand trembles in mine; he's shaking everywhere. I pull the duvet over Comet's body and our legs and press the side of my body against Theo's until we're flush from foot to shoulder.

"I don't want to die." His voice cracks. A tear falls down his cheek, and when he tries to yank his hand out of mine to wipe it away, I tighten my grip.

I lean my temple against his, our noses close enough to touch. "Then why don't you go home, Theo?" I whisper as the world around us falls apart.

"I can't. There are eight billion people on Earth—what have I done to deserve to survive?"

My heart breaks. "You don't have to earn your life."

"Everyone else in the bunker did. It'll be full of doctors and scientists and world leaders and me, a depressed nineteen-year-old who was given a fake bullshit title from his parents."

I tip his face toward mine so he knows how serious I am when I say, "You don't deserve to die."

"Neither do you, but you don't have a bunker to hide in." His face crumples. "Neither does Penny." His voice is nearly a whisper.

The breath rushes out of me. "Penny isn't going into the bunker?"

Pain fills Theo's eyes. "It belongs to the government, and she didn't make the cut. Never mind the fact that she's as good as family. Never mind that Charlotte and Andrew love her more than anything. Never mind that she sacrificed *everything* to raise us. But because her blood isn't royal, she doesn't get a place?" He closes his eyes and leans his head back against the headboard. A large swell tips the boat sideways. I grip Theo's hand.

"You're the heir to the throne!" I say, scrambling to think of a plan, to save him from this grief. "If you ask—"

"I asked. I *fought* for her. All I got was a canned response about rations and space and oxygen. The list is the list—no exceptions. It's all just a bunch of bloody bullshit." Tears run into the stubble dusting his cheeks. "I don't want to live in a world—and I sure as hell don't want to ever run a country—that treats some people as disposable while others are revered for nothing more than being born titled. No one even cares that I'm missing; they just care that the *heir* is missing."

I hate the resignation in his voice. "You're going to be the king. You could change things."

"Not fast enough to save Penny. And if Penny dies, it will destroy Charlotte and Andrew. They need her more than they need me. If I'm not in the bunker, there's an opening. Henry promised he'd do everything in his power to make sure it goes to Penny."

"Your brother knew you were leaving, and he was okay with it?"

"He understood. And he'll make a better king than I will. His brain isn't messed up like mine."

My heart sinks. "If Penny loves you half as much as you think she does, she won't want to take your place."

His jaw clenches. "But she'll do it. When the clock runs out and it's time to seal the door, she'll do it."

The violent rocking of the boat has only gotten worse. I don't think we can ignore the storm any longer.

"If we were capsizing, they'd tell us, right?" I ask.

"Yes," Theo says, his jaw tight. I feel a tiny bit better for a tiny amount of time, until another giant swell tips us onto our backs and he adds, "But maybe not until it's too late. We have to get off this boat." He rises to his feet and hooks Comet's leash to his collar.

"Now?" I'm shaking everywhere and my pulse is racing. Comet and I are a trembling mess.

"*Now*. If we're not off this boat by the time it starts taking on water, we'll drown."

I hop off the bed and take the leash from Theo, but no matter how hard I tug, Comet whimpers and refuses to budge. He buries his shaking body under the duvet. I throw my arm around him and whisper into his ear. His body stills as he cocks his head, like he's listening. I place a firm kiss behind his ear and gently tug on the leash. He jumps quickly off the bed and when Theo throws the door open, Comet leads the charge down the hall.

It's chaos. People are everywhere. The pregnant woman from earlier looks like she's in labor. Theo screams to everyone we pass to get off the boat and I knock wildly on every closed door as we race up to the main deck. We're almost there when an alarm finally blares and an announcement crackles through old speakers. Theo translates. They want everyone to rush to the starboard side of the boat because the port side is dangerously close to taking on water. A passenger has opened a closet filled with orange life jackets. I clip one around my torso while Theo does the same, and when no one's looking, I grab a jacket for Comet.

Jackets firmly in place, we rush to the indicated side of the boat. Theo bypasses the crowd and pushes open the door that will take us to the open deck.

"Are you sure?" I call over the whistling wind.

"We'll die if we're on this boat when it capsizes."

"What about Comet?" I tug on the leash because he's going wild by my side. He doesn't want to go into the storm, and I don't blame him.

"What about him? He's coming with us." Theo holds the door open with his palm flat against it, bracing it against the wind. Comet refuses to move, so I pick up all ninety shaking pounds of him and push our way into the storm.

Driving rain stings my skin, and my ankle nearly buckles under Comet's weight. I assume adrenaline is the only reason I can still walk. Theo holds the door open for more passengers, but despite his desperate yelling, no one follows. He lets go of the door and it snaps shut in the wind. He bends to help me carry poor Comet, who's trying wildly to break free.

"I'm sorry, boy. You're a good boy. The best boy," I whisper into his ear as we make our way quickly across the slick deck. The starboard side of the boat is precariously high in the air and the angry midnight sea is a long, long way down.

"Are you sure about this?" I scream to Theo over the wind. Part of me still thinks the wind will calm down any minute, the sea will flatten out, and the boat will be fine. Jumping feels like a risky variation of the plan that we don't have to take—not yet. "If we jump too early, we'll be stranded in the middle of the sea."

"If we jump too late, we die."

The steel in his eyes and the set of his shoulders confirms that this was never a suicide mission. He doesn't want to die, and neither do I. The deck is almost perpendicular to the water now, and I know he's right. We take turns holding a shivering and terrified Comet while we climb over the safety railing on the side of the boat, until we're both sitting with him in our arms and one strong gust of wind away from sliding into the sea.

"What if I lose you out there?" I scream. There's no horizon in the night-black sky, nothing to separate the violent water from eternity.

"Swim like hell, American girl."

"On three?" I ask. He nods and holds up his fingers. *One. Two.*

I hold my breath and jump.

CHAPTER 22

I wrap my arms tightly around nearly one hundred pounds of soaking wet fur as Comet and I fall. When we hit the water, he's ripped from my grasp. I choke on freezing cold salt water as I plunge toward the sea floor. My chest seizes frantically with each second underwater. I kick hard, and after an unbearable amount of time, my life jacket tugs me toward the surface.

I've inhaled a lungful of rainwater and I can't see anything. "THEO!" I scream. All I hear is rain and wind and thunder. "THEO!" Something slams into my back. I spin toward it, terrified, but my heart melts with relief as Comet pants heavily in my face. His paws scramble against my arms and jacket as he searches for purchase. I hook my arm through his life jacket. "Good boy," I croon. "We have to find Theo."

Comet tugs me away from the thrashing boat. "Theo!" I scream again. A wave surges over my head and I swallow another lungful of briny water. When I'm back on the surface, I try to wipe the water from my eyes, but the rain makes it useless. "Theo!" I scream until my throat is sore.

"Wren?" Theo's voice carries from a distance, and Comet's ears perk up the instant he hears it. I have no idea where the sound is coming from, can't orient myself in any direction except away from the boat, but Comet yaps and frantically tugs me to follow him.

"Theo?" I call, my voice so hoarse, I'm surprised anyone can hear it.

"WREN! OVER HERE!" I still don't know where "over here" is, but Comet does. He barks in excitement and charges toward the sound. "Wren!" Theo's voice is so close, I swear I could touch him. I roll off Comet's back and thrash through the water until I collide with Theo. I wrap my arms around his neck and sob into his shoulder as relief racks my body, the salt of my tears mingling with the sea. He stares at me for a long moment, his black pupils blown wide, blacker than the sea around us. He leans his head close to mine and whispers in my ear.

"I think someone recognized me."

"What?" I blurt in utter confusion, because how could someone—but then I get it. He grins wickedly, if tiredly, and I kiss him. The heat of his tongue quickly warms me, the slick water between us feeling like nothing at all. I hold on to him with shaking arms, and I'm not sure if I'm trembling from fear or cold or *him*. All I know is that I never want to let go.

When Comet nudges his nose against my cheek, I break away from Theo with a laugh and give Comet a hug for bringing us back together. "I owe you the biggest steak in Greece," I promise him as I stroke his wet fur. He seems to understand because he nuzzles my hand affectionately.

The three of us hang on to each other while we watch the ferry teeter back and forth in the water. With every swell I hold my breath and prepare for it to capsize, but it doesn't. And when the rain and wind get a little less driving and the waves flatten out and the boat is *still* floating, I glance sideways at Theo to see if he's as mortified as I am.

"I guess it's not going to sink," I say slowly.

"Good. That's good, obviously. That's really, really . . . good," he says, his expression as baffled as I feel.

"Of course!" I agree. "It's great!"

We float in silence, staring at the ferryboat as it sails into the black.

"It might be better if we were *on* the boat, instead of floating alone in the middle of the freezing sea."

"No arguments here," he agrees.

"How long can we survive in this temperature of water?"

"We'll be all right until help arrives."

"*If* help arrives," I counter. "The boat didn't sink, so . . ."

"Someone will come," he says. "And until they do, we'll be fine. The water's not dangerously cold."

"The hypothermia is making you insane," I say through chattering teeth. I don't know how it's possible to be both numb and freezing cold at the same time, but I've managed it. I can't even feel my legs, which are hooked tightly around Theo's waist.

He huffs a laugh, his hot breath fanning deliciously against my ear. "Now that you mention it, it probably wouldn't hurt to use our collective body heat to stay warm." He tightens his grip around my back.

"And if help doesn't arrive?" I ask in a quiet voice. I tug myself tighter against his chest.

"Then we float under the stars for as long as we've got," he says in a solemn voice. I tip my head back to see the sky. The storm is a distant, terrible memory, the clouds chased away by a full moon and a sky blazing with starlight. I press a kiss against Theo's temple.

"Thank you," I whisper.

"For what?"

"For being my starlight."

If he questions me, I'll claim hypothermia-induced insanity. But he only tugs me closer to him and presses another long kiss against my lips, and I realize if there are boats out there, they will find us, with the way his electricity is crackling through my veins. A bright spot in a dark sea. A glimmer of warmth and hope and goodness in the blackest night.

✸ ✸ ✸

The golden thread of dawn is just weaving across the horizon when I jostle Theo. "A boat." My voice is hoarse and even those two words tear like flames along my throat. "A boat. Look!" I point to a tiny speck in the distance.

Theo squints at it. "It's probably just deck chairs or something that fell off during the storm."

"No. There's a flag. Look!" I point again and I know the instant Theo sees it because every muscle in his body goes rigid. He drops his arms from around my neck and waves them in the air. We both shout for help at the same time, and Comet joins in with his booming bark. The small fishing boat draws closer, and I give Comet a good scratch behind both ears. "I knew I loved you," I tell him, which makes Theo smile. "You love him too—admit it."

He slowly lowers his hands and his blue eyes smolder at me in the hazy dawn light.

"Admit it." I nudge his foot with mine.

"I love the dog," he says softly.

The boat draws closer and an old man with olive skin and a bushy gray handlebar mustache throws a rope into the water and yells something I don't understand. I grab the rope and he tows me in. My muscles are too spent to pull myself over the edge, but he reaches for me with both hands and hauls me out of the water and into the bottom of the boat like it's nothing. I cough up the salt water I swallowed while he was towing me in as I lie on my side next to what smells like a bucket of dead fish. My stomach is too sensitive to look over the side and confirm. Another man, even older than the first but with the same olive complexion, passes me a towel to wrap around myself and chatters at me in what sounds like Greek. Hope blooms in my chest.

"I'm sorry. I only speak English."

"Boat?" he asks.

"There was a storm. We—we fell off." I'm not about to admit that we got spooked and jumped.

His brow furrows in a moment of confusion before he stands and mimes a storm and a rocking boat. I nod vigorously.

"You're from one of the ferryboats?" the man with the mustache asks as he pulls Comet through the water in a rope harness fashioned by Theo. "They don't usually come this far east, but it was a nasty storm. You may have been blown off course." He lifts Comet over the edge of the boat and the dog immediately flops next to me. His head collapses in my lap and his eyes fall shut. "I know the feeling," I whisper to him, absentmindedly stroking his wet fur.

"Are you from Santorini?" I ask as the bubble of hope in my chest grows. In the distance, I see land.

The old man shakes his head and the bubble bursts with a violent pop. "Amorgos." He throws the rope back to Theo and drags him through the water. Theo's palms grab the edge of the boat and his biceps flex as he pulls himself out of the sea and into the boat.

"They're from Amorgos," I say sadly.

"Can you take us to Santorini?" Theo asks, but the man with the mustache waves off his request.

"We go to Amorgos. You'll rest there. Now lie down. You all look half dead."

I want to argue with him, to insist that he take the prince to Santorini posthaste (!), but I don't have an ounce of fight in me. I fall back against the hard wooden slats of the boat and let Theo take half the towel to pull over himself. We stare at each other with wide eyes for a long time before he finally says, "I think that bucket next to your head is filled with fish guts." It's the last thing I hear before the world goes dark.

CHAPTER 23

DATE: UNKNOWN
LOCATION: UNKNOWN

ITINERARY: UNKNOWN
DAYS UNTIL THE COMET HITS: UNKNOWN

There is a creature panting hot, stinky breath directly into my nose. I open my bleary eyes. *Comet.* His paws are resting on my arm and he's waiting impatiently for me to wake up and play with him.

"Who's the best boy?" I rasp, and holy hell, my throat *hurts*. Lesson learned. Talking is off-limits. I'll never do it again. I try to swallow, but my mouth is filled with sand. Everything hurts. My *eyelashes* hurt. I lunge for the cup of water next to the bed and almost die. Every muscle in my body protests such a stupid, thoughtless decision. It seems moving is also off-limits, which is a fun surprise.

I gingerly lift the glass and take huge, gasping gulps. Water sloshes over the side and down the front of my striped Parisian shirt. The once soft material is stiff and rough against my skin like a cat's tongue.

Next to the bedside table holding a decorative stack of books and an old Polaroid camera with a layer of dust on top is a wicker chair with a fresh change of clothes. I slip out of my salt-encrusted leggings and T-shirt and pull a sleeveless, flowy pale blue dress over my aching body. I also ditch my bra because bras are a torture device, and if I only have a few days left to live, I'm *not* wearing underwire.

I eye the window across from the bed and weigh the effort of getting there against what appears to be a spectacular view. My ankle seems to be slightly better, but that might just be because everything else is worse. But even with a less swollen ankle, I'm not sure my muscles will support my weight across the room. I stand, and yeah, no. Not happening. I sink to my knees and crawl across the sun-drenched tile floor. I lay my arms on the windowsill with my chin resting on the back of my hands, and for a split second I almost think it's all been worth it for this blue-and-white view. White: the house I'm in, built right into the side of a mountain. Blue: practically everything else. All I see is clear azure sky filled with marshmallow clouds and a sea that glitters under heavy sunlight. It's so blue, it reminds me of Theo's eyes, which is something I cannot deal with right now. I could deal when his eyes reminded me of the sea, because yeah, they're super-duper blue. But when the sea reminds me of his *eyes*? I'm in trouble.

Chattering voices float through the open window on a breeze. I crane my neck to get a better look. The top of Theo's head is just visible. I ignore the way my veins feel electrified and focus on what's on the table in front of him. *Food*. Enough of it to make standing and moving worth the effort. I limp down a curved set of tile steps and out onto the patio.

I stop short as a dozen pairs of eyes turn to me. Theo's sitting at the end of the table, the only spot I could see from my window, but every other seat is filled with people of all ages. I recognize the two men who rescued us in their fishing boat: the older one with snow-white hair and the other one (also old) with a bushy handlebar mustache.

"Hey," Theo says, capturing my attention. His eyes are twinkling as he gives me a searching glance that makes me uneasy.

"Is everything okay?"

"Better now that you're here," he says, making me blush furiously. I glance at all the eyes on us. Why is he flirting so shamelessly in front of everyone?

"What's going on?"

His smile turns wolfish. "Wren, this is the Castellanos family. Everyone, this is Wren. My fiancée."

Um. What?

I don't have time to respond with anything other than slack-jawed confusion before a chubby-cheeked preschooler with angelic curls, his tiny fists wrapped around demolished slices of tomato, squeals, "Puppy!"

Sure enough, Comet's at my heels. The boy leaps out of his chair and gleefully feeds Comet a chunk of grilled fish from the table.

The family pulls me into a loud and friendly round of introductions. Mr. "Call me Nicholas!" Castellanos is the man with the mustache who saved us. His father is the older man from the boat, who doesn't speak any English. Nicholas and his wife, Mrs. Castellanos, have three daughters, three sons-in-law, and a handful of grandchildren. A teenage girl named Eleni, with big eyes and long pigtail braids, watches me carefully. Her mom introduces herself as Stefanie. I try to keep all the names and faces straight, but it's hard to retain many details when one single word is hovering in my brain like a bomb about to detonate.

Fiancée.

What is Theo doing?

An overflowing plate of pasta and vegetables is placed in my hands by a woman with a baby on her hip. I survey the tight quarters for an empty chair—there isn't one—and am about to sit on the ground when Theo puts his hands on my hips and tugs me into his lap. He wraps his arm around my waist and rests his chin on my shoulder. A shiver runs up my spine.

I turn my legs sideways across his lap so I can see him. "Don't you think we're a little young to be talking marriage, honey?" I whisper through a big, fake smile that is hopefully masking the absolute riot of emotions in my chest.

"Oh, one hundred percent. We're out of our minds." He grins up at me.

"What are you doing?"

He twirls a strand of my orange hair around his fingers. "We're so madly in love, in fact, that we're running away to Santorini, where we want to get married on the beach before the comet hits. If Mr. Castellanos here likes us enough, he might even pilot us there on his boat." He winks and tucks a loose strand of hair behind my ear and kisses the end of my nose, for show. It's lucky I'm sitting because my body turns to jelly under his featherlight touch.

I'm gonna pass out. "You couldn't think of any other way to ask for his boat than to pretend we want to get married?"

"We're running out of time and options here, American girl. Can *you* think of a better reason he should waste half a day driving us to *another* beautiful Greek island so we can die there instead of here?"

"Other than the truth?"

"I was looking for something that wouldn't betray my access to a private plane and runway, just in case it made them ask questions we don't want to answer."

"They don't know who you are?"

He shrugs. "I introduced myself as Blaze Danger. They haven't asked any questions or been weird about it."

"They haven't been weird about the name Blaze Danger? Something is definitely wrong."

"Ha ha."

"Wait—do you know what this means? We found the one place where no one recognizes you. Is your ego going to be okay?" I press my palm to his forehead. "How will you survive?"

He simply smiles in return. "I think we're in the clear."

"*If* we can get to Santorini."

"Hence the show. Now eat up, honey. I want you to have strength for our wedding ni—"

I stab his thigh with my fork.

"What?" he asks, eyes big with faux innocence. "For our wedding night *dance*! That's all I was saying." A smirk plays on the corner of his lips and I'm struck by the urge to kiss it.

"I hate you," I say, which just makes him laugh. It's impossible not to realize how happy he is like this, eating a big family meal without any of the royal pomp and circumstance. He wasn't lying about his love for the Greek islands. He's transformed before my very eyes. Gone is the tension in his muscles. In its place, laughter and easy smiles. My heart suddenly feels like it's too big for my chest.

"This is delicious. We can't thank you enough," I say, turning my attention to the Castellanos family. I glance out at the sea and try to reorient myself, but I still don't know what day it is. When I ask, they tell me it's June 16. I didn't lose more than half a day sleeping upstairs. "Did you watch the news about the missile?" I ask, realizing I still don't know what happened.

Stefanie answers my question. "They launched the missile, what was it—yesterday?" She turns to her husband for confirmation. "I swear time has become meaningless. Anyway, they launched the missile in near-perfect conditions, but just as it was about to leave the atmosphere, it exploded. No one knows why. Just one of those weird freak accidents. It never even got near the comet."

Theo's hands tighten on my hips. His skin sears through my thin dress. It takes me a long time to speak. "It's official. We're all going to—"

"Eat ice cream for dessert!" Mr. Castellanos booms as his wife covers one of the kids' ears with her hands. The children follow their grandfather into the kitchen.

"They don't know?" Theo asks Stefanie.

She shakes her head. "No use getting them all upset and worked up over something we can't change. They won't understand anyway."

"How are the rest of you so—" I wave my hands in the air as I search for the right word. This boisterous family is so full of life. So *happy*. Like I was on our road trip through France. But looking at all these faces, I can see it's clear they have more to lose than I do.

"We're happy because we love each other. We're with family. We're the lucky ones."

Theo covers the back of my hand with his, threading his fingers through mine. I wrap both of our arms around my waist and struggle not to cry.

"You two are lucky as well, to have survived falling off the ferry," says Stefanie.

I nod, barely trusting myself to speak. "Do you—" I clear the emotion out of my throat and try again. "Do you have a phone I could use to let my family know I'm still alive?"

Stefanie hands over a phone and shows me how to call or text out of the country. I know I'll fall to pieces if I call, so I send a proof-of-life text to Mom, whose number I have memorized, and ask her to forward it to Naomi. Then I pass the phone back to Stefanie.

Nicholas ushers the children back outside, each of them clutching a large bowl of ice cream in their hands. "Theo tells me you two want to get married!" he booms.

I nod again and wrap Theo's arm tighter around my body.

"I think fate might be on your side," Nicholas winks at us. He has flecks of pink ice cream in his mustache.

"Why? Do you know how we can get to Santorini?" I ask hopefully.

He waves away my questions. "No, no. You don't need to leave. I'm a priest. I can marry you!" He beams with pride.

My heart stumbles. "No. No. No. You don't have to—We couldn't possibly—We're going to Santorini."

"Who's marrying you?"

Theo's face is pale. "We don't have the details locked down yet, but—"

"What if you can't find someone to do it?" Nicholas demands.

Theo and I blink at each other in silence. He's as shocked by this turn of events as I am. "Who will be your witnesses?"

"Well—" I rasp. I guzzle water from the cup in front of me. "The thing is—"

"Please let us do it!" Stefanie pleads. "It'll bring us so much joy! We can do it tomorrow on the beach!"

This is a disaster. They're getting way too invested in this ridiculous plan. "We don't have that much time. And we really want to go to Santorini, even if we can't get married there. It's . . ."

"It's where we met!" Theo interjects. He sounds as desperate as he did last night on the boat. He *really* doesn't want to marry me.

"Yeah. Exactly!" I place a quick kiss on Theo's forehead. "That's where we want to be when the comet hits."

"I understand," Nicholas concedes. "I'll grant your wish and take you to Santorini."

Theo and I simultaneously wilt with relief. "Bullet dodged," he whispers into my ear.

"Consult me the next time you have an insane idea," I whisper back. I straighten and address Nicholas. "Thank you! You have no idea how much this means to us."

"Of course. Tomorrow we go to Santorini. Tonight you get married." He holds up his hands as Theo and I sputter protests. "I'm not taking no for an answer. You two kids deserve a little happiness. We all deserve a little love and joy. It's settled." He claps his hands on his thighs and stands. "Alert the town! We're having a wedding at sundown!"

CHAPTER 24

DATE: THURSDAY, JUNE 16
LOCATION: AMORGOS, GREECE

ITINERARY: CONVINCE THEO TO MARRY ME
DAYS UNTIL THE COMET HITS: THREE AND A HALF

We're not getting married," Theo announces as the door shuts behind us in the room where I woke up less than an hour ago.

"Shh!" I gesture to the open windows. "Why shouldn't we?"

"Don't be absurd."

"This is your fault! I don't remember agreeing to be your fake fiancée."

His face hardens. "There's a world of difference between pretending to be engaged and actually getting married."

"Is there?"

"It's not happening, Wren."

"Who cares if we get married? It doesn't mean anything. Nothing means anything when we'll be dead in three days anyway."

"Bullshit."

"No, seriously. It doesn't matter. Wedding, no wedding. It's meaningless at this point." I don't even stop to think about whether I believe what I'm saying. The fact is, I can't let Theo quit so close to the finish line. I'll say whatever it takes.

"If you believed that, you wouldn't be here right now."

"What does that mean?"

He rubs a hand over his face. "Why'd you dye your hair?"

"Because I wanted to. What does that have to do with any-thing?"

"Why'd you take all those pictures of Paris?"

"It's pretty."

"Why'd you practically cry eating that spaghetti Bolognese in France? Why'd you kiss me last night like the world was burning? Why'd you call me your bloody starlight?"

My knees wobble. The force of his gaze is too much. "What do you want me to say?"

"If it's all meaningless, why are you trying so desperately to get back to your family?"

"Because I love them!" I shout.

He takes a swift step toward me, crowding me against the bed. "And that love matters."

"Fine, yeah, you got me! I love my family. Good work, De-tective."

"Why did you risk your life to drag that dog across the boat with us last night?"

Comet pants protectively against my legs. "Because he was scared and confused, and no one should die alone. Not even dogs. *Especially* not dogs!"

"Exactly." Theo's chest heaves. "It matters. It all matters.

Every bloody moment matters, and I'd love if you'd stop telling me it didn't."

"But—" I sputter, completely unable to refute his point. "But the wedding wouldn't even be legal! They think your name is *Blaze*. It'd just be a means to an end, and because that end is so close—"

"We're all born, we all die. And every fucking thing that happens in between those moments *matters*. That's what makes up a life. I don't see how us knowing that second date makes any of the rest of it less true. And not to be all woe-is-me-my-sad-rich-boy-life-sucks, but I've spent almost every single day of my life doing things because other people told me to. Because I never had the power to say no. So, you'll excuse me if I need a minute to process the fact that my *wedding*—the only one I'll ever get in my life—is going to look different than I imagined."

"You imagined your wedding?" I ask softly. I have too, in a vague I-hope-I'm-happier-than-my-parents sort of way. They fight more than seems normal, and while I don't doubt that they love each other, I also don't know if they're *in love*. I never wanted to end up like that.

"Only because royal weddings are the pinnacle of our insanity. I knew it'd be over the top, monstrously expensive, and broadcast across the globe. I'd have hated every second of it."

I swallow the lump in my throat, so completely out of my depth. None of this is fair. We're still teenagers. We shouldn't have to grieve the life we thought we'd have. Theo needs to talk to someone who can make this better, and as much as I wish that were me, I'm not built for this. The best I can do is hope to make him laugh. "We can set up a TikTok live video and broadcast the ceremony, if it'll make you feel more at home." I hate myself for the stupid fake smile I give him.

His shoulders slump. "Blimey, Wren. Are you capable of having a conversation that's not buried under a thousand layers of sarcasm and banter?"

He has no idea how much I wish I could. "I thought Brits loved banter?"

"There she goes again! The girl so scared of her own emotions, she won't let herself feel anything other than mild amusement, even on her deathbed."

I step back, physically moved by the bruising force of his words. It takes a moment to catch my breath. "Ouch." It shouldn't hurt so much. He's only confirming what I thought was true. And yet, knowing he sees the very worst in me is a pain I'm not prepared for.

"I'm sorry, are you going to acknowledge that I hurt your feelings, or are you going to shove this conversation in your super-secret scary feelings box?" His eyes are the bleakest I've ever seen.

My throat burns as I fight the onslaught of incoming tears. "I didn't think you'd use that against me." The weight of his disappointment is crushing. I have to redirect this conversation before I suffocate under his bad opinion of me. "We don't have to do this. We can find another way," I force myself to say.

"How?"

"We'll steal a boat. It worked with the car." Even as I say it, my stomach flips uncomfortably. I hate the idea of stealing from the Castellanos family after they've been so kind to us, especially after Theo's "it all matters" speech. I think I'm a good person, but if I'm about to be sorted into Heaven or Hell, I don't want grand theft auto *and* grand theft boat on my permanent record.

"Do you know how to pilot a boat across the sea? Do you even know which direction takes us to Santorini?" he asks.

I shake my head, and the gloom in his eyes tells me that he doesn't either.

"I'd stay here, you know," he says at last. "It's not the house where I spent my summer holidays, but it's pretty damn close. I could be happy to die here."

It's me, then. The only reason we can't rest is because of me.

A soft knock on the door interrupts my thoughts.

"Come in," Theo says.

Stefanie opens the door. Next to her, Eleni's arms are loaded with a pile of fabric. "Let the wedding preparations begin!" Stefanie points at Theo. "The groom must leave." He gives me one last desperate glance, but I don't know what to say. I'm the girl with backup plans for her backup plans, but I'm so tired. I'm empty.

I just want to go home.

Stefanie shuts the door in Theo's face and gives me a quick once-over. "First, we choose a dress." Eleni carefully lays out a dozen dresses in every shade and style across the bed. I can't bring myself to care about any of them.

"The one I'm wearing is fine." I smooth the wrinkles in the pale blue dress.

"But the groom has already seen it!"

"It honestly doesn't matter. We don't care about stuff like that."

"Trouble in paradise?" Stefanie tilts her head sympatheti-cally, and even though the woman before me looks nothing like my mom, I wish I could pretend she were mine. Just for today.

"What? No. We're fine."

"We heard the shouting," Eleni murmurs as she runs her fingers along the hem of a shockingly pink strapless dress.

"It's complicated. Do you think—would your grandpa still take us to Santorini if we *don't* get married?" I ask her.

Eleni's mom puts an arm around my shoulders. "Do you want to talk about it? It's normal to get cold feet."

"I think we're both tired and stressed and way too young to be getting married, if we're telling the truth," I say, which makes her laugh. "If Eleni wanted to get married right now, what would you tell her to do?"

Stefanie looks at her daughter, her eyes brimming with love. "Whatever makes her heart happy."

"So cheesy, Mama." She rolls her eyes and tugs uncomfortably on her pigtail braids.

Back when I stole Dirk's car, I said I'd do whatever it took to get home to my family, because that's what makes me happy. They're the ones that matter. When I think about it that way, the answer is simple. Who cares if I have to put on a dress and say a bunch of words that I don't mean? It's the simplest way to get home. "What if the thing that makes me happy isn't the thing that makes him happy?"

Stefanie smooths her hands over my shoulders and the touch feels so good, I want to cry. "He cares about you. I could see it in his eyes during lunch, and again just now when he left. The next few days are going to be really, really hard, but you two have come this far together."

I know she's talking about the life and relationship she assumes we have, the one that doesn't exist. But I can't help but think about how far Theo and I *have* come together. Five countries in five days. From holding hands in the dark to stealing cars to him pulling me off Stella's couch when I was ready to give up. He held my freezing body all night in the sea, whispering encouragement into my ear when it seemed easier to give up. He kept a grip on Comet's life jacket when my painfully cramped hand threatened to let go.

I don't want to care what happens to him, don't want to have to deal with one more painful goodbye. I just want to follow through with the plan. Get to Santorini—whatever it takes.

I swallow the lump in my throat and run my hand over the swaths of fabric lying on the bed. If we do this one last crazy thing together, by this time tomorrow, I'll be on a plane home to my family.

"Let's choose a dress."

⁂ ⁂ ⁂

The next two hours are a swirl of dresses and makeup and women running in and out of my bedroom while chatting excitedly to each other (always in Greek) and to me (sometimes in Greek). The younger people seem to have an easier time remembering that I speak English, but almost all of them can switch over quickly when I shake my head apologetically. I realize early on that I don't really need to understand what's happening, because I have no opinions on the event other than "get it over with and get me out of here." I even let the women of the house (and several neighbors) pick my dress. They fall in love with an ivory one-shoulder chiffon one with an empire-waist cut that makes me look like an ancient Greek goddess. Strappy leather, gladiator-style sandals are slipped onto my feet and three women are frowning at my hair while Eleni dusts light shimmer powder across my cheeks.

"Close your eyes and I'll do your eyelids," she says. She swipes makeup across my lids, and I have to admit that this is the best I'll have looked since Theo and I met. It's nice to feel pretty one last time. "I could be your maid of honor, if you want."

"Oh!" I exclaim. "That's really nice of you to offer. How old are you?" The women behind me get to work untangling my hair.

"Only sixteen. How old are you?"

"Eighteen."

Eleni sighs wistfully. "I'll never get to be eighteen. Or have a boyfriend."

"I don't have a boyfriend either," I say without thinking. My eyes fly open and she's looking at me with her brow furrowed. "Because I have a fiancé now," I finish pathetically, like I'm rubbing my happiness in her face. "Sorry. This is weird for me. I never thought I'd get married so young. And now we're here."

My eyes stray to the window behind her head, where the sun is moving quickly across the sky. Time has never flown as fast as it has since I agreed to this scheme. Down on the beach, small figures rush about, setting up chairs for the wedding guests. My stomach flips unpleasantly; I try to find something else to focus on. "Does that camera on the table by the bed work?" I ask, pointing over my shoulder in the general direction of the Polaroid camera I saw when I woke up.

"I think so. Why? Do you want me to take your picture when you're ready?"

"No. Well, maybe. But I was wondering if I could, um, have it. To use for the night. Taking pictures calms me down." Not to mention it's the only thing I have left from my old life.

Eleni retrieves the camera from the table and snaps a picture of me. A black-and-white square ejects from the camera. She hands it and the camera to me. "It's yours."

I watch the picture materialize and am shocked to discover I still look like me. I feel like a completely different girl than I was even one week ago, but I still have the same brown eyes and the same stubborn set to my shoulders. I hug the picture to my chest, indescribably relieved. "Thank you."

"If I were dating Blaze, I'd take pictures of him all the time," Eleni says as she returns to her stool and picks up a makeup brush. "He has nice eyes."

"He does," I agree. Nice eyes that are going to hate me forever for hijacking his dream wedding. *If* he even goes through with it.

"So can I be your maid of honor?" she asks again. Behind me, two sets of hands tug my hair into a complicated braid.

I hesitate, which makes no sense. None of this is real. It won't even be legal because Theo didn't tell anyone his real name. This is just a show to appease the family before they drop us on the shore of Santorini. I don't even care about weddings! And yet, I guess I always thought it'd be Brooke. In that vague of-course-it-will-be-Brooke kind of way. It feels wrong to let it be anyone else, even if it's not real, even if it doesn't matter.

I realize there's more truth in what Theo said than I realized. If it didn't matter, I'd let Eleni be my fake maid of honor. I wouldn't be near tears at a single picture of myself, and I wouldn't flinch every time someone says "wedding."

But for some reason it does matter. I only have a few days left, and it all matters so much, I can't breathe.

"I don't think I'm going to have a maid of honor," I say eventually. Comet shifts at my feet, giving me an idea. "Comet and I will walk each other down the aisle!"

Eleni frowns, and I can see that she thinks I'm choosing a dog over her. Which I am. Just me, my dog, and the crown prince disguised as a guy named Blaze, having a fake sunset wedding on the beach. What could go wrong?

CHAPTER 25

DATE: THURSDAY, JUNE 16
LOCATION: AMORGOS, GREECE

ITINERARY: GET (FAKE) MARRIED
DAYS UNTIL THE COMET HITS: THREE AND A HALF

Nothing in my life will ever be as surreal as the moment my adopted apocalypse dog drags me down the beach toward my apocalypse wedding. No matter how many times I tell myself it's fake, it's not real, it's not even *legal*, I can't shake the nerves that something will go wrong, and we won't make it off this island alive. I think maybe I could have handled it if I'd been stranded at Heathrow, but to get this close to home and fail would be unbearable.

Comet strains on his leash toward the small crowd of people sitting in chairs a hundred yards away, but I hold him back until I get the cue that it's *go time*. In addition to the official wedding guests, there are dozens of people watching from balconies and rooftops of the houses set in the cliffside. People have been stopping me all afternoon to tell me how happy this has made them, how nice it is to have a distraction from the inevitable. It relieves some of the sting of being a teenage bride and a liar.

Not that I regret what I'm doing. I just wish we weren't in this position at all. I wish Theo were safe in his bunker and I were in Chicago with my family. I wish I could throw my arms around Wally's neck and tell him that he's the best boy in the world and that I didn't abandon him. I wish I could talk to Theo now and feel his electric warmth next to mine. I could use a little of his starlight.

Comet's restless and my ankle is throbbing by the time Eleni runs across the sand. "Finally," I breathe, shuffling from foot to foot to get some of the feeling back in my legs and distract myself from the pain that started in my ankle but is now radiating everywhere else. "Are we ready to start?"

Eleni bites her lip and tugs on her braids. "Not yet. We have a problem."

"I promise I don't care about the food or the music or the decorations or any of it. As long as this wedding happens, I'm happy."

"That's the problem. It doesn't look like the wedding is going to happen."

"Why not?"

She pulls even harder on her braids and glances around desperately, like the Bad News Fairy is going to climb out of the sea and deliver the news for her.

"Just tell me, Eleni. I'm not going to be upset with you."

"We can't find Blaze."

It takes a long moment for me to digest this information—to remember that Theo is Blaze. And when I do, I laugh. I can't help it. If you'd told me a year ago that at eighteen years old I'd be left at the altar by a guy whose passport says *Blaze*, I'd have laughed my ass off.

Eleni watches me warily. "Are you okay?"

"When was the last time anyone saw him?" I ask, even though I know it's useless. He's not coming.

"A few hours," Eleni admits, confirming my suspicions. He told me he'd be happy to stay here, and there's plenty of room on this small island for him to hide out for a few days.

I fulfilled my half of the bargain, and he called it quits.

"What should we do?" Eleni asks. "Should I tell everyone to go home?"

My eyes rove over the guests. Raucous laughter carries easily across the water, and I hate to ruin what might be their last good night.

Backup plans for my backup plans. I need to think of something to get the attention off me and Theo and keep everyone here—especially Nicholas—in a good mood. They want a wedding? They'll get a wedding.

"Hold Comet. I'll be right back." I hike up my dress and run through the sand. All eyes snap to me when people see me coming. I drop the hem of my dress and wave my hands in a crisscross motion. *No wedding! Nothing to see here! Stop looking at me! Seriously—stop looking! Have you never seen a jilted teenage bride before?*

I find Eleni's mom and pull her aside. "How do you feel about getting married tonight?"

She frowns. "What do you mean?"

"I'm not getting married, but that doesn't mean the celebration has to end. You and your husband should renew your vows tonight. Followed by anyone else who wants to."

"I don't understand. What happened?"

"Blaze is gone. He's not coming."

She places a hand on her heart. "Oh, Wren—"

"It's okay!" I insist in a strangled voice. "I swear! It's okay! Please say yes."

"Yes, we'll do it! I wish I'd spent more time on my hair, but oh, I guess that doesn't matter now." She runs her fingers through her long dark hair, looking flustered and excited and then, when she glances at me again, worried. "Are you sure you're okay, my dearest?" She cups my cheek with her hand.

Her tender mothering brings a lump to my throat. Tears burn the backs of my eyes, and I'm not even sure why I'm crying this time, or if it's for all the reasons stacked one on top of another.

Theo is gone.

I'm not going home.

I'll never see my family again.

I'm about to die.

"I'm fine. I'll be fine."

She tucks a loose strand of orange hair behind my ear. "It's okay, dear. You'll stay with us." I start to protest, but she silences me with a tight hug that breaks the dam in my chest. "I won't take no for an answer," she whispers.

Quickly wiping the tears from my cheeks, I back away from the wedding while she makes an announcement in Greek. Expressions turn curious and then excited as couples raise their hands to get in line for the vow renewal extravaganza. My last successful plan.

I take Comet's leash from Eleni and tell her to go enjoy the vow renewals and the party. She hesitates, clearly debating just how sorry to feel for me. "I'll be okay," I lie. She gives me a quick squeeze before leaving Comet and me to fend for ourselves. We take a long walk where the water meets the sand until my body drops. Waves rush over my feet, soaking through the bottom six inches of my dress. I lie on my back and let my shoulder blades sink into the soft sand as I stare up at the sky.

I've never felt so far from home.

Comet snuggles next to me and places his head on my stomach. I think he has a sixth sense. He hasn't left my side once today because he knows I'll fracture into a million pieces if he does. I curl my fingers into his soft, warm fur, and it gives me the courage I need to finally open the off-limits box. For the first time in five days, I'm not scrambling to get shelter or food or sleep. This is it. My plan failed. It doesn't matter if I fall apart now, because I've reached the end of the line.

Sunset turns the sky into a pink-and-orange Creamsicle that makes me ache for home all the way to my bones. As gorgeous as the Greek sunset is, splashed across the white stone houses built into the mountains, I can't fool myself into thinking it's the prettiest sunset of my life. Not when I've spent a lifetime watching Chicago sunsets from my own backyard, the fevered riot of color that paints the surface of Lake Michigan every summer evening.

On a night like tonight, I might be lying on the beach with Naomi or bugging her to let me stage photoshoots so I could get practice. I'd be listening to Mom and Brooke debate boring lawyer stuff while Dad and Cedar play guitar in the other room, or I'd be watching *New Girl* on Netflix, or doing any of a thousand mundane things that have added up to make my life. But the truth is, I think it's most likely that I'd be alone in my room studying Northwestern's course catalog and planning my future from my first 8:00 A.M. lecture to my last 5:00 P.M. lab with a tight, unyielding grip. And if I'd known my plans would be shot to hell at age eighteen by a comet careening through space, I'd like to think I would have come out of my room a little bit more, spent less time making backup plans for my backup plans until my eyes were bloodshot and I had stress canker sores from worrying about things I couldn't control or things that wouldn't happen for another four years.

I wish I had thrown out the itinerary every now and then. I wish I had been flexible. And most of all, I wish I could have one more of those mundane nights with the people I love. As soon as I can pick myself up from this beach, I'll call them and refuse to hang up the phone until the comet hits, even if it's scary and uncomfortable to say goodbye.

The soft padding of footsteps drags me back to the present. I turn to see Eleni walking toward me. "Can I sit?" she asks. When I nod, she sits cross-legged next to me and digs her toes into the sand. We stare out at the water for a long time without speaking.

"How's the party?"

She shrugs one shoulder and scrapes her fingers into the sand. "It was fun at first, and I'd forget for a few minutes. And when I remembered, I felt so mad, I wanted to scream."

"I get that," I say, remembering all the times I felt that way with Theo. "But it's okay to have good moments even when things are bleak."

"I'm sorry Blaze left."

"Thanks."

"You can sleep in my room tonight if you don't want to be alone. And tomorrow I can show you a cool spot on the other side of the island. There's this cave with a beautiful view."

I'm out of options. It's over. My plans and backup plans failed. I'm numb with disbelief and grief and suffocating panic.

"I need to call my family first, but sure. Yeah. That sounds great, Eleni," I say in a dull voice.

We sit in silence for a while longer before she leaves, and I'm about to stand and follow her when Comet lifts his head and stares into the darkness. He pushes up to his feet and pants excitedly. My chest tightens. Over my shoulder, a familiar figure approaches in the dark. He's hunched over, his head down, his hands in his pockets.

Comet leaps away from me and bounds toward Theo like he's returning from war. Traitor.

Theo crouches to meet Comet and accept a sloppy kiss on the cheek. "What are you doing here?" I ask in a shaky voice.

He holds my gaze for a long moment. "I'm sorry I made you wait."

I turn my back on him and face the water as heat rushes through me. "I get it. You don't have to explain."

"Look at me."

"No."

"Please, Wren."

"It's fine. I don't want to talk about it." I swipe a stray tear from my cheek.

"We don't have to talk. But if we don't go now, we'll be late."

I spin to face him. His expression is unreadable in the dark. "Late for what?"

"Our wedding."

CHAPTER 26

DATE: THURSDAY, JUNE 16
LOCATION: AMORGOS, GREECE

ITINERARY: GET (FAKE) MARRIED (FOR REAL THIS TIME)
DAYS UNTIL THE COMET HITS: THREE

It's almost midnight. Theo and I stand across from each other, waves lapping onto our toes. We're as far down the beach as we could get without running into rocky cliffs. Away from the noise and the celebration and all those people. He visibly relaxed as we moved away from the crowds, and I feel silly for not realizing how traumatizing it would be for him to put on this show with half the town watching from their roofs. Now it's just us, Nicholas Castellanos, Comet, and Eleni and her mom to act as witnesses. Eleni's holding a bouquet of flowers I've never seen before, so I think she might be my self-appointed maid of honor after all.

Theo is wearing khaki pants and a white linen shirt with the top button undone and the sleeves rolled to his elbows, his disheveled hair falling across his forehead like midnight silk.

The moon casts dark shadows across his face, and I've never wanted to take his picture more than I do now. Not because he's beautiful (though he is) but because he looks like himself. I can't understand the riot of emotion in his eyes, can't begin to fathom why he's agreeing to this, but the relaxed set of his shoulders and the intense way he's staring at me isn't anything like the rigid way he holds himself when he's *the prince*. Right now he's just a boy who's looking at me like this was always the plan. He and I barefoot on the beach, making our last wishes come true.

Thinking about how natural he looks makes me fidget in my dress. Crusted sand clings to the hem and my once intricately woven braid is slipping sideways on my head, thanks to the wind, the crying, and the sand. I self-consciously try to tug my hair back into place, but when another chunk slips loose and blows across my face, I give up.

"You look beautiful," Theo says. The second time he's said it. The butterflies in my stomach wake up.

"Even my tragic hair?"

One half of his mouth kicks up in a sad smile. "I don't mind a little tragedy, American girl." He reaches out to tuck my hair behind my ear.

"We don't have to do this," I whisper for what feels like the millionth time since he pulled me up from the beach and said he wanted to get fake married—for real this time.

"You'll take us to Santorini in the morning?" Theo asks Mr. Castellanos. The old man has cake crumbs in his mustache and sways a bit on his feet like maybe he's a little drunk, but he agrees. Theo turns back to me. "I want to do this," he says. He glances at my hand and hesitates. "I don't have a ring."

"I don't need one," I say quickly.

He threads his fingers through mine and squeezes tightly, bringing me back to the bed we shared in Paris. Tears sting my eyes again, and this time I'm not even sure why. All I know is that when I saw his face in the dark, it was like the clouds had parted. Starlight.

Mr. Castellanos stumbles over his words in English before sighing. "Between us, I'm too drunk to translate this in my head. Do you mind if we do it in Greek?"

Theo and I shake our heads. Somehow both of my hands are gripped tight in his. I don't remember if I reached for him or if it was the other way around.

Mr. Castellanos speaks for a few minutes in Greek before nodding once to me. "Orkous agapis."

"It's time for your vows," Eleni translates.

There's a pressure behind my breastbone, crowding my chest until it burns. I'm not prepared for personalized vows.

Theo leans so close that his lips brush my ear. "I told him we wanted to do our own so we wouldn't have to lie. Do you want me to go first?" He seems so unruffled by this situation that I feel terrible for my panic. Surely, I can think of something to say. And anyway, Mr. Castellanos is drunk, and Eleni and her mom are standing far enough away that it feels a little bit like our own private moment.

"No, I can do it." My hands shake in his and he squeezes them tight. I take a deep breath and push away the pressure of what this is "supposed" to be and say the first thing that comes to mind.

"I met you on the worst day of my life."

His answering smile breaks open something in my chest.

I can do this. All I have to do is tell the truth.

"But because of you, the days after haven't been as bad. I

don't know what our world is going to be like in a few days. I've tried very, *very* hard not to dwell on it. But I know I'll be grateful I met you for the rest of my life. When I dragged you through Camden Market, I thought I was saving you—the spoiled rich boy who couldn't fend for himself." Theo cocks an eyebrow and I grin in response. "So imagine my surprise when you've been saving me every day since. You've held my hand, made me laugh, put up with my dog, and kept your promise. Not bad for a spoiled rich boy." I wink, and Theo suppresses a smile. "I'm forever grateful, and . . ." I'm not sure how to finish this. I'm worried anything else will sound too earnest or cheesy. "I owe you one."

Mr. Castellanos nods to Theo to indicate it's his turn. My stomach churns with such violent anticipation that I'm worried it might be dangerous.

"You might be the only girl in the world who would take the piss out of me in our wedding vows—" he starts.

"Please, I beg of you. Be a little less British right now."

Theo rolls his eyes skyward, no longer able to conceal his smile. "There she goes again," he says.

"I know, I'm sorry. I'm a bully at heart and I can't help myself," I say.

"It helps keep my ego in check. Besides, *you*, Wren Wheeler, are not a bully. You're good. You remind me that there are good things in this world. You remind me that there are families that love each other, dogs worth saving—"

"All dogs are worth saving."

He exhales a long-suffering sigh. "Are you gonna let me do this or what?"

"Sorry. Please continue."

"You reminded me that there are futures worth fighting for.

If I'm starlight, you are daylight, chasing the shadows out of my mind. You think I saved you? I think we saved each other. I've felt more alive and freer in the days I've known you than all the ones that came before it. A less romantic person might call that circumstance, but I think it's something else. Something more powerful." His dazzling gaze lights my skin on fire, and everything else stops. Time. Space. My heart. I suddenly can't recall if I've known him for five days or fifteen years. "I call that fate. You and your plans stepped into my life at the darkest moment and dragged the sun in with you. I promise not to give up on you, for whatever time we have left."

Theo slides the black ring off his finger and slips it on mine. And for all my protests about this wedding being fake and not needing a ring, I already know I'll never take it off.

I'm relieved I went first, because my feeble IOU pales in comparison to his poetry. I had no idea he was such a romantic, that he believed in fate. And now my racing heart is splintering for all the other things I'll never know about him.

Mr. Castellanos says a few more words in Greek, and then Theo and I kiss. Short and sweet and still electric. Like a flash of heat lightning in a distant summer sky.

Eleni and her mom clap and hold a marriage certificate out for Wren Wheeler and Blaze Danger to sign while Comet runs circles around us. With the certificate pressed against Theo's back, I sign my name as Comet shoves his head between my legs. My hand slips and the pen punches through the paper once. *It's fake, fake, fake,* I remind myself as I grip the pen tightly and force a shaky approximation of my name. And then it's Blaze's turn. I feel the paper pressed against my shoulder blades and the swoosh of the pen. And then it's done. A quick round of hugs for everyone, an extra-long one from Eleni, and then she's walking back up the beach with her mom and grandpa and my dog, who doesn't want to go but reluctantly allows himself to be led up the beach when I promise they'll give him a treat.

Theo and I are alone. Married, but mostly not. Friends, but maybe more. Alive, but only for a few more days.

I swallow, blood thrumming painfully in my veins. "What should we do now?" I ask in my breeziest voice. I am the personification of casual indifference. The relentless tick of the doomsday clock is getting louder and closer with each passing hour, but I'm chill. I'm not obsessing over the nice things he said in his vows and my insides aren't a swell of desperate longing and rising panic. And I definitely don't want to jump his bones and make out with his face.

(I'm going to die a liar.)

"We could go to the party." He answers my question just as casually as I asked it.

"Okay." My feet are anchors. It's impossible to move.

"I don't really want to go to the party," he confesses. "I hate parties. I hate the expectation and the attention and the pressure."

I too hate the idea of going to a party tonight. I don't want to share Theo with anyone. I'm not only a liar, but a selfish one at that. "I don't want to go either."

His eyes burn bright. They flick across my face with interest before settling on something just over my shoulder. Maybe a rock. The world's most fascinating rock, for how hard he's staring. "We agree, no party." He clasps his hands behind his back, his shoulders stiffening in that formal way they do when he's *the prince*. I hate that he's doing it now, here, when it's just me and him. I reach out and shove him gently on the shoulder to get him to loosen up. He leans back and then springs forward again like one of those toy punching bags with all the weight in the bottom. It seems his feet are also anchors. We'll still be standing here when the comet hits, staring at each other, tied down by all the words we're too afraid to say. On my left ankle is a tether that says: *I like you too much.* That's the main problem here. I've gone and developed an apocalyptic crush while I was just trying to get back home. On my right ankle is a rope and a confession: *I wish you'd get in the bunker.*

The words are braided tight, mirroring the twisted misery in my gut as more unspoken words snake together and yank tight tight tight on my lungs.

I wish you'd take me with you.

I wish you'd save Mom and Dad and Brooke and Cedar and Wally and Comet too.

I'm full of impossible wishes.

"You're being weird. Why are you being weird?" I demand.

"I'm not," he counters.

"Yes, you are. Your shoulder bones are made of steel. That only happens when you're nervous or having your photo taken." I put my hands on his shoulders and shake them. His eyes are saucers. He's baffled. I've baffled him.

"*I'm* being weird," I say. Sometimes I find it helpful to say the obvious out loud. I let my hands drop and immediately wish I hadn't. "We could get some sleep!"

"Do you want to go to sleep?"

"No." I never want to go to sleep again. I want to drink nothing but Red Bull for the rest of my life. "We could swim!"

"In the freezing cold sea that almost killed us last night?"

An idea hits me. I gasp with delight. "We could go skinny-dipping!"

He raises his scarred eyebrow. I don't want him to think I'm propositioning him. (I am.) I need to keep talking to lessen the impact of that suggestion.

"We could climb these rocks or search for seashells or, or— build a sandcastle. I've never built a sandcastle. What's wrong with me? I've been to the beach. Why didn't I do that?"

I know why. I thought I'd have all the time in the world to build sandcastles. I thought I'd have all the time in the world for . . . *all of it*. Everything in my plans and then some. The vise on my lungs cranks tighter tighter tighter. My lips go fuzzy and numb as black spots burst across my vision. It's possible the comet has already hit, that the world is falling apart. I crouch in the sand and gasp big gulps of briny air that skip my lungs on their way down. The more air I swallow, the less I can breathe.

"Wren? You all right?" Theo crouches next to me, his voice thick with worry. He puts a finger under my chin and gently tips my face up, his eyes searching.

I shake my head, recognizing the symptoms of another panic attack. "I'm dying and you're dying and there's not enough time left."

He leans forward and kisses my forehead before pressing his to mine. "Come here, American girl." He shifts so that he's behind me, then wraps an arm around my chest, anchoring me to him. His chest rises and falls, his breathing deep and slow. It reminds me that breathing is supposed to be easy.

I stop fighting the air and inhale slowly through my nose. I focus on the weight of Theo's arm, the span of his chest against my back, the heat of his breath on my ear.

It helps. The black spots disappear. I tip my head back against his shoulder as my muscles unwind and I allow myself to melt into him.

"We can do all those things," he says in a low voice against my ear.

Goose bumps fan across my neck. I shiver despite the heat of him. "Even skinny-dipping?"

"If you'd like," he says. "But first, let's stay like this for a while."

I want to. He has no idea how badly I want to, but there's still a pressure crowding my chest. "There's no time." We have to do as much as we can as quickly as we can. "Do you have a pen and paper? I need to make a list." First, skinny-dipping.

He's quiet as he drags his fingers through my hair, destroying what's left of my braid. The pressure of his fingers scatters all my thoughts. "Do you want to know what I think?" he asks at last.

Desperately. And also: *not at all*. The tone of his voice makes it clear he's not about to shower me with compliments.

"I don't know, do I? Keep in mind that my ego is bigger and more fragile than yours. I built my entire high school identity and life plan around proving I'm as smart as my sister."

"I think you're making plans and itineraries to keep yourself distracted."

"From what?"

"You tell me."

I freeze, wondering if he knows all my unspoken thoughts. "Can you blame me for wanting to distract myself from the end of the world?"

"Of course not. But I think it might make you feel better to at least acknowledge some of the feelings you're avoiding."

"I tried," I say miserably. "That's what I was doing when you found me on the beach. It was terrible, and I don't want to do it again. Especially not now that—" I press my fist against my mouth.

He shifts me to the side to get a better view of my face. "Now that what?"

Now that I've acknowledged my feelings for you. I won't say it. He can't make me. It'll be worse once I've spoken it out loud, because if he meant even half the things he said in his vows, I think he might have feelings for me too. And I'm not interested in playing Juliet to his Romeo.

"C'mon now, Wren. I thought we decided to be friends."

I shake my head. Nope. Not happening.

He sighs. I feel the vibration of it in my back and a shiver rolls down my spine.

Damn it. I'm gonna say it. I can't stop myself. "I'm scared." I hope maybe he'll interrupt, but of course he doesn't. He waits for me to continue. "I'm scared of all the things I've never done, the places I've never seen, the life I haven't lived. You're right. I do make plans and itineraries to distract myself from my fears. I've always done it because I hate the idea that there are things I can't control."

He takes his time replying, choosing his words carefully. "I think you're being too hard on yourself."

"Spoken like a boy who's had every opportunity, and therefore done everything."

"Hello. Virgin. Right here." He points to himself.

My cheeks burn so hot, they contribute to global warming. Now that one of us has mentioned the elephant on the beach, it's impossible to ignore. "Do you regret waiting?"

He hesitates. "I won't pretend like there aren't experiences I want to have before I die, but no. I always told myself I'd wait for the right moment, with the right person." He holds my gaze for a long time until it's impossible to imagine he's talking about anyone other than me. "Life's more than a list of to-dos to scratch off. Who cares if you never built a sandcastle? I doubt that's what you'll be thinking about when the comet hits."

He's not wrong, even if I still wish I were more of a diver than a wader. I can't get into cold water without slowly and excruciatingly hitting all the body checkpoints. First a toe, then an ankle. Knee, thighs, belly button, shoulders, head. Slow and steady. It's never not agonizing, and I fear I spent too much of my life wading into, well, everything.

If I'm ever going to jump in, now would be the time. "I'm scared of losing you." I squeeze my eyes shut and bury my face in my hands.

He laughs softly, which makes me wish the comet would hit now.

"Is that what you were so scared to tell me?" he asks.

"Well . . . yeah." I venture to open one eye and sneak a glance at him. His eyes blaze with heat as he stares at me.

Oh. I've never been looked at like that.

"If it wasn't clear from my overly honest vows, I fancy you, Wren Wheeler."

"Are you trying to kill me?" I wheeze.

He smirks and trails his fingers along my bare back. "I thought you might appreciate that."

I fancy you. Brooke was right to be scared. *Those* words, in *that* accent? I never stood a chance against Theo's charm or his chivalry or his desert-dry sense of humor.

As the comet has been hurtling toward Earth, Theo and I have been sprinting just as quickly toward each other, and the inevitable collision will be a bright, hot bone crush. Losing Theo is going to hurt worse than I'm prepared to handle. He doesn't fit into any of my carefully curated plans, but somewhere between jumping off a ship and the wedding, that stopped being a good enough reason to avoid this.

"There is one thing I'll be sad if I die without doing," he whispers.

"Only one?"

I feel the curve of his lips turn up in a smile. "In my defense, it's one very distracting thing."

"Skinny-dipping. I knew it. You seem like the type."

He smirks, his eyes darkening as he slips his hands around my waist and draws me in until our bodies are flush together and every atom in me sparks like a live wire.

"This time, when I kiss you, it won't be because someone else is watching or because we almost died in a storm." He presses his lips against my neck, just below my ear. I'm struggling to think coherently now. He slowly, softly presses another kiss against my neck, one on my jawline, one on the corner of my mouth. I tilt my head until my lips meet his. When his tongue brushes against my lips, that distant heat lightning strikes my bones and fuses us together.

He braces his hands on my hips and lifts me up, perching me on the edge of a rocky outcropping. I wrap my legs around his back and pull him to me, slipping my fingers into his silky hair as his hand rakes through mine. We kiss as the world spins, the hard planes of his body fitting perfectly against my soft ones, everything inside me turning to molten gold, drowning me in impossible promises of the future we could have had, if everything had been different.

When we finally break away, I'm flushed everywhere. Fevered. My internal temperature is skyrocketing, and I think I might be dying, actually. I look past him out into the black water. "Let's get in."

"You were serious about that, huh?"

"I've relinquished my hold on sandcastles and rock climbing. Let me have this one thing."

He runs a hand through his hair, indecision all over his face.

"What, are you scared?" I taunt, unable to remove my hands from his shoulders. And then something hits me. "Do British princes learn how to swim? If not, I'm quite good at mouth-to-mouth."

"Quite," he agrees, leaning in to kiss me again, dragging his tongue slowly over the roof of my mouth until I'm quivering. He finishes the kiss with one closed-mouth peck and backs away with a smirk that tells me he knows that the electricity in my veins has short-circuited all my breakers. "The palace has a private swimming pool," he drawls as he slowly unbuttons his shirt with deadly lung-collapsing precision. I watch as he drops it to the sand, and then I stop watching as his hands move to the button on his pants.

"Wait! Do my zipper before you get in." I spin and pull my hair up off my neck. Theo curses softly under his breath as he drags the zipper down.

"I'll tell you when I'm in so you know it's safe to look," he says. His pants hit the sand, the sound thudding in my ear like a shot fired at point-blank range. Followed by a splash.

He swears loudly. "It's cold!" I sneak a glance out to the water, but it's too dark to see him, which I assume means it's too dark for him to see me. I finish what he started and slip off my dress. After a minute of debate, my underwear goes on top of the pile. The cool night air feels dangerous and a little bit bad. Like something I would never, ever plan for.

"I'm coming in!" I shout. And then I put my hands over my

own eyes and run, shrieking at the first splash of cold water under my feet. I hold my breath and dive in headfirst.

$$\ast \quad \ast \quad \ast$$

We don't last long in the water. Theo runs out first, and I watch his silhouette under the night sky as he steps into his pants.

"Your turn!" He picks up my wedding dress and shakes out the sand. I'm already freezing, and I know the night air on my wet skin is going to be even worse, and yet the sight of a shirtless Theo waiting for me gives me all the courage I could ever need. I take a deep breath and sprint out of the water as goose bumps run the length of my body.

He meets me at the sea's edge and helps me step into my dress, which clings everywhere. As soon as the zipper is up, he grabs my hand and pulls me across the sand toward the soft glow of our would-be reception's string lights. "Where are we going?" I ask, pushing strands of wet hair out of my eyes, worried he's about to march us soaking and disheveled into the dwindling celebration, but he dodges the party and instead leads us to the Castellanos family's cliffside home.

"Quiet," he whispers as the front door creaks open. He glances over his shoulder, a wicked gleam in his eye. I bite my lip and hold my breath, worried that the sound of my heart will wake the whole house. We climb the stairs in a fevered sprint, two steps at a time, both of us shivering. We burst into the room at the top of the stairs and I clap a hand over my mouth to keep from laughing as I close the door gently behind me.

I spin and am almost knocked sideways by the nearness of him. Moonlight streams in through the open window, glinting off his raven hair and cobalt eyes. My breath hitches as heat spreads low in my belly. Unable to go another second without touching him, I press my lips hard to his. Without breaking contact, he propels me backward and presses me into the door.

I moan softly against his lips, and he grinds his hips against mine, making me dizzy with want. I rake my fingers through his damp hair and shiver as cold drops of water trail down my fingers. Theo steps back, his chest heaving, his eyes nearly black. "Do you want to dry off?" he asks. I swallow the painful, nervous lump in my throat and nod. "I'll get you a towel," he says, turning toward the bathroom.

I take his hand, my eyes locked on his. With my free hand, I reach back and pull down my zipper. I slip the strap of my damp dress down my arm, letting it fall to the floor and pool around my feet.

Theo shudders out a breath, his eyes closing to half-mast.

"Follow me," I whisper, and lead us to the bed. I slip under the sheets as Theo shucks off his pants and slips under with me.

He speaks first. "We don't have to—"

"I want to," I say quickly. "I'm nervous, though." This feels entirely different than last time, when having sex was just an item on a to-do list.

"*You're* nervous?" He draws my hand to his chest, and we lie like that for several breaths, Theo's rapid-fire heartbeat in the palm of my hand. "*I'm* nervous. I want you to have everything you deserve, and you're stuck with me." One side of his mouth tugs up in a self-deprecating smile.

"Don't do that," I whisper. I close the remaining space between us until we're lying nose to nose. "I'm with you because I—" *I love you.* The words appear unbidden, and I don't know what to make of them. "Because I want to be," I say instead, one hundred percent certain it's true.

Theo tips his mouth to mine and kisses me again, this time soft and slow instead of frenzied. "What a coincidence," he whispers against my mouth. "End of the world or not, I wouldn't choose to be anywhere else, or with anyone else, right now." He presses a hot kiss to the sensitive spot below my ear before trailing kisses down my neck toward the hollow of my throat.

Nothing about this moment feels like completing a bucket list.

No, this feels like my body is on fire, like I might die from the ache of wanting more. His lips find mine again and I kiss him hard as his weight presses me into the mattress.

A soft moan escapes his lips. "Wren. You're perfect," he breathes.

Theo. I love you.

My own voice filters in through the haze. I don't intend to think it—but it must mean something that I do.

We're lost for a long time in sighs and touches and whispered words. Then his hand drifts between my thighs and his breath tickles my neck as he asks, "Can I?" and I whisper, "Yes, yes, *please.*"

After I have fallen off the edge of the cliff, I want to take him with me. He leans over the side of the bed, rummaging in the pocket of his pants and retrieves a square foil. He spins the condom between his fingers. "This was slipped into my hand this afternoon by a very old man with a wink and what I'm assuming was a very dirty joke in Greek."

I laugh. "Do you think he knows the world is ending?"

"Absolutely not." Theo grins. "But we should probably use it . . . just in case." Moonlight illuminates the sliver of hope in his eyes, and my heart sticks in my throat for how much I love this boy, and how he can still find it in his soul to hope that maybe we'll live to see the other side of this disaster.

"Agreed."

He unwraps the foil and we slowly fit ourselves together in the dark, whispering and kissing and holding eye contact the whole way through. And when it's over, I kiss him again, certain that even if we had all the time in the world, it would never be enough.

One day, one year, one lifetime with Theo—it wouldn't matter. I'd never get used to being this happy.

CHAPTER 27

DATE: FRIDAY, JUNE 17
LOCATION: AMORGOS, GREECE

ITINERARY: BOAT RIDE TO SANTORINI, PRIVATE
    PLANE RIDE HOME
DAYS UNTIL THE COMET HITS: THREE

The sunrise over the Aegean Sea makes my heart hurt. It is beautiful and over too quickly. It's the beginning of the end.

I trace the word "home" in the sand next to my legs and stare at it for a long time, unsure if I should put a frowny face or a smiley face next to it. I've never wanted two conflicting things as badly as I do now. I want to stay here, curled up against Theo's body until the world falls apart. I want to go home. Both things are true.

Theo is sprawled languidly against a seaside cliff with my head resting on his bare shoulder. We snuck out of our room and down to the beach at the first hint of dawn, and though we've fallen into a natural silence as we've watched pink and gold steal across the horizon, my voice is still hoarse from talking all night.

"Are you awake?" I ask.

His head is tipped back and his eyes are closed. "Yeah."

"Last night was . . ." I swallow, nervous again for the first time in hours. Last night was *perfect. Magical.* All the clichéd words I used to describe my first time, but this time, they're true. This time, they're sorely inadequate.

"It was . . ." I try again. Fail again. It's harder to be honest in the light of day. "It was the best night of my life."

Without opening his eyes, he reaches up to my hand—the one resting on his bare chest—and curls his fingers around mine. He picks it up and kisses my palm.

"I was thinking the same thing, and it's not even a close contest," he says. His voice is pure gravel. A bowl of gritty, good-for-you Grape-Nuts. "Last night with you is here"—he holds our hands up above his head—"and just below it is the time I took home the first place trophy in a welly-wanging contest when I was eight." He moves our hands to chest level, a twinkle in his eyes.

"I don't have any idea what that means, but I think I fancy you."

"Oh, you think, do you?" His lazy smile grows.

"Can I take your picture?"

"Whenever you want, American girl."

I reach into the bag I brought with us to the beach and retrieve the Polaroid camera. My hand trembles slightly as I point the lens at Theo. I wait for him to drop his lazy grin and adopt his rehearsed camera smile, but he doesn't. He's relaxed and perfectly himself as he lounges with his head resting on the rocks, facing me. His hands are loosely clasped over his bare stomach and his feet are covered in sand. His hair is delightfully disheveled. My throat dries.

He trusts me. He dropped his shield and is letting me see *him*.

Snap.

I anxiously shake the picture to mask the now violent tremble in my hands as I piece together fragments of truth in my mind.

He trusts me.

I promised I wouldn't give up on him.

We've been saving each other.

And the scariest one of all—*I think I love him.*

The clock has run out. I can't put this off any longer. "Can I ask you a question?"

"Can I see the picture?" he asks.

"You want to?" I'm surprised by the request. It's the first time he's asked. He nods, and I toss the picture into his lap. He studies it intently, the ghost of a smile playing around the edges of his mouth.

"I like the way you see me. It sounds crazy, but sometimes I think you're the only one who does." He shakes his head as he returns the photo, his cheeks stained sunrise pink.

"It doesn't sound so crazy." I tuck the picture and the camera into the bag. "So. My question."

"Ahh yes. The reason you look like you've got an earthquake trapped inside your body." He eyes my hands knowingly and I stuff them under my armpits. "Ask away, American girl."

"I love when you call me that."

"I know." His smile turns smug.

"So. The fake wedding." I'm stalling for time.

"I remember it well."

"How much of what you said last night was true?"

"All of it," he says without missing a beat.

Hope surges through me. "So you meant it when you said that there are futures worth fighting for."

"Yes."

"Including yours."

He raises an eyebrow. "What are you trying to say?"

I clasp my hands together. I unclasp them. I spot my scribbled word in the sand and drag my fingers through it. I'm freaking out. I'm a rubber-band ball of emotions, bouncing all over the place. "You need to go home, Theo."

He's confused for a moment, and then the magnitude of what I'm asking him to do shudders through him. He rakes a hand through his hair. "I didn't mean—I just meant—if things were different, *we* could have had a better future."

"Things can be different."

"No," he says dismissively. He climbs to his feet and pulls his shirt over his arms. He buttons it aggressively. I didn't know that was possible, but he punishes those buttons as he pushes them through their little holes. He's *furious* with them. He wants to strangle their tiny little button necks. (It's possible the body earthquake shook something loose in my brain.)

"Theo—" I use my most measured voice. The one I use on Wally when he slips off his leash and is about to bolt.

"I'm saving Penny's life. My brother will have told her by now. Arrangements are being made. Bit insensitive of me to barge back into the bunker and kick this fifty-year-old woman out on her arse, don't you think? Not to mention Charlotte and Andrew, who will literally never speak to me again."

I can't fault him for his chivalry, but I refuse to believe this is the only way to save Penny. "Admittedly, I don't understand very much about how royalty works, but you're the heir to the throne. Give them an ultimatum—you'll come home *if* they make room for Penny."

"No."

"Theo." I reach for his hand. He pulls it away.

"What about you?" he asks. "How do I save *you*? How do I save Will and Raoul and Stella and everyone else who deserves it at least as much as I do?" His eyes spark with the sharp pain of what must be some kind of pre–survivor's guilt. I throw my arms around his neck and squeeze. He reaches behind him and removes my arms with excruciating tenderness, swiping the tears off my cheeks with his thumbs as his own fall onto the sand.

"I'm sorry," I whisper.

"I once told my mum I feel trapped in the palace, and she told me if I feel trapped in eight hundred thousand square feet, I'll feel trapped everywhere. I thought she was right—until I met you. This week has been hell, but it's also been heaven. It's the first time I've ever been allowed to make decisions that have an impact on my life—the first time I've ever made my own plan. That bunker offers me exactly one future, and it's not one I want. Whatever happens next, at least I'll have chosen my own fate."

The resolve in his eyes is something I can't argue with, so I do the only thing that feels right: I press a kiss to his cheek and thread my fingers through his. Together, we set off to complete the last phase of our itinerary.

We're so close to the end. I can't believe we're here, that the plan *worked*. And my part is done. After five days of non-stop running, the end is in sight. Nothing can go wrong now. It doesn't feel nearly as good as I thought it would. I've never wanted to carry out a plan less than this one.

We're trudging up the sand when I trip on a rock and twist my ankle, *again*. I wince as pain lashes through me. Zero out of ten, would not recommend. Theo grabs my hand with his and holds me upright. When my life inevitably flashes before my eyes, this stupid everlasting injury better not be included.

"Do you think our lives will flash before our eyes as the comet hits?" I ask. Theo looks at me warily. "It's not a trick question. I'm not going to spend our last day together fighting with you."

"Does that mean you accept my decision?"

I grind my molars. "Yes."

He closes his eyes and exhales in relief. When he leans down to kiss me, guilt swells like a balloon in my chest, but I kiss him anyway, wrapping my arms around his neck because I can't bring myself to stop. When he breaks away, he swipes another stray tear off my cheek. "I hope there are certain memories, and, um . . ." He clears his throat. "Certain people who are on my mind before it's over."

"Certain people?" I bat my eyelashes and flutter my hand in front of my face. "Whomever could you mean?"

"You," he says evenly. His eyes have taken on a new intensity that I've never seen before. It stops me in my tracks. He takes a deep breath. "Wren, I think I—"

"There you are!" Eleni bounds down the beach toward us, Comet on a leash beside her. I call his name and he yanks his leash out of Eleni's hand and sprints toward me, knocking me back in the sand. He licks my face twice and then abandons me for Theo.

Eleni's braids are fuzzy and disheveled like she slept in them. I can't imagine what I look like. It hasn't occurred to me to be self-conscious about it until now. "Pappous is getting the boat ready. He sent me to find you." She hands me a white bag filled with food. "For the trip."

"Point the way," Theo says. He stretches out his hand to help me up. Once I'm up, he doesn't let go. Eleni points down the beach to a small marina with a long dock. Theo wraps Comet's leash around his free hand while I slip mine away. He glances at our fingers, a frown sketched across his features.

"You go ahead. Eleni, do you have a phone I can borrow? My parents haven't heard from me since yesterday afternoon."

"I'll need to use it too," Theo says. When I shoot him a questioning glance, he leans close and whispers, "The pilot needs to know we're on our way."

My stomach flips. We're only a couple of hours from Santorini. Depending on how fast the pilot can get the private jet ready to fly, Theo and I are nearly out of time.

Eleni takes a phone from her pocket and hands it to me. "You can use this. Blaze can use the one up at the house."

I push up on my tiptoes to kiss his scruffy cheek. "I'll meet you at the boat."

He bends and answers my kiss with a long one on the lips. His warmth washes through me and it's too easy to sink into the kiss, into him, into the daydream of forever. I wish more than anything that I could, but the one thing Theo and I have never had is time.

My heart tears in half as I pull away from him, two warring sides battling in my chest. One half that wants to make him happy, the other that knows he deserves something more. "Go! Go! I'll be quick. I'll leave a message if they don't answer."

"All right. See you soon. Let's go, Comet." He turns.

"Wait! What were you saying a minute ago? Before Eleni came?"

He stares at me for a long moment, his eyes full of unsaid words. "We can talk about it later."

When the shape of him has faded from view, I take a deep breath and dial Mom's number. The plan is to let my family know that I'll be home in twenty-four hours.

After that, there's only one call left to make.

CHAPTER 28

I knew leaving the island of Amorgos would be hard, but I didn't expect the lump that forms in my throat when the entire Castellanos family lines up on the dock to wish Theo and me farewell. After battling the crowds and chaos across five countries, we landed here like a couple of strays and found a family willing to take us in. No amount of thank-yous could ever be adequate, and when I try, Eleni and her mom shake their heads and wrap me in a tight hug before ushering me aboard the boat with Mr. Castellanos, Theo, and Comet.

Comet is lounging luxuriously near the back of the boat, living his best life as Mr. Castellanos gives him belly scratches. In contrast, Theo is nervously rubbing his thumb over the spot where his ring used to be.

He pushes himself upright when he sees me. "Did you talk to your family?"

"Yeah." I rub the leftover tears from my eyes. I sat on the beach long enough to spend a few minutes talking to Mom, Dad, Brooke, and Cedar, and then Naomi. Even though we didn't have to say a final goodbye, I sobbed through the entire thing.

"Are you all right?"

"No, but at least I get to see them again."

Theo frowns and turns his face toward the water, and I can't help but assume he's thinking about his own siblings and his decision never to see them again. He nudges Comet away from his side and makes space for me to sit next to him as Mr. Castellanos shoves the boat away from the dock. Theo drops his arm around my shoulders and tucks me into his side, clearly eager to forget our argument on the beach.

And while I would love nothing more than to relax my head on his shoulder and zone out, my brain won't shut off. "How long will it take to get to your house? And how long for your pilot to get the plane ready?"

"It's a couple of miles from the marina to the house. We'll have time."

It's impossible to be as confident as he is when the rest of my life can be counted in hours. "Do you know what time the comet is supposed to hit?"

"Monday."

"Right, but what time on Monday?" The uneasiness roiling in my stomach is unpleasantly familiar. It's the feeling I get when I sit down for a test and I haven't studied hard enough. I should have asked these questions earlier.

"I don't know," Theo says. "Early, I think." He drags a hand through his hair, and I can see the tension around his eyes and in his shoulders.

"I feel like an idiot for not paying attention to the news at all this week. I don't even remember *where* the comet is supposed to hit. Somewhere in the ocean? And when it does, is the whole world going to die immediately, or will some of it be aftermath stuff, like the dinosaurs who died off because there weren't any plants for them to eat?" Now that I've started addressing the questions, a new one pops into my head every two seconds. I can't believe I ignored what was happening for so long. It didn't seem important at the time. Or that's what I told myself when it was too scary to think about. "Theo? Do you know any of this stuff?"

A muscle twitches in his jaw. "Can we just ride in silence?"

My lungs squeeze painfully. After last night, I thought we were closer than ever, but everything we've said to each other this morning has felt *off*. What happened to our whispered feelings in the dark? Why does Theo feel more like a stranger to me now than he did when we first met? "Message received." I slip out from under his arm and sit on the other side of the boat with Comet, embarrassment rushing through me. I have no idea how to chase away the awkwardness that has nestled between us.

The three-hour boat ride is silent and miserable, and by the time Mr. Castellanos drops us off at Vlikhada Marina, I'm desperate to get off the boat and put some space between Theo and me. The abandoned marina is small, with shallow teal water and a curved dock. There's not a soul in sight. It was probably beautiful once, but now the dock is charred and crumbling, the boats singed black and submerged in water. Theo winces as his eyes rove over the destruction.

"What do you think happened?" I whisper as we walk through the eerie, empty marine graveyard.

"I don't want to know," he says.

Comet, Theo, and I walk parallel to the coastline as we climb farther into another one of those caldera cliffside developments like the one in Amorgos. Unlike Amorgos, we don't see anyone, and I can't help but wonder how many of these dwellings are vacation homes that currently stand empty. The farther we climb, the bigger the villas get, and I'm having a hard time keeping up. Theo doubles back and plucks my bag off my shoulders, transferring it to his without a word. I lift the camera around my neck and snap a picture of him in profile. His jaw is clenched, but not in a fake, posed way. He's just stressed, and for some reason that allows me to relax a little. I haven't lost him just yet.

We walk all the way to the top of the caldera and stop at a tall wrought-iron gate. Beyond it, down a long driveway, is Theo's summer home.

"What's the code?" I ask, pointing to a keypad that opens the gate.

"We can't use the code. It'll send an alert to Mum's staff." His eyes scan the property. "We keep a few people on-site to take care of the house while we're away, but it doesn't look like anyone's here now. I'm counting on the fact that they left when news of the comet broke."

At the mention of staff, the hair on the back of my neck stands up. "And if you're wrong?"

"Let's find out." He pushes a button on the keypad. "This buzzes up to the house but won't alert security. If someone is in the home, they'll answer."

We stand in tense silence for several long seconds. When no one answers, I think we're in the clear, until my eyes follow the lines of intricate wrought iron to a security camera perched on the far edge of the gate. Its lens is pointed directly at us. "What about the cameras?"

His dour mood briefly disappears as he flashes me a quick grin. "I happen to know those were disabled when we went on holiday here this spring, and as of last week, they hadn't been fixed yet."

"How were they disabled?"

"Let's just say family holidays get a bit claustrophobic and I wanted the option to visit the beach at night by myself." He slings our bags up and over the gate before linking his hands together.

I place my good ankle in his hands. He boosts me up and I glance back down at him.

"We've come full circle," I say, flashing back to the fence we jumped a lifetime ago.

"I'm sorry about your ankle," he says.

"It was worth it." I smile down at him as he gazes up at me with stars in his eyes. Then, without warning, I'm pushed up and over. I grip the fence with both hands and slide slowly down to save myself from another injury.

Once Theo and I are both safely on the mansion grounds, I whistle and take in the view. The massive home has white-washed walls that almost hurt to look at in the bright sunlight. At our backs, the Aegean Sea shines just as bright. A large, square infinity pool overlooks the coast. I drop Comet's leash and he leaps for the pool, diving right in.

While I'm gawking at the house, wondering how long it takes the staff to clean the dozens of gleaming windows, Theo unearths a spare key from a rock in the garden (Royals! They're just like us!) and unlocks the door.

"Home sweet home," he says with a surprisingly strained expression. No one would ever guess what he sacrificed to be here. "Feel free to do whatever you want. You can shower—"

"Is this your way of telling me I smell?" I joke, hoping to pull him out of his sour mood before it's time to leave.

"No. But I know how madly in love with showers you've fallen during this trip."

"I'd marry a shower if I could."

He ignores my quip. "There's an empty room down the hall where you can take a nap. Or you can swim in the pool. I'll turn the hot tub on if you want."

"I don't have a swimsuit. Although that didn't stop me last night . . ." I raise my eyebrows.

He turns his back to me.

"Are you seriously going to ignore my blatant flirting? That's how this is ending?"

"Huh?" He spins toward me, the blank look on his face making it obvious he hasn't heard a word I've said.

"Never mind. As amazing as a shower and a nap and a swim sounds, do you think we'll have time for all of that?"

He blinks at me, his expression frozen in that same pained grimace he's been wearing all morning.

"So . . . can you go call your pilot? Is the electricity still on?"

"Yeah." He flicks the nearest light switch on as proof. "So I guess I'll go . . . make the call." His feet don't move.

"I'll see you when you get back."

A flash of pain flits across his brow, and then he spins on his heel and stalks away. I stand in the middle of the airy room for five minutes, trying to decide what to do first. I want to do everything Theo suggested and more, but I'm afraid if I make myself at home, it will be that much more painful to leave. Eventually I turn the TV on.

Every channel is covering Comet Watch (with short interruptions covering the destruction and crime already happening in major cities across the world), and the news is not great. (Understatement of the century!) It's still on course to hit Earth and destroy everything, etc. The news station has a countdown clock with fewer than sixty hours on it. Theo must have been right about the comet hitting early on Monday morning.

The reporters say it's a guarantee that ninety percent of life on Earth will be wiped out immediately. And those that die will be the lucky ones, considering the nightmarish hell that will follow. A few thousand select doctors, scientists, geniuses, and miscellaneous rich people who have been squirreled away in underground bunkers in several countries won't be able to emerge for years. A horrible tremor travels through me. *Theo would be so unhappy.*

I'm going to die knowing that Theo hates me. It's inevitable. I can't take back what I've done, but I can pull my head out of the sand just this once and force whatever conversation he's avoiding, because I don't want to leave Greece with this unspoken tension and confusion between us. When I'm back at home, I don't want to regret all the things I didn't say.

He enters the room, his expression stricken.

"We need to talk," I say before I can lose my nerve.

He winces and stuffs his hands into his pockets. "Did you overhear?"

"What? No. This isn't about the flight home."

"Oh. We *do* need to talk about that, though."

"We will," I insist. "But first my thing."

"Right. Of course. You go first."

"You've been kind of a jerk today," I say.

He frowns. "Have I?"

"Yeah. I don't know what happened or why you're suddenly acting so weird, but I hate it. I'm good at shoving unpleasant thoughts aside and ignoring hard conversations and generally not dealing with shit. It's what I've done for the last week, and it's the reason I bury my head in planning for the future. It would be so easy for me to get on the plane and ignore the weirdness between us and pretend it doesn't matter because the world is ending, but I don't want to do that."

"Okay." He nods warily, like he's not prepared to hear what I have to say.

"I want to tell you that despite how horrible this week has been, I wouldn't trade meeting you and going on this adventure. Even if it meant getting home a few days sooner, I wouldn't change it. My life has literally never been worse, but at the same time, I've never met anyone like you." His eyes soften, giving me the motivation I need to continue. "I care about you, Theo. More than anyone I've ever met. As hard as I tried to not let myself fall into this, I fell anyway." Admitting this is scarier than our fake-not-fake wedding vows, and I hold my breath while I wait for his response.

Theo crumbles. "She's not coming," he rasps, like saying the words causes him physical pain.

"Who?"

"The pilot didn't answer her phone."

My heart stutters. "What?"

"She's not coming."

"Call her again."

"I called three times this morning and twice just now. I left voicemails. She's not picking up because she's not coming."

"That's why you were acting weird," I say, trying to wrap my brain around what's happening. We had a *plan*. I did my part. It can't fail now.

"I know," he admits, his chest heaving. "I didn't want to worry you unnecessarily because I hoped she'd answer when I called from the house. If I've been distant and short-tempered this morning, it's not because I regret last night. It's because I knew there was a possibility that I wouldn't be able to keep my promise to get you home." His eyes glow with desperate sincerity.

"I don't understand. *Where is she?*"

He pushes his hand through his hair, looking tortured. "I don't know."

"But . . . you promised she'd be here. I asked back at the pub if she was a flight risk and you said no. Did you even talk to her?" The awful possibility that he's been lying to me this whole trip thunders through me. "Did you tell her we were coming?"

"Yes," he insists. I raise an eyebrow, and he blanches. "Well, sort of."

Oh. The breath whooshes out of my lungs. I'm an idiot. *Brooke was right. I've been played.* It's bad enough that I trusted Theo. It's worse that I let myself fall for him, that I believed his delusional "vows." No matter how many pretty words he says or bogus promises he makes, he doesn't have feelings for me. If he cared at all, he wouldn't have lied while dragging me halfway around the world. I should have stopped trusting him when I learned about the bunker.

"I have to get out of here. Comet? Comet!" I brush past Theo. Outside, my dog cocks his head from his position on the patio, decides moving is not worth the effort, and collapses back down, closing his eyes.

Theo blocks my path, his hands up in a gesture of conciliation. "I swear I talked to her. I didn't tell her I was coming, but I told her *you* were and asked if she'd do me one last favor and fly you home. She agreed. But we're late. And she promised this before the missile launch failed. I'm sorry, Wren. I didn't know what to do. I didn't know how to tell you."

"You just tell me!" I shout. "You tell the truth even if it sucks." A tear rolls down my neck and I realize I'm crying. "I trusted you." My voice breaks.

"I know." Theo wraps his arms around me. "I'm so, so sorry, Wren. I've never felt worse about anything in my life." He takes a deep breath and my heart wobbles like an unsteady top. "I think I lo—"

"Don't say it." I push myself out of his arms and back away to the other side of the room. I'm not ready for this. Not now. Not like this. The backs of my legs slam into the white couch. "Please don't say it," I whisper through tears. Soon enough, he'll wish he hadn't.

He ducks his head. "I'll keep calling. I'll figure something out."

I stand unmoving as he walks out of the room. I don't let myself think about what he almost said, or how my heart went wonky in my chest when he almost said it, because it would have hurt too much to hear the words only to have him take them back a few minutes later.

Before I can make a new plan, he's in front of me again, every trace of soft fondness wiped clean. I expect his eyes to burn, but it's the opposite. He's a matchstick blown out.

"What did you do?"

CHAPTER 29

*W*hat did you do?" Theo asks again.

"I—" *I blew the plan to hell. I tore it up, I went off script, I ignored our pact.* "I called your family," I whisper.

"When?"

"Before we got on the boat this morning."

His eyes widen in disbelief. "You have the nerve to yell at me for keeping secrets when you sold me out for a ride home?"

"No!" I'm seized by sudden panic—I have to make him understand that this has nothing to do with saving myself. "Why would I? I thought my ride home was *here.*"

"Then why did you do it?"

"Because I don't want you to die! Because I—I . . ." This time the words stick in *my* throat.

"How'd you contact them?"

I wince. He'll hate me even more if I admit that I memorized the phone number on the business card I tore up in France. After placing that call and admitting what I knew, it was surprisingly easy to get the right people on the phone. I guess it helps that there's a ticking clock no one can deny. They no longer had the luxury of writing me off as crazy. "Does it matter?"

"It all matters," he insists. I flinch against the words, because this time I know he's right all the way down in my bones. It's why I made the call. "Were you planning this the whole time? Were you using me to get to Greece, only to send me back to prison the second you got what you needed?"

"If I didn't care about you, I'd leave you here to die alone."

"No, if you cared about me at all, you'd let me make my own decisions. Shite, Wren." He pushes his hands through his hair and paces the room. "I thought you were different from all the other people who only bothered with me because I'm a fucking *prince*."

"I am!" I insist, battling tears. "That's not what this is about. This wasn't the plan, but after last night I can't *not* save you!"

"I don't want to be saved!" he roars. "You can't save everyone!"

"But I can save you," I whisper. "*And* Penny. I told them I'd only disclose our location if they made space for her in the bunker."

"How soon are they coming?" His eyes dart to the exits in the room and the whiplash is extreme. We're back in front of the World's End, and he's trapped. Except this time, I'm feeding him to the wolves instead of helping him run. I can't look him in the eye.

He steps toward me, crowding me against the couch. "Listen— what if they're wrong? What if they launch another missile? Maybe it'll be okay, and I don't have to be *the prince* anymore and you don't have to live in your sister's shadow. We can just be Theo and Wren and—"

"Stop." The future he's proposing is impossible in every sense of the word. "They're already on their way."

Outside, car doors slam. We both know what it means.

"You take the plane," he says.

"As much as you hate to admit it, in the eyes of the monarchy, the country, and the world, your life is worth more than mine. Your mom's security detail won't take me home."

"That's not fair!" he snaps. Uniformed figures appear through the window behind him. "Sending you home has been the plan from the beginning."

My gut swirls miserably. "Plans change, Theo."

It's the last thing I say before half a dozen bodyguards in black suits and sunglasses throw open the doors and station themselves at every exit. I hold my breath and wait for Theo to fall apart, but he doesn't. The moment he registers the guards, it's as if he rebuilds himself brick by brick. Steel poured into every inch of his frame; all emotion is gone from his face in a blink.

"Gentlemen," he says in a voice I don't recognize. He nods toward the biggest guard, the man now standing at his side.

"Your Royal Highness. Are you ready to go home?" A pair of shiny handcuffs hangs from his belt. Theo was right. The Firm is prepared to drag him home kicking and screaming.

Theo cuts me a glance. I don't recognize the boy I see because this isn't my Theo. This is the *prince*, and he's furious, hurt, and terrified.

It doesn't change how I feel. "I love you," I say.

A war of emotion plays out on his face before he sighs. "Wren, I—"

"You don't have to say it back," I say hastily. "I would have regretted not saying it, though."

He wavers, mistrust and indecision etched in his expression.

"We don't have much time, sir," his bodyguard says apologetically.

Theo draws himself up, gives me one final heartbreaking glance, and sweeps out of the room with all the authority of the future king of England.

"How'd you know I turned you in?" I call to his retreating back.

He pauses. Doesn't turn. "I called my brother Henry. I *was* willing to do anything to find you a ride. We had a deal, remember?"

And then he leaves, and I'm left stunned and alone, watching him go. As Theo ducks into the back of a dark car with blacked-out windows, Comet rises to his feet and cocks his head. He barks once at the unfamiliar men. My heart spasms as one final idea materializes unbidden. I sprint outside and throw myself in front of the car, banging on its hood until the driver rolls down the window.

"I get one favor," I say breathlessly. The burly man in the driver's seat blinks at me. "The Queen promised to grant a favor to any person who had information that led to the—" I cut myself off. I almost said "capture." ". . . *recovery* of the prince."

"I don't know if that applies to you, considering you helped him escape," the man says evenly.

"I saved the prince's life. I deserve one favor."

"What is it?"

I can't save myself. I already bargained for Penny's life. It was part of the deal of giving Theo up. "Save my dog. His name is Comet. He's a good boy."

The driver looks in the rearview mirror. "Up to you, sir." I wish I could hear Theo's response, but a few seconds later the driver nods. "Where's the dog?"

At the sound of my whistle, Comet runs headfirst toward me. This is the only goodbye I'll get to say, and I want to make it worth it. I throw my arms around my perfect apocalypse dog and bury my face in his neck. Before I'm ready, the driver opens the door to the back seat and ushers Comet inside. "Wait! I—I need another minute."

"There's no time." He hands the end of Comet's leash to Theo, who gently calls my dog up into the car. Comet happily jumps in and lays his head on Theo's lap while my heart collapses. Theo won't even look at me. I sit in numb disbelief as the driver slams the door shut and peels out of Theo's long driveway.

I didn't even get to say a proper goodbye to my dog.

I don't know how I make it back inside Theo's mansion, but I find myself sobbing on the white couch for so long that I lose all sense of time and space. All that exists is me and the puddle of tears and snot on this formerly pristine couch and a confusing tangle of emotions that I'll never have time to unravel. Before Theo found out that I'd called his family, he was going to say he loved me. If I hadn't stopped him out of fear that he'd take it back, he would have said it. I could feel it. But when *I* said it first, he didn't say it back.

So maybe it was never true.

The deep, throbbing ache in my chest is desperate to believe what we had was real, but I can't forget the way he lied about the pilot and left me to die alone in Greece. I hate that I'm spending my last hours wallowing over a boy I didn't know this time last week. I hate that he hates me for saving him. I hate that his life is so miserable. I hate that I'm going to die with ugly hair. I hate that I never figured out who I wanted to be.

It's all so fucking unfair, I can't breathe.

Hours pass. I put off calling my family because I don't want to break their hearts. I can't ignore it forever, though, and I'm bargaining with myself to stand up when a bell rings. I ignore it. It rings again, followed by a hammering on the door. For a few impossible seconds I think it might be Theo. My faithless heart leaps—until I remind myself that *no, actually. I don't want to see Theo.* I want him to be safely on a plane to the UK by now.

I drag myself to the front door and wrench it open. Standing on the porch is a small olive-skinned woman wearing a nervous expression, her hair pulled back in a sleek bun. "Wren Wheeler?"

"That's me."

"My name is Melissa Petridis. You may call me Lyssa. Are you ready to go?"

"Who are you?"

"I thought you knew. I'm a pilot. Prince Theodore has asked that I fly you home. Today. Now."

My heart races—a traitor until the very end. Did he call her again and somehow convince her to come here? "When did you talk to him?"

"He left me several messages."

"But . . . why are you here *now*?"

She hesitates. "Does it make a difference?"

"Yes! It all matters!"

"He and his fleet of bodyguards arrived at my door quite unexpectedly. He was insistent and I found myself unable to say no."

I go completely still. "How did he seem? Furious? Sad? Did

he say anything about me? Does he forgive me? Did he leave me a message?"

Did he get me a flight home because he loves me, or because he was upholding his end of the bargain one last time?

Lyssa's brows flit together in confusion, and I know she doesn't have answers to my questions. All she has is an order from the royal family and a high degree of loyalty.

"I'll grab my bag." I retrieve my backpack from the hall. Empty now, except for a Polaroid camera and a few snapshots. I pull it over my shoulder and step onto the porch, closing the door behind me. "I'm ready to go home."

CHAPTER 30

My neighborhood is unrecognizable.

After a fifteen-hour plane ride and an eight-hour time difference, my brain is so foggy that I'm convinced I've been brought to the wrong place. I don't even know what day it is—in Santorini *or* Chicago—when I'm dropped off. I glance back at the driver only to find he's already gone. When Lyssa informed me that she'd scheduled a car to pick me up at the empty airport, I didn't question it. If I were more awake or less about-to-die, I might have demanded answers about how she'd arranged that so near the end. But as it is, I mumbled an unintelligible thanks. She looked like she wanted to say something, but instead she just nodded to the runway, where a man held a sign with my name on it.

He drove me here, left me on the end of the block, and now I'm home.

Allegedly.

CLOSED STREET signs block cars from entering the neighborhood. Behind the signs, the road is littered with furniture. Couches, recliners, and tables weighed down with food are everywhere. The Beasleys' painstakingly manicured lawn has a dining room table sitting in the middle of it. Mrs. Beasley once yelled at Cedar for picking hollyhock from her garden, and now the pink and purple blooms are crushed under the weight of sturdy dining room chairs while she laughs with the Singhs over a melted ice cream sundae.

The pack of boys who haunt the neighborhood all summer long are darting between the furniture, leaping over the backs of couches, armed with Nerf guns, water guns, and sometimes both. I think I see a glimpse of Cedar's hair, but then it disappears behind a love seat.

Several big-screen TVs have also been moved outside, and though they play footage of various news stations, no one seems to be paying attention to the doomsday countdown clock. At the far end of the block, right in front of my house, a band is playing, and this time I'm positive I see my dad and his Sunburst electric guitar.

I move toward him, weaving through chairs and couches. A splash of water hits my arm as a group of determined parents wrench the top off a fire hydrant and everyone cheers when a geyser of water shoots into the street. Kids flock toward it.

I'm halfway to the band when I hear my name. I spin to see Brooke barreling toward me just before she tackles me. The smell of her coconut shampoo hits me square in the chest and my knees collapse. We both fall backward onto a mattress.

Suddenly I'm crying harder than I ever did in Europe. It's funny how that happens. My body has been wound tight and ready for battle all week, and now that I've finally accomplished what I set out to do, I'm shaking and sobbing like I just found out about the comet.

"I can't believe you're here," Brooke gasps. "I can't believe you made it."

"I love you and I'm sorry about our fight."

"I'm sorry too. I love you and I was so scared." She hugs me tighter. "MOM! DAD! CEDAR!"

An electric guitar stops mid-strum, followed by a crash and a screech of microphone feedback. Footsteps thunder through the street, but Wally gets to me first, and if I thought I was crying before, it's over now. Seconds behind Wally is the rest of my family. I'm passed around from family member to family member, still too weak to hold myself up. Everybody cries. Dad holds me the tightest, Mom the longest. The circles under both of their eyes are four dark purple bruises, and I wonder if they've slept at all in the last week. When I ask, they tell me it doesn't matter. I'm home now. Cedar hugs me last, his skinny arms snaked around my middle until I can't breathe. And it's all so much better than the reunions in my imagination.

When I look up, I see another familiar face. Naomi stands in front of me, one hand clasped tightly around Levi's. It turns out fate did have a plan for the two of them after all. For a heartbeat, I remember her choosing Emily and Tatum over me in London, and I'm not sure what that means for us. We talked on the phone, but it's different to see her in person.

"Wren?" She stares at me like I'm a ghost before she shrieks. She drops Levi's hand and throws her arms around me. As soon as she does, I realize Emily and Tatum aren't part of this reunion. This is about me and my best friend.

"Surprise!" I say.

"Your hair—"

"It's horrible—"

"I'm obsessed. I love it."

"I hate it."

"We hadn't heard from you in so long—"

"I was on a plane—"

"I missed you so much—"

We trip over the words as we sob into each other's shoulders. People around us start to whisper and the whispers turn to shouts. My name passes over everyone's lips until I can't ignore them any longer.

"What is going on?" I ask the obvious question, gesturing to our neighbors and friends. "Are we going to party until the world ends?"

"You don't know?" Brooke asks.

My gaze snaps to hers. "Know what?"

"Come look."

I'm swept in a Wheeler family tidal wave and carried to our old gray sofa, which is sitting in front of the neighbor's seventy-inch TV. Brooke finds the remote control and unmutes the news. Wally climbs on the couch and splays out across my lap, pinning me under him.

"I don't want to watch comet stuff," I protest. I don't want to spend my last day on Earth thinking about how it's my last day, not because I'm avoiding it, but because there are so many better ways to spend this time. I want to load a plate with food and gossip with Naomi about her and Levi. I want to dance in the spray of a fire hydrant and shoot Nerf guns at my little brother and play Frisbee with Wally. I want every mundane moment with the people I love.

"They're gonna blow the comet up!" Cedar shouts, and everything inside me is drawn tight in anticipation until I'm a rubber band ready to snap.

"What?"

Dad turns the volume up on the TV, but my ears are buzzing and my eyes are blurring. "What are they talking about?" I wheeze. I grip my trembling fingers in Wally's short chocolate-brown fur.

"There's a ship with explosives on board," Dad explains. "They're going to launch it into the comet and blow it apart into small enough pieces that will burn up upon entering the atmosphere."

"I thought they already tried that."

"That was a missile launched from the ground. This is a space-craft armed with nuclear weapons. It's a suicide mission for those on board, but if they're successful, it'll save the world."

"What are the odds?"

"NASA has it at fifty-fifty."

A fifty percent chance that I'll live. It's more than I thought I had five minutes ago, but suddenly it's not enough. The need to survive claws at my chest, desperate, furious. "When will it happen?"

"Not for hours," Mom says. She picks up the remote and mutes the TV. "We want to hear the whole story. What happened after you left the airport in London?" A few neighbors move closer to hear the story of my miraculous return.

I realize immediately that I want to keep Theo to myself, so I take a deep breath and tell them an edited version of my trip. I include stealing a car in France and jumping off a ferryboat in the Mediterranean Sea. I don't include the cliffside beach wedding.

When I get to the private jet flying out of Santorini, Brooke blinks at me, slack-jawed. "Who is this guy you traveled with?"

"His name's Geoffrey. I never got a last name."

"Yeah, but who *is* he if he has access to private jets on Greek islands?"

I shrug. "No one important. Just some rich kid."

Naomi's eyes narrow, and when the crowd's collective attention returns to the TV for an update, she takes my hand and tugs me after her. We climb the steps to my front porch and sit on a swing overlooking the party.

"You. Levi. Holding hands. Tell me everything!" I insist.

"I will, but I want to show you something first." She taps on her phone, pulling up a TikTok video of what looks like a crowded train station. It plays for a few seconds before she pauses it. Then points at a dark-haired figure. My stomach drops. "That's Prince Theodore," she says.

"Oh—okay," I stammer.

She points to the girl next to him. "And that's you." Stella told the truth: most of my face is obscured, but my best friend recognized me anyway.

"How long have you known?"

"As soon as this video went viral, but you weren't responding to my texts, and when you finally did, it seemed more important to make things right between us. But, Wren, I'm dying to know—what the hell happened in Europe?"

Without warning, I burst into a fresh round of tears and fill in all the gaps from my story, including the wedding, our honeymoon on the beach, reporting him to his family, and telling him I love him before he walked out the door.

"He just left you there?" she gasps. "I *hate* him."

I spin the black ring on my finger. "Not exactly. He forced the pilot to fly me home, but I don't know if it's because he cares about me or because he felt like he had to."

"Call him and ask."

"I can't."

"Sure you can. It's not like anything else important is going on in the world right now." She hands me her phone.

I roll my eyes at her outstretched phone and wonder if I could get ahold of him if I tried. Both of our phones were abandoned on that ferryboat, but as the girl who saved his life, I should be entitled to some access to the prince. *Right?* One last phone call before I die.

But I can't bring myself to take it and try, just like I can't unglue my legs from this bench, my eyes from the TV across the street, or my heart from a bunker halfway across the world.

Naomi fills me in on the Levi story, which is beautifully straightforward. When news of the comet broke, she texted him asking if he wanted to meet up. He'd been about to ask the same thing. They met in the park, admitted their feelings for each other, and haven't been separated since. I love that she gets a happy ending.

Eventually we find ourselves back at the party. Plates of chips and dip, brownies, pie, deep-dish pizza, and every other food I could ever want are passed from table to table, couch to couch. Brooke slips me a beer that I quickly pass on to Naomi because the memory of my Italian hangover is still painfully fresh. The day passes unbearably quickly as we talk and laugh and dance and sleep for short bouts of time. Hours pass in a blink, and then, it happens. The ship hits the comet. The comet explodes.

And we still don't know if it's enough to save the world.

Hours later, we do. With my family gathered on the couch, clutching each other tightly, the debris from the comet enters the atmosphere and burns up.

The city explodes anyway. Fireworks color the sky in blues, greens, yellows, and reds. Car horns honk, people shout and celebrate from streets and rooftops, and the party continues, this time with even more food, more music, more laughter, and more lightness, all because we've been granted more time.

⚹ ⚹ ⚹

The party is showing signs of slowing down when I sneak inside for a long shower. My muscles ache with exhaustion, but my brain is buzzing. I lie in bed and stare at the glow-in-the-dark stars that Brooke and I stuck to the ceiling more than a decade ago, and I suddenly know why I can't sleep.

I need a new life plan. I climb out of bed, grab a notebook and pen, and stumble downstairs and out the front door. It's time to start brainstorming.

The party on our block has mostly died down, though the street looks like a trashed Pottery Barn showroom. I never imagined I'd see Mr. Beasley passed out on his front lawn, but he's not the only one. I step over sleeping bodies and find Brooke sitting on the sidewalk in the dark, her face lit by the glow of a TV, a bag of popcorn in her lap.

"Can't sleep?" she asks.

"I don't know what I'm going to do with my life."

"Same."

"You're going to be a lawyer."

"Yeah." She sighs and scrubs a hand over her exhausted face. "Maybe. I don't know. The whole end-of-the-world thing really puts, like, everything into perspective."

"No kidding." I take a handful of popcorn. "It turns out I've been blindingly jealous of you my whole life."

She rears her head back. "You have?"

"Obviously! You're the smartest person I know."

"You're smart too!" she protests.

"Thanks, but I never felt like I was succeeding *enough*, be-cause it's impossible for a mere mortal to succeed as much as you."

"Oh." She blinks, trying to process this revelation.

"And then when I thought I'd study photography, you made it painfully clear how you felt about that."

"I was trying to help—"

"I know. But making me feel silly about the one thing I want to do with my future wasn't actually very helpful."

"Shit." She laughs weakly. "Okay, yeah, I can see that. I shouldn't have given you such a hard time. I've always thought doing well in school was the most important thing in life, but look where that got me."

"A scholarship to the law school of your dreams?" I guess, although I have a feeling that's not where she's going with this.

"Not quite. When I thought I was going to die, I just kept thinking—am I *happy*?" She looks at me. "Did you think that too?"

"I mostly thought about getting home." *And then I fell in love with Theo, and I was happy.*

"Lucky you," she whispers.

"Lucky both of us," I say. "Now we can make the future look however we want." I flip open to the first blank page in my notebook and poise the pen over the paper. "I'm going to make a list of all the Northwestern majors that sound interesting to me in alphabetical order. Do you want to help?"

"In the morning."

"But—"

"Wren, close that notebook or I swear I'll burn it. Your fu-ture can wait until the morning."

"I guess." My fingers clutch the edge of the notebook, itching to open it and fall back into old habits. But she's right. My plans can wait until tomorrow or the day after that or maybe even until the end of the summer. I can spend the next two months hanging out with my sister instead of making plans and burying myself in course catalogs. I have time, and anyway, nothing about my future will ever be set in stone because nothing in life is guaranteed except the moment I have now.

"Hey, you haven't told me what you thought of England. Did you love it?"

"It was different than I expected. Almost nothing went according to plan."

"You must have been miserable!" She chucks a piece of popcorn at my face.

"I didn't even eat breakfast at the World's End because it was closed for renovations."

She frowns. "I don't think the World's End serves breakfast. It's not that kind of place."

My jaw drops. "You told me it was the best breakfast you ever had."

"Are you sure?"

"Positive."

She pulls up the restaurant's website and downloads the menu. "No breakfast!" she says triumphantly.

"I don't know why you're so happy when this makes you a liar."

"You're so dramatic." She rolls her eyes. "I didn't *lie*. I must have made a mistake."

"That *mistake* is the reason I didn't make my first flight home!"

"Well." She shrugs and pops a handful of popcorn in her mouth. "Maybe it was fate."

"Not you too."

"You don't believe in fate?"

My mind flashes to Theo under a starry sky on a Greek beach. If Brooke misremembering the World's End menu and sending me there for breakfast led to me meeting Theo on the brink of the apocalypse and crossing western Europe with him, only to have the world *not* end wasn't fate . . . what was it?

Brooke gets tired of the silence and unmutes the TV—the news again—and I groan.

"Do we really have to—" The words die on my lips as I stare at the screen. My heart stops. "Is this real?"

"Sad, isn't it? She was so young."

The banner reads: *Queen Alice Dies of Heart Attack. Prince Theodore Assumes Throne.*

A picture of Theo exiting a private jet fills the screen. His night-kissed hair obscures his face, and he's wearing the same button-down shirt and pants as when he left me in Greece.

"Who's that?" Brooke asks. "Is that the new king?"

My stomach free-falls as I grab the remote and turn the volume all the way up. "That's my husband."

EPILOGUE

Northwestern's course catalog lies untouched on my desk under a pile of photographs. I haven't opened it once since the world didn't end, even though classes start in a few weeks. I haven't registered for a single class or freshman orientation, either, but I'll get around to it eventually.

In between dodging Mom's and Dad's questions about my future and third-wheeling Naomi and Levi's dates, I've been photographing everything in sight. People, but also buildings and landscapes. Weird shadows and interesting plants. Candids are still my favorite, but nothing is safe from my lens. My family is fully sick of me, but I can't bring myself to stop. I photograph Mom when she's drying her hair and Dad when he's folding the laundry. (I *don't* photograph them when they're having tense whispered conversations about finding a marriage therapist. The therapy boom is in full swing and they're on at least three waitlists.)

My bedroom walls are covered in Polaroids and digital prints, every spare inch now papered with memories. "Serial killer chic," Brooke calls it. I consider it proof. If something happens to anyone in my family, at least I'll have these pictures as evidence that for one summer after my senior year of high school, we lived a million wonderful mundane moments together.

The only picture Brooke doesn't actively loathe is the one she found in my backpack after the not-end-of-the-world. Shirtless Theo on a beach in Greece, looking at the camera like he's in love with it. I shrieked and tore it from her hands before she could recognize the new king of England.

After I told her that he was my husband, she looked at me like I'd lost my mind in Europe, so I laughed and pulled the stupidest "just kidding!" of all time. I was kidding, though. It's not like he's really my husband. We were married as Wren and Blaze, and I'd sooner die than claim a husband named *Blaze Danger*. My family would disown me, as would be their right.

I'm eighteen. I don't know what I'm doing tomorrow, let alone with the rest of my life. *Marriage?!* I laugh when I think about it, chasing away the tears that threaten every time I think of the way Theo never even said goodbye.

The only reason I still have that picture of him tucked away in my dresser drawer is because I haven't figured out how he could look at my camera like that when he didn't care for me at all. It's a trick of photography that I haven't been able to repeat yet. I'll keep the picture until I do, until I figure out what exactly makes this one so perfect. It's not the subject, but it might be that special magic hour light. I don't know. I'm working on it.

There's a soft knock on my door frame. "Come in," I call, scrolling through my latest photo shoot on my laptop.

Brooke opens the door and pops her head in. "Are you finally registering for classes?"

"Nope."

"What are you doing?"

"Editing pictures."

"The good classes are going to fill up, and the bad classes with good time slots will too. You're going to end up with nothing but 8 A.M. lectures and 5 P.M. labs."

"Are you just here to scold me?"

She winces. "Sorry, no." She's been trying not to do that anymore, and I've been doing my best to not compete with her. "You have mail." She holds up a manila envelope with my name and address scrawled on the front in messy handwriting I don't recognize.

"Who's it from?"

"It doesn't say, but it has a ton of stamps on it. I think it's from overseas."

My fingers freeze on the black ring that I've moved to my right hand. "Overseas where?"

"Doesn't say. Do you want me to open it for you?"

"No!"

It's *not* from Theo. We haven't had contact since he left Santorini. And if I occasionally read *Daily Mail* articles about him, it's only because they sometimes mention Comet the Apocalypse Dog. On a good day, there are pictures. I focus every ounce of my energy analyzing how happy Comet looks and ignoring how *unhappy* Theo appears. I'm not a body language expert. How would I know whether he's happy?

I take the envelope with trembling fingers and tear it open. Inside is a single sheet of paper. I turn it around and my heart stops.

It's the marriage certificate from our fake ceremony in Amorgos, complete with the tiny hole I punched in it when I was signing my name. "Is this a joke?"

"What is it?" Brooke plucks the paper from my fingertips. The color drains from her face as she examines the paper. "Wren, did you get married in Greece?"

"No. Of course not." I push my brown-again hair out of my face. "Why would you ask that?"

"You signed this marriage certificate." She points accusingly at my signature. *Wren Wheeler.*

"It was fake. We needed a way off the island. The guy I was with signed a fake name."

"That Geoffrey guy? I still can't believe you spent an entire week with him and didn't find out his last name! Have you tried looking him up online? And why don't you ever talk about him?" She asks the questions but knows better by now than to expect an answer.

Her eyes travel to the groom's signature and her body relaxes. She drops the certificate onto the bed. "Well, that's a relief. No one would believe for a second that you married the king of England."

My heart pounds uncertainly in my chest as she leaves, and it takes me a minute to figure out why. She shouldn't know about Theo. She should be mercilessly mocking me for pretending to marry someone named Blaze Danger. I pick up the certificate with trembling fingers and stare at the groom's signature.

In messy script is written *Theodore Geoffrey Edward George, Prince of Wales.*

My head spins, my vision tunnels. My throat is packed with sand.

What did he do?

I can't move or speak or even think straight. I might not know anything about the royal family, but this feels like kind of a big deal.

I think I'm married to the king of England.

ACKNOWLEDGMENTS

The process of writing a book is different every time. Some books are a struggle from the first word to the last, while others are a joy. Most books fall somewhere in the middle of this sliding scale of frustration, but *The Prince & the Apocalypse* somehow exists outside the spectrum completely. This book was nothing short of a gift. Wren and Theo's story came to me in a flash, and drafting it felt like magic. Nothing in publishing is ever a guarantee, but from the first moment I sat down to write, I believed in this story about celebrating life amid unthinkable tragedy. I'm truly grateful for everyone who made this book possible.

Thank you to my editor, Sarah Grill, who fell in love with these characters (especially Comet the apocalypse dog) and made my dream come true by bringing *The Prince & the Apocalypse* to Wednesday Books. From our initial call to her first edit letter and beyond, I knew she was going to be not only an amazing collaborative partner but also a tireless advocate for this book. Together we made *The Prince & the Apocalypse* something I'm so proud to have written.

Thank you to my agent, Katelyn Detweiler, who trusted my vision when I told her I was writing a book about the end of the world, but in a *fun* way. Her endless support, wisdom, and encouragement have been invaluable to me. Katelyn is my perfect agent match, and I'm so thankful to have her in my corner. And nothing but gratitude to Sam Farkas, who has been instrumental in bringing my books to readers around the world. Thank you. The entire team at Jill Grinberg Literary Management is one I'm honored to work with.

A hearty thanks to everyone at Wednesday Books who had a hand in bringing this book to readers in an exciting and unique way, including Sara Goodman, Eileen Rothschild, Jen Edwards, Olga Grlic, Eric Meyer, Cathy Turiano, Carla Benton, Devan Norman, Soleil Paz, Meghan Harrington, Lauren Ablondi-Olivo, Alexis Neuville, and Brant Janeway.

Thank you to Mary Pender, Olivia Fanaro, and the team at UTA for championing my books in Hollywood.

Thank you to some of my favorite authors who read and blurbed an early copy of this book, including Kass Morgan, Emily Wibberley, Austin Siegemund-Broka, Rachel Lynn Solomon, Kristin Dwyer, Alex Light, and Diana Urban. And thank you to all my friends who have helped me through writing crises both minor and catastrophic, and for keeping me going when writing and/or publishing felt bleak. To Joanna Ruth Meyer for being Wren and Theo's first fan, and for listening to my writing and publishing rants while our boys ran around together at Krazy Air. To Kimberly Gabriel, who didn't laugh me out of existence when I told her what I planned to do with this book (specifically chapters 25 and 26). To Monica McDowell for your constant enthusiasm and encouragement. And thank you to Nicole Adair, Kelly Coon, Sophie Gonzales, Jenny Howe, Amalie

Jahn, Gretchen Schreiber, Ruth-Anne Snow, Erin Stewart, and Lillie Vale, for the friendship, advice, and support.

Thank you to my family. To my mom and dad for being the best parents a girl could ask for. And thank you to my siblings, Sandy, William, Michael, and Tommy, for making me laugh, loving my kids, and supporting me with each new book release.

None of my books would have been possible without the unwavering support of my husband, Scott. He is a true partner in every sense of the word, and no one has been more supportive of my career than he has. Scott, I love you and I'm grateful for the amazing husband and father you are. And finally, thank you to Owen, Graham, and Emmett for being the absolute joy of my life. You are all perfect exactly as you are. I love you.

ABOUT THE AUTHOR

Kendyl Hawkins

Kara McDowell is the author of *The Prince & the Apocalypse*, *One Way or Another*, *This Might Get Awkward*, and *Just for Clicks*. She lives with her husband and a trio of rowdy boys in Mesa, Arizona, where she divides her time between writing, baking, and wishing for rain.